VILLAINS ARE MADE

GODS AMONG MEN SERIES

ALTA HENSLEY

DEDICATION

For every reader of fairytales who wanted the Villain to get their happily ever after.

WARNING

Enter this tale at your own risk. It's dark. It's dirty. It's the love story of a villain.

I know how villains are made.
I've watched their secrets rise from the ashes and
emerge from the shadows.
As part of a family tree with roots so twisted, I'm
strangled by their vine.
Imprisoned in a world of decadence and sin, I've seen
Gods among men.
And he is one of them.

He is the villain.
He is the enemy who demands to be the lover.
He is the monster who has shown me pleasure but
gives so much pain.
But something has changed...
He's different.
Darker.
Wildly possessive as his obsession with me grows to
an inferno that can't be controlled.

Yes... he is the villain.
And he is the end of my beginning.

CHAPTER

ONE

Apollo Godwin

"You shouldn't have come," my brother says as I approach, not trying to hide the sound of my boots mucking their way across the rain-soaked ground.

Ares Godwin stands where I expect to find him. He's stoically planted with his hands in his pockets on the edge of the cliff overlooking the Salish Sea. Olympus Manor—our family estate—to his left, and the tree of forgiveness to his right.

He doesn't turn to face me, but keeps his eyes focused on the water crashing into and over the rocks below. "Does the family think I'm going to skip out on bail and leave the country? Is that why they sent you?"

I huff as I stand next to him, mimicking his

stance. "Hardly. And *they* didn't send me. You should know better than that."

Through the corner of my eye, I see the side of Ares's mouth lift in a smirk. "Scared I'd jump to my death then?"

"I wouldn't blame you."

"But you knew I wouldn't."

He's right. I know he won't. He's a Godwin. Godwins don't give up.

We are gods who walk the earth. We are the monsters, the beasts, the villains in the story. We are the vipers who strike our enemies when they least expect it. The Godwin family wields the mighty thunderbolt like Zeus, and yet...somehow the powerful have fallen.

There is a chip in our shield. A crack in our protection. We are vulnerable now, and for the first time in my life, I see my family is human. Flawed. Even weak. Everything has changed.

My brother—my identical twin brother—is going to jail for the rest of his life for murder.

"But you were an asshole for taking the helicopter by yourself. I had to travel here by boat like a true savage," I say, trying to cut through the thickness of our air with jest.

The island of Heathens Hollow, hidden in the fog of the Puget Sound, beckoned to my brother in his last hours of freedom, and I can completely understand the pull. I knew he'd come, and regardless of how I had to travel, I'd be here by his side.

He sighs. "Part of me wishes they'd insist on the death penalty. I think that's far less severe than having to live in a cage for the rest of my life. Hard to imagine I'm never going to see this view again."

I turn my head and look at the old willow tree that has stood on the edge of this cliff for centuries. "Have you asked the tree for forgiveness yet?"

Ares chuckles. "I'm not in the mood to whip myself or kneel on rice hours before sentencing, thank you very much." He shifts his weight, releases a deep breath. "What I've done, even that tree can't forgive."

The tree of forgiveness... The bane of my siblings' and my existence. Both our parents forced us to come to this tree to punish ourselves whenever we did anything wrong. They didn't believe it was their duty to teach us the lesson, rather it was our job to search our inner selves to find the lesson and learn from it ourselves.

I walk over to the leather strap still hanging from the lower branch. "Maybe I should be the one to whip myself." I look over my shoulder at Ares. "I should be the one going to jail today. Not you."

"Stop," he snaps. "We've had this conversation over and over, and I'm sick of it."

"You didn't kill that man. I did." There's a part of me that wants to throw myself off the cliff just so I don't have to live with this guilt any longer. "I can't let you take the fall for me. I don't care what you, Athena, or my father say. I can't."

"I'm not going to jail because of you," Ares adds, his attention going back to the sea. "I'm going to jail because my sins caught up with me."

"You've sacrificed your entire life for this family. There isn't anything you wouldn't do for them. But you don't have to for me. I'm not asking you to."

"Listen to me," he says with a voice of fire as he storms toward me. "I'm going to say this one last time so we can put this topic to rest. I'm not taking the fall for you. When they first thought I killed that man, they got my DNA. They were able trace me back to all the murders I *did do* in the past. I'm going to jail for all those hits, regardless. Not just the single one you did. There is no reason for you and me to both go to jail. It's inevitable I'm going down. You don't need to." He shrugs. "I couldn't be the family hit man and not expect to get caught, eventually."

"You can tell me this until you're blue in the face, but if I didn't kill that man at Medusa Enterprises—in the goddamn boardroom—you'd never have been arrested. It's because of me you got caught. I was the reckless one."

"No, it's because someone was setting you up. Someone took video of that incident and went to the authorities with it. You had no way of knowing you weren't safe in our building. You had no way of knowing. If anyone is to blame, it's Medusa security. Footage of you killing someone should have never gotten out the front door. Our family business, our family empire, should have been impenetrable." He clears the distance between us and places a hand on my shoulder. "This isn't on you."

Ares looks over his shoulder at Olympus Manor, and my eyes follow. There is slight movement to the curtain that hangs from the attic window. I smile knowing the manor's ghost is watching two brothers discuss life and death matters. I wouldn't expect anything else. This island is full of ghosts. They are the backbone of Heathens Hollow. It's almost as if the dead rule over all of us.

However, hundreds of people *live* and do work on the island and have for centuries. But the Godwin family still owns Heathens Hollow. The land is ours and the people merely lease it, never truly owning what ultimately is ours. The Godwins have owned this island since the Victorian era. It's a fishing town, just under four hours from Seattle, that houses the rich, the middle, the poor, and then the Eastsiders. The people who live on the Eastside of the island don't even have enough to be considered poor.

Though the island is so close to such a big and thriving city, the fact it remains cloaked in hazy fog for most of the year keeps it somewhat a secret. Rarely do people speak of this secretive place. Tales are told, but reality is never known. Truth of what happens on this island is...murky. The only way to reach the island is by sea or air, and the isolation only adds to the hidden shadows of this place. It's dark, dank, gloomy, and even after a rain, a rainbow never forms. This island is not for the fragile or for the man who can't endure the harsh storm. The full-timers are weathered, cut to the bone, and if someone really wants to know Heathens Hollow, all they have to do is look into the eyes of one of the old fishermen who work the boats at the harbor. Everything you want to know is expressed.

And then there are the wealthy. Not Godwin family wealthy. No one can match us. But there are the second vacation homes, the mansions only visited when the occupants want to swim in dark seclusion. There are still parties fueled by fame, liquor, and sex, but on this island the pace is often slower. The heartbeat of the Pacific northwestern island pauses, beats loudly, then pauses again.

Heathens Hollow is the island of gods and monsters. Innocence is drowned early in life by the crashing waves. Heathens Hollow is...home. Though we live and run our family empire—Medusa Enterprises—from Seattle, Heathens Hollow will forever be our resting ground.

Olympus Manor has served as a beacon, a legacy, a symbol of our family lineage. Though we all have houses in Seattle, this is most definitely our family home. Our ancestors haunt the hallways of the house, they wander the grounds, and they stand over us in protection, even now.

"Remember when we were kids, and we'd stand here on the cliff and howl like we were wolves," Ares says, clearly reflecting on his past in his last hours of freedom.

"Father hated that," I say as I see the vision like it was yesterday. "He hated when we acted feral."

"He hated a lot about us. We weren't allowed to be kids."

"We were Godwins. The expectations were—"

"Unrealistic. Always have been," Ares interrupts.

"You know there still may be a chance Father gets you out of this," I say. "Troy Godwin never loses."

Ares smirks. "Maybe. But doubtful. I think the inevitable is pretty set in stone on this one." He looks down at my left hand and notices what's missing. "Where's your wedding ring?"

I run my thumb over the bare skin of my wedding finger. "It's complicated."

"Simplify it for me. What's going on with you and Daphne?" he asks. "I've been so wrapped up in my own shit, that I clearly didn't get the memo."

"No memo... Things are just shit between us," I confess. "We both want out. A divorce."

"But you know you can't," he finishes for me.

"Godwins don't divorce," I parrot the words of my father. "But we're both tired of living this lie. We don't love each other, and I don't think we ever did. I married her so I'd have arm candy at events, and it felt like what society wanted. She married for money. It was essentially an arranged marriage. But we now want to sever the agreement but can't."

He points to my hand. "Taking the ring off makes you feel better?"

"It felt like it was scorching my finger," I admit. "But we aren't here to discuss my lame issues. A shitty marriage is nothing compared to what we need to face today."

"Still... I'm sorry, man. I thought Daphne was one of the good ones."

"She is," I confess, not wanting to bash someone who truly has a good heart. "I don't hate her. I just don't love her. And she feels the same."

"That sucks. I hope you can figure it out. Because as you said, Godwins don't get divorced."

Hating how the helpless feeling of our fucked up lives threatens to suffocate me, I take a step back and examine my brother's appearance and the fact that he's only wearing casual slacks and a black T-shirt. "Tell me you aren't wearing that to court."

Ares looks down at his clothing. "Who cares what I wear. I'll be in an orange jumpsuit soon enough."

"Unless Father somehow works his magic." I loosen my tie and pull it over my head. "In which case, you need to look good. Here, we're going to switch outfits."

Ares and I, though twins, couldn't be more different. He's the ruthless hitman in the family. The rebel, the dark and mysterious. I, on the other hand, am the Chief Financial Officer of Medusa. Strait-laced, always in a suit, and never a hair out of place.

Numbers are my life, and money makes my dick hard. Ares is the brother who cleans up the messes, even though he's dirtier than all of us combined. We were both born and groomed for these roles. Our father had a master plan for this family, and we are merely soldiers in his war of domination.

The one time I stepped out of our roles and killed someone before Ares had a chance, our empire fell to the ground. I'm the reason for the demise. I should have kept to the numbers.

"I'm not wearing your clothes," Ares says, shaking his head, but smiling at the idea.

"Yes, you are. Because we're going to take that chopper back to Seattle, and the minute we land, the press is going to be surrounding us and focused on you. You need to look like a Godwin. Power. Prestige. You are not a broken man. We rise above." I hand him my tie and then take off my suit jacket. "Strip."

When he takes my coat from me, he notices the extra weight and reaches into the pocket. Pulling out my passport, wallet with my I.D, and a large wad of cash, he shakes his head and says, "I'm not leaving the country. I'm not going to run. It will destroy our family and Medusa, and you know it."

I continue undressing, ignoring his words.

"I'm not leaving," he repeats. "Medusa is powerful, but it won't survive the shitstorm me being on the run will cause. As it is, you guys are going to have your hands full trying to pick up the pieces by having a serial killer in the family. I don't need to keep the wound open by being on the run. Plus," he adds, "none of you need the Feds breathing down your throats. We don't want Athena sharing a cell with me, and you and I both know that she's damn close to being there."

When I'm standing in nothing but my underwear, I finally say, "I had a feeling you'd say that. But I had to try." I point to him. "Get undressed, fucker. I'm cold."

"Fine," he says. "But we're going back to Seattle. I'm going to face this head on."

I sigh deeply and give a clipped nod. "I still have faith we'll figure a way out of this."

"I love you, brother," Ares says to me. It's uncharacteristic for him to be so...sensitive, but then again, his life's about to end.

"I love you." I point to the tie that he's ignoring. "You're a Godwin."

"What does that mean? Have you ever asked yourself that?" he asks as he does what I say and places my tie around his neck.

"I think you're about to show us."

"We need to head back to Seattle," Ares says, inhaling deeply. He's taking in the last of Heathens Hollow into his lungs.

I look to Olympus Manor as we slog through the mud to the chopper. "Do you want to go in and say goodbye?"

"I already did. Frankly, that house may be more of a prison than the one I'm going to."

CHAPTER

TWO

Daphne Godwin

I wish the red lipstick I wear, and the red nail polish of my manicure were laced with my enemies' blood. Maybe then I'd have the courage and self-confidence needed to face her. Warriors of tribes used to do that, and they'd come out victorious, but I doubt my outcome will be the same. I don't know how to intimidate. I don't know how to scare. I'm not a true Godwin, and it's clearer to me right now as I breathe deeply to calm my shaking hands.

Blood with menace does not run through my veins.

But it runs through Athena Godwin's, and as I enter her office at Medusa Enterprises, I'm very aware of that fact.

When my sister-in-law lifts her eyes from her laptop to stare at me, the look on her face is as if she smells shit. But then again, that's how she always looks at me. She examines me from head to toe, no doubt assessing if my designer clothes are fashionable enough, if the extra pounds I gained in the past months are concealed well enough, and if my appearance is worthy to enter Medusa as a Godwin, even if I only hold the name by marriage.

Athena and I could actually pass as blood sisters since we both have dark hair, even darker eyes, and our features are similar. Godwins have an exotic, mysterious, almost vampiric appearance. Every single one of them has eyes that haunt you, leave you silently begging for mercy as they captivate you as theirs. Their company name—Medusa Enterprises— is fitting since every member of the family can almost turn you into stone, incapable of moving from their clutch until they say you can.

Athena and I are both curvy and muscular. But I go to the gym to fit into the ballgowns and to burn calories I consumed at last night's party. She works out so she'll never need a man to kick someone's ass because she can always do it better. We may look the same, but nothing is similar between us. Athena possesses something I don't... Command.

I'm diamonds. She's daggers.

I attend banquets. She pays for them.

I sleep with the wolves. She howls at the moon right before she shreds her prey.

Athena is a goddess nobody wants to fuck with because she has the devil backing her bet.

She swipes at the corner of her mouth as if she just drank blood from someone's neck. "Last I checked, you weren't on my calendar for the day. Is there something I can help you with?"

"I know you're probably busy," I begin as I take a seat across from her. I'm trying my best to give off the confidence needed for me to be in this room.

Her eyes narrow. "I am."

Buzzing with regret for even coming, I know I have to continue on. No turning back. "I was hoping I could talk to you about something important."

"You couldn't have just texted me?" She looks over my shoulder through the glass windows of her office at her secretary. I didn't stop to ask permission to enter, and it's clear by the way Athena glares through the window that her secretary is in deep shit for not playing pit bull.

Knowing I'm running out of time, and Athena's patience will only last so long, I ask, "Have you spoken to Apollo at all?"

"Of course I speak with my brother. We run Medusa. We can't exactly do that without speaking." She releases an audibly loud sigh. "Can we just get to the point, please? I have a board meeting I need to prepare for."

"Our marriage is...miserable. For the both of us. And I was hoping you could help me. Speak with your father about allowing a divorce."

She smirks, closes her laptop, and leans back in her leather chair. "And you thought I'd help you, why?"

"If anyone can make Troy Godwin change his mind on anything, it's you."

Her smile remains, but there is a sinister darkness in her eyes. "You knew the rules when you spent an ungodly amount of Godwin money on a wedding dress, dry chicken, flowers, wedding photos with fake smiles, and champagne. Divorce is not an option. A Godwin will be a widow, but never sign divorce papers. You know this."

I nod. "I do. I did. But..." I take a deep breath. "We're not even friends anymore. We're enemies."

"Enemies can make the best lovers."

"Surely, you want to see your brother happy. He's not."

"Then make him happy."

"It's not that simple."

Athena rubs her temple as if my very presence is giving her a migraine. "It is. Suck his dick, spread your legs, continue going to those charity luncheons you attend, spend his money on expensive clothes and jewelry you'll only wear once, and shut the fuck up. Pretty damn simple if you ask me."

When I open my mouth to argue, she cuts me off.

"And before you spout words of love and romance to me," she begins, rolling her eyes, "know that you're speaking to the wrong person. I will not approach my father with anything regarding you, because I agree with the family dictate. When you said those vows, you agreed to be a Godwin until you're in your grave. It's our rules, and we didn't exactly hide those terms from you. So stop being a rich, spoiled wife who wants to run away with half of everything like the other rich bitches you lunch with."

"I don't want anything. I'll leave with the clothes on my back if it means—"

Athena stands, places her hands on her desk calmly, and says, "This conversation is over. Sorry you wasted your time coming downtown to discuss this with me. But if you don't mind—"

"Athena, please. Your family doesn't even like me. You didn't think I was good enough to marry your brother to begin with."

"No one is good enough to marry any of my brothers. But regardless, I approved of you because I knew a stray dog would always be loyal. And that's what you were. A stray dog from the Eastside of Heathens Hollow. So take the bone I'm giving you and leave my office. I won't tell my father, or *your husband,* that you came."

"Why are you such a bi—"

"Bitch?" she cuts in. "You bet your ass I'm a bitch. It's far better than being a victim like you."

"Fuck you," I hiss. "I'm not a victim."

She gives an evil grin. "No? You sure as hell are

acting like one sitting across from me, begging. You came from nothing. Less than nothing. You were nothing but an Eastsider living in a shack with your sister and piece of shit abusive father. You were just a poor kid with a constant black eye with fantasies of what you have now. You owe my brother everything you have. So I don't give a fuck if you're miserable or not. Maybe Apollo isn't the best husband. But one thing he has done for you is give you a life others would dream of. So stop being a goddamn baby and suck it up."

Athena can cut me to the core with her words alone. She has that wicked eloquence over all her opponents. And in her life, every single person she knows is her opponent. Athena doesn't have friends. Friends make you weak. She has enemies. Just not everyone knows that fact when they meet her. She's led by fire, and poisonous water courses through her veins, making her one of the most vicious and dangerous women I know. But she's powerful, and I had desperately hoped she'd use some of her ascendancy to help me.

How wrong I was.

I'm suffocating.

I'm fading.

But Athena will only stand there and watch me fall to my demise and simply consider it a good day's work.

"Are we done?" she asks. I can see her annoyance that I'm not picking up on the fact that this conversation was over before I even took the seat across from her.

There's a knock on her office door and her assistant peeks her head in. "Ms. Godwin... I have a call you need to take on hold."

Athena scowls at the poor woman. "I'm busy. I'll call them back."

"He says it's urgent," the woman pushes. I feel bad for the secretary because most likely she won't have a job by the end of the day for not instantly doing as Athena ordered.

"What part of 'I'm busy' do you not understand?"

The woman swallows but doesn't back down. "Ms. Godwin, you are going to want to take his call."

Athena's eyes narrow, but she reaches for the phone as the secretary scurries away. "Yes?"

Whoever is on the other line has accomplished the impossible. They've chiseled at Athena's stone exterior. It's a small chip, but I see it. Her eyelashes flutter, her lip quivers ever so slightly, and her breath hitches.

"Daphne's with me," she says, but her voice cracks. She takes a breath and adds, "We're on our way."

I tilt my head in question. After the conversation we just had, I have no intention of going anywhere with her.

She hangs up the phone and reaches for her purse. "There's been an accident. Ares and Apollo were flying to Seattle from Heathens Hollow. The helicopter went down near Whidbey Island."

I've heard the saying *my hearts stops* but never really knew what that meant until now. "Are they—"

"We need to get to the hospital."

THREE

Ares

Living like kings can come with a ransom. Every time we rode on that helicopter, we were rolling the dice. You can't soar with eagles, fly too close to the sun, and not have your wings eventually melt.

My eyelashes act as binds, preventing me from opening my eyes. Molten fire seems to ooze down my throat with every swallow. I hear beeping, machines humming, and distant voices I recognize and also ones I don't.

Someone squeezes my hand. "It's okay. Take your time. We're here."

Not caring if I rip every eyelash off, I pry my eyes open and see hazy images of people towering over me, around me, swarming me. I blink away the fog and notice my brother's wife sitting to my left, holding my hand.

Why is Daphne holding my hand?

"Give the man some goddamn space," I hear my father's voice command.

I see the hazy figures step back as if the seas are parting, but Daphne only squeezes my hand harder and remains in place. A bold move to go against an order of my father's.

"Where am I?" I somehow croak, realizing I'm laying in a bed and my body doesn't want to move. It's screaming at me as I try to sit, demanding I stay in place.

"You and your brother got into an accident," Daphne says, pushing against my chest so I have no choice but to lay back down and stop trying to fight the gravity that weighs heavier than normal. "The helicopter went down. You're in the hospital, but they say you're going to be just fine."

My vision is clearing enough that I can see the worry on her face as she rubs my arm with the free hand that isn't holding my other. I'm not sure why she's touching me in such a way, but I'm uncomfortable with it. She's my brother's wife, and this feels more than just how a sister-in-law would comfort her family member. When I pull my hand free from hers, I see a flicker of...pain? She places her hands into her lap, looks down at her feet, scoots her chair back, does what my father first asked, and gives me some space.

My father approaches the bed. "You're lucky to be alive, son."

I suppose I am alive, even though my body still questions that fact. Everything fucking hurts.

"The helicopter crashed?" I ask, not being able to remember it doing so.

"It looks like you flew into some weather coming back from the island," my father says.

I blink the last of the fog away and scan the room. Athena is leaning against the wall, appearing cool and collected, but I know my sister. The dark circles under her eyes, and the way she chews her bottom lip, tells me she's been worried; maybe still is. The nurse is checking the machines, and writing something down on a clipboard, and the doctor has just left the room as I only see his back before the door closes.

"Where's my brother?"

No one answers, but they all dart their eyes from one another. Apollo was in the chopper with me. If it went down, then he did too.

"He didn't make it," my father finally says, not even pausing to ease into the icy cold water of truth.

Daphne scoots her chair back to my side and touches my arm as she says in a much softer tone than my father, "He died in the accident."

Oh, Jesus... That explains the pain in Daphne's eyes. The reason she's touching me for comfort. She just lost her husband—

My brother...

My brother...

Oh god no. Apollo? This can't be—

No.

I try to sit up to hunt him down and prove this is all a mistake, but the tidal wave of shock and grief is paralyzing me. My heart breaks into a million pieces, and I can't even fall apart and cry since everyone is staring at me. Everyone is watching my every fucking move. Godwins don't cry. We only show one emotion —rage.

This is all a mistake. This is me being drugged. I'm hearing this wrong. I'm hallucinating. I'm in purgatory between hell and heaven, and this is somehow a test. This is wrong. Wrong!

"Prepare for a crash landing," the pilot shouts over his shoulder at us.

Apollo looks out the window at the water below and then back at me. I don't see fear. I see acceptance.

"Fuck," I say, scanning the area for land that doesn't exist. The helicopter is going to crash on water. It's going to hit and sink and we're going to fucking die.

Apollo reaches out and takes my hand. He gives a knowing nod and squeezes. "See you on the other side, brother."

My body shakes as the memory of the helicopter crash starts coming back to me. My father bends down, his face close enough that I clearly see his eyes. "*Ares* died, but you survived. There's a reason, son. Ares is no longer with us, but *you* are."

I don't know if it's the ringing in my ears or the pounding of my heart. But his words aren't making sense. Did he just say *Ares* is dead?

I'm here.

Or at least I think I'm here.

I'm not dead.

I wiggle my toes, and I inhale deeply just to prove to myself that I am indeed laying in this hospital bed.

"Both Ares and the pilot didn't make it. The rescuers pulled both of their bodies from the wreckage shortly after your rescue. You somehow got free and floated long enough for help to arrive," my father continues.

"I don't understand," I begin.

Daphne takes my hand again. "You have some minor injuries. Some cuts and bruises. You do have a head wound, and you've been unconscious for a few days. The doctors were hopeful you'd wake up, but they said confusion and memory loss could be a side effect. So, it's okay to feel this way."

Confused? Memory loss? This has nothing to do with my head injury. My fucking father is telling me I'm dead when I'm alive. They're telling me my brother is dead but—

"Apollo?" my father says. "Did you hear Daphne? You're going to struggle with memories. You may have some confusion. But you came out of this alive."

"My brother—"

My father pats my arm, an unusual sign of affection. "He's dead, son. He didn't make it. Ares is dead."

Athena, who hasn't said a word since I woke up, turns on her heels and goes to leave the room. "I'm going to have the doctor come back and take a look at him." She doesn't wait for anyone to say anything and leaves.

"Daphne," my father says, "make sure Athena doesn't tear down the nurses' station or hurricane her way around out there. I'd like a moment with my son."

Daphne, with tears in her eyes, stands from her chair and does what he asks without argument.

When the door closes, my father turns his attention on me. "I know you're feeling a lot of different emotions right now."

"I'm not Apollo." I rasp the words out, knowing this news has to come as a shock to my father. He thought one son survived the crash, and the other died. He got it wrong. It's backwards. "I'm Ares."

"No, you are Apollo," he says firmly.

When I go to shake my head, he cuts me off.

"You listen to me. I will not lose one son to death and the other to prison. So you are going to grieve your brother however you choose, but then accept the fact that you are now him. You are not Ares anymore. You are Apollo."

"What the fuck are you talking about?" My head

spins, and I suddenly want to go back into the coma I was in.

"Everyone—including the authorities—believes Ares died in that crash. They believe you died, and your brother lived. I don't know why you were wearing his clothing, or why you had his identification on you, but you did. So as of right now, everyone believes that the man who was going to spend the rest of his life in jail is now dead. But Apollo, the strait-laced, good Godwin son, somehow survived. *You* are now that son."

"They all think I died? Everyone?"

He takes a calming breath. My father doesn't like to repeat himself, and he has zero patience for anyone, but he is once again acting uncharacteristic and repeats, "Focus on what I'm saying. You and I are the only ones who know Apollo was the one who died. But the world believes Ares died. We will not allow Apollo to die in vain. If we can use his name and identity, then we will."

I close my eyes, take a deep breath, and try to shake off the drugs, or the brain damage, or whatever is making my father's words seem unreal.

"When they brought you in to the hospital, you were in your brother's clothes. You had his wallet and passport. There was no reason for anyone to think you weren't Apollo. And at first, I even believed you were him until I noticed your pinky finger."

My eyes open and lower to my crooked pinky on my left hand that resulted from an injury as a child that never healed properly. I had broken my finger playing rough with my brother and my father had told me to man up rather than letting me splint it or set the bone back into place. So, it was the only part of me that was slightly different than Apollo. It would take a father's eye to notice. Not to mention the fact no one can pull anything over on Troy Godwin for long.

My father continues with, "There was no reason for me to correct anyone on the assumption that you weren't Apollo. Why? What good would that do? They'd only let you recover long enough to send you to prison for the rest of your life. But," he gives me a wicked grin, "if you rise from the ashes like a motherfucking phoenix and become Apollo, then you are a free man forever."

Grief from losing his favorite son must have made him lose his goddamn mind. "I can't just be... my brother."

"You can. You will. There is no other choice unless you want them to come into this room and handcuff you to the bed."

"I feel like I'm going to puke," I say, closing my eyes, not being able to process his words.

"It's a lot. But you and I both know that Apollo would want you to do this. He wouldn't want you to go to jail for...for what *he* did."

"I can't do this. It's so fucked up." I've never gone against an order of my father's. When he says jump,

I've only strived to jump the highest of them all. But this request... "This can't be real."

I open my eyes as my father leans even closer to me. "Your sister and *your wife* are about to come in here. You are going to morph into this new identity. You are going to be reborn, son. This is your second chance at life, and you sure as fuck will not turn it down because you suddenly have morals."

"You want me to lie to everyone? To lie to our family?" I pause and think about the poor woman who was holding my hand, thinking I was Apollo. "You want me to have Daphne believe I'm her dead husband?"

His eyes and the firmness in his jaw answers this question for me. "You know your brother better than anyone. You can do this. And you always have the head injury to fall back on if you come across a situation you don't know how to handle or get asked a question you aren't sure how to answer. You'll fake amnesia if it means you're no longer going to prison."

His words are sinking in. "You want me to go to his house, his bed—Jesus fucking Christ. He has a wife. Am I supposed to just—"

"Fuck her. Yes. Their marriage is shit, by the way," my father interrupts. "So fix that. You are going to need Daphne by your side to help you with this ruse. And besides... Godwins don't divorce."

"This is insanity."

My father stands to full attention. His shoulders

are back; his spine is stiff. "From this moment on, you are Apollo Godwin. Ares is dead. The name Ares is dead, and I will never call you by that name again. You will not respond to that name ever. Apollo," he dictates. "Apollo Godwin."

He's serious. This is serious. My father wants me to become my twin brother. He wants me to embrace this mistaken identity. He feels this is my only choice unless I want to be locked in a cage forever.

And fuck me... He's right.

CHAPTER

FOUR

Daphne

"Sorry, sorry," I say to Apollo as I drive over another speed bump in our gated community too fast, causing the car to jolt more than I intended.

I don't know why I'm treating him as if he's fragile and can break any second. Every bump we hit on the road has me apologizing and glancing over to see if I caused a grimace or if I added to his pain level in any way. When the doctor released him from the hospital, I was relieved but also worried that I wouldn't know what to do or how to care for him. The doctor gave him orders to take it easy and allow his wife to "love on him." Ha. Like that would happen. Clearly, the doctor doesn't know who Apollo Godwin is, and that he doesn't *allow* anyone to do anything for him. But I was still willing and eager to do whatever the doctor said. The man nearly died, was in a coma, lost his brother, and now he gets to come home as if nothing happened and he was in tiptop shape.

But how could that be? How could he walk away with a few wounds and a gash to the head while his brother and the pilot died? Apollo should have died. Any mortal would have. But then again... He is a god among men, and maybe Zeus himself has kept him on earth with us mere mortals for some reason yet unknown.

As we pull up in the driveway and I park, I rush over to Apollo's side so I can assist him out of the car. Although not a patient man, he's beaten me to it and is already out. I don't know if I should offer my arm or—Apollo marches toward me and swoops me into his arms, cradling me against his chest.

"What are you doing?" I squeal, not resisting in fear that I'll hurt him. "Apollo!"

"I'm showing you I'm not a piece of fine china. A few cuts and bruises are not something to worry about."

He carries me to the house and pauses before the front door. "Keys."

Feeling as if I weigh a thousand pounds, I quickly fumble with my purse, find the keys, and open the door, all while he holds me against his chest. He then turns the handle and kicks the door the rest of the way open. Acting as if I weigh nothing, and not even winded in the slightest, he then walks across the threshold with me still in his arms as a groom would do to his bride on their wedding day. Something he never did on that day, however, so this act is even more alarming.

"Put me down before you hurt yourself!" I hold on to his neck as if that will help lighten my weight. He turns on the light in the foyer as if what he's doing is completely normal. "You've lost your mind."

"That may be," he says as he continues toward the kitchen. "But my head is the only thing that may not be one hundred percent. My body is fine. I'm fine. So stop acting like I'm not." His eyes lower to mine and he adds, "Got it? Stop treating me like I'm weak. I'm not."

Wiggling in his hold for the first time, I agree. "Yes. Now put me down."

He places me on my feet by the kitchen island and looks around the space as if it's the first time he's seen it.

"I bet it feels good to be home," I say.

"It feels odd."

"For me too," I admit. "I only came home to shower and change clothes, and then I went straight back to the hospital." I look around the kitchen like he is doing. "Funny what a few days away can do."

He turns to me and arches an eyebrow. "You stayed at the hospital the entire time?"

"Yes." Regardless of how our marriage is, the thought of losing him was— "I'm still your wife."

"Right. You are still my wife." He pauses. Studies

my face. Then adds, "Thank you. For being with me at the hospital."

Apollo has never thanked me for anything before, and the foreign words feel...nice.

"The doctor said you may have some headaches, possible memory loss, heightened emotions, and maybe even some depression."

He tilts his chin and then nods. "Things are a little foggy. I don't really remember the accident. I don't remember a lot. Maybe I blocked it out for a reason."

I wonder what were the thoughts he had while crashing to the sea. Did he think he'd die and never see the inside of the house again? Did he think his life was over and everything flashed before his eyes? Was I in his last-minute visions? Did he see me at all?

He runs his fingers along the white marble countertop. "My brother never came to the house. He never was inside." Though Apollo is speaking the words, it doesn't feel as if he's saying them to me.

"You both spent your time at Medusa or Olympus Manor," I say, not sure why I'm even speaking. He knows this, so why I feel the need to say it is just...odd. I feel so awkward and out of place that my mouth just moves without me thinking it through. I walk to the refrigerator. "Do you want something to eat?"

He's still glancing around the room, examining.

"I let the housekeeper have some days off since we were both in the hospital. I didn't see the point for her to keep coming." I'm nervous now that he's maybe seeing dust and finding the condition of the house unsatisfactory. "I'll have her come first thing tomorrow morning." I open the refrigerator and see that it's mostly empty. I now feel as if I'm a complete failure as a wife. This isn't the homecoming I was hoping to give him.

"I'm not hungry," he says, throwing me a lifeline.

"I'll try to get to the store after the funeral tomorrow. If there is anything you want—"

"The funeral is tomorrow? My brother's?"

"I thought your father told you." Apollo's stiffening and the widening of his eyes tell me how wrong I am in thinking that. "Troy didn't want to have the funeral until you were out of the hospital. He wanted you to be there."

I shift from one foot to the other, waiting for him to say something. Anything. I feel as if I just revealed some secret I wasn't supposed to.

"Athena handled all the arrangements," I continue. I can't stand the silence in the room and decide to fill it with chatter. "All we have to do is arrive. And if it becomes too much for you, or you don't want to go—"

"Of course I want to go," he says a little too quickly and harshly. He takes a seat at the counter, pauses for several moments, and then adds, "Sorry, I didn't mean to snap."

"I can only imagine what you're going through." I want to reach out and take his hand to offer comfort, but I'm not sure how he'll take the unfamiliar act. It's what a wife would do, but Apollo and I aren't exactly the normal definition of wedded bliss. "It's late. Maybe we should get some sleep. The doctor said you need to take it easy."

Leaning on his elbows, he locks his eyes with mine. "Do I need to carry you up the stairs too?" He smiles, letting me know his comment is in jest. "No more talk of what the doctor said. I'm fine. I need you to believe that."

"Got it," I say, rolling my eyes. "The mighty Apollo has spoken," I tease. I head toward the stairs, with him following behind. "You may not need sleep, but I do. My body is stiff from all the nights in that chair beside your bed."

When we reach the landing upstairs, I turn to head to the primary bedroom, surprised when Apollo follows me and doesn't head to the guest room where he's been sleeping for the past months. "Is there something you need in the room?" I ask, stopping and turning to face him.

His head flinches back slightly. "To sleep..."

My eyes dart over his shoulder toward the guest room. "Okay...but..."

He follows my stare and glances over his shoulder. He then looks back at me but says nothing.

"Do you not remember that you moved into the guest room a few months ago?" I ask, surprised that this is something he'd forget or that would be washed from his memory because of the accident.

"I...remember," he says. "But you and I are married, and that's not how married people act. We won't be sleeping in different rooms." He moves past me and enters my bedroom—our bedroom—without waiting for me to argue.

My slight hesitation to follow him into the room is just the time he needed for him to shed his clothes. He's lifting his shirt above his head, revealing his six-pack abs I used to love so much. There's bruising around his rib cage, and a few bandages, and regardless of how he's claiming he's fine, I doubt he is completely pain free.

As he unfastens his pants, he looks at the bed. "Did you change the side of the bed you sleep on while I was in the other room, or is that still the same?"

I point to the left side. "Still my side." Feeling uncomfortable that he's now wearing nothing but his underwear, I say, "I'll get your pajamas from the other room."

I quickly leave, not sure why I feel so... uncomfortable. It's been a long time since I've seen him without clothes on and an even longer time since feeling any kind of desire because of it. But tonight...is it desire I'm feeling?

Grabbing gray satin pajamas I once got him for Christmas, I head back to the room with my mind and emotions spinning. There's a reason he moved to the guest room. There was a reason we no longer slept together. Nothing has changed, or has it? Did a near death experience change a failing marriage? Is it as simple as that?

When I hand him the pajamas, he looks down at them and chuckles. "Okay..."

"You told me you liked them when I bought them for you," I say, feeling as if I'm just now being let in on a secret that he actually hated them.

His eyes lift to mine as he stops laughing immediately. "I like them. I do." He then dresses, and for some odd reason, appears completely awkward and out of place wearing them. "I was just laughing as I remembered what they had me wear in the hospital."

I watch him climb into his side of the bed and wonder if I should be the one to head to the guest room. But I'm exhausted, and I'm sure he is as well. I don't feel we need to have some long, drawn-out marriage talk tonight. Clearly something is different, and I don't think he, nor I, have the energy to approach the topic of where we go from here. Heading to the bathroom to get ready for bed, I do everything I can to get the image of Apollo's body out of my mind.

FIVE

Daphne

I can't sleep. I hear Apollo's breathing, and what used to be a calming sound to me when we first wed, is now causing a sort of electric currant to flow through me. I feel his heat, even though we aren't touching. I feel a sense of closeness, even though we haven't connected at all.

Or have we?

He touched me tonight for the first time in...ages.

He held me. He carried me. His eyes looked into mine.

But more importantly, he spoke with me. We had a real conversation in the kitchen. Yes, it was awkward, but we at least spoke. And he made a dictate we'd no longer sleep in separate rooms. It was a command I wasn't prepared for but one I wasn't going to protest.

I was grateful he was already asleep when I came out of the bathroom once I was ready for bed.

Or was I?

Was there a part of me that was disappointed he wasn't laying there waiting? Waiting for his wife.

Maybe…

So many conflicting thoughts and feelings running through me, but one thing is for certain—I can't stay in this bed any longer. I need a moment to myself. I need to—

I climb out of bed as gently as I can so I don't wake him and tiptoe my way out of the room and head down to the living room. Flipping on the gas fireplace to heat the chilly room, I sit on the couch and stare into the flames. It feels like a lifetime ago when Apollo and I got married. He had promised me the world. He had sworn to protect me and give me anything my heart desired. He had offered me a life of a princess on a golden platter, and I was so desperate to take it. He was a Godwin, and growing up on Heathens Hollow, I knew exactly who they were and what that meant. The family not only owned Medusa Enterprises, but they owned the entire island I lived on. Poseidon Shipping provided the majority of employment to the people of the island, and though that division of Medusa was run by Leander Godwin—Troy's brother— and his daughters, I most definitely knew the name Apollo Godwin.

And just when I thought I didn't want anything to do with the Godwins again, and had started to plan my exit strategy, the accident happened. I saw a family dynasty nearly fall. The powerful Troy Godwin had pain in his eyes and tears threatening to escape as he said goodbye to one son while hoping the other fought to survive. When I once wanted nothing to do with Apollo, I suddenly couldn't leave his side. He was my husband. I took vows. I made a promise in front of everyone. The Godwins were correct in their belief that divorce wasn't an option.

I was wrong in wanting out. I was wrong in so many ways.

Did I love Apollo? Do I love him now? No...I don't think so. But he was the first man I ever had sex with. He was the first man to care about me and to offer protection. He saved me. So, maybe the problem was me. I needed to learn to love him. And as I sat beside him in that hospital, holding his hand in mine, I swore I'd try. I'd try to love this man who has done nothing more than offer to share his power with me.

Athena had told me to spread my legs and all would be fine, and when I watched Apollo undress tonight...well, it didn't sound like such a bad idea. My body still buzzed from the thought of what we could do if only exhaustion and tense reconnection didn't get in the way.

My body is *still* aflame, and there is no way I'm

going to be able to return to bed feeling this way unless...

I take the hem of my nightgown and lift it up above my hips. I then lower my panties to my feet and kick them out of the way. I feel the heat of the fire against my bare flesh, and I bring my finger to my clit and slowly circle. Closing my eyes and picturing Apollo being the one to touch me rather than me, I moan as my body thanks me for finally giving it the pleasure it's been craving.

"Daphne..."

My heart flips as I look over my shoulder to see Apollo approaching the couch lit up by the fire.

"Have you come yet?"

"What? No...I uh..." I pull down my night gown as fast as I can, standing up and walking toward the fireplace as if it's heat can protect me from the cold splash of water Apollo's entrance just caused. My face has never felt so hot. Mortification nearly suffocates me. I feel as if the flames from the fire are licking my body.

"That's a shame." He sits down on the couch and pats the seat next to him.

"What are you doing?" I ask, feeling butterflies flap around in my tummy. I don't understand why he won't simply walk away and allow me to die in my embarrassment.

"Come over here and let me show you how it's done."

"What? Apollo...*what?*" Did he just imply what I

think he did? No way could I have heard him correctly, and yet his serious face, the casual way he sits on the couch with a seductive smirk, tells me I heard him correctly.

"Lift that nightie back up, come spread your thighs, and let's finish what you started. You'll come this time," he says in a calm and even tone.

Although my thoughts and emotions are swirling in chaos, the man has full control of his, and though he caught me in the most private and compromising position, he's not teasing me. There is no jest in his words. He appears completely at ease but also determined to do as he's saying. He even appears dignified and nearly regal, sitting on the chair with his intent to perform his *husbandly duties*.

I try my best to seem calm. This is complete madness, and yet I'm not running out of the living room. I'm not saying no. Do I actually want him to do as he's suggesting? I literally can't remember the last time he ever has. We've never been that couple. We don't...well, we just aren't like this.

He pats the couch again. "Now, Daphne."

"It's fine. We really should get to bed. You're still recovering, and we have the funeral tomorrow. I don't know what got into me." I let out a forced laugh. "It's been a long time, and I was trying to relieve some stress and—"

"Now."

My heart beats so loudly in my ears, I'm sure he

has to hear it as well. "You don't need to show me how—"

"If I have to get up and drag you over here, you will regret it. Now get over here and spread those legs."

Jesus, the man is serious. Dead serious. And even though his threat sounds aggressive in the wording —and completely unlike him—his tone remains calm and firm.

Not sure what else to do, as nothing I'm saying to defuse the situation is working, I stand up and take the first step toward him. Have I gone insane? Am I really walking toward Apollo so he can finish what I started? Did he just want me to lie there and...come? I can't remember a time we'd ever done anything sexual if it wasn't in the bedroom. The light cast from the fire is bright. He'll be able to see everything if I truly spread my thighs like he's commanding. The darkness from our room won't conceal me from his view. Am I seriously even considering this? I could simply say no. It's not like we've had sex in what feels like forever. Months... Maybe even a year.

But I continue on. With each step I take, my resistance seems to dissolve, and I am morphing into...willing... Or maybe just accepting of what my body desires. My body wants to come. Or maybe it's that the embarrassment and shame of this entire situation is just too much, and I simply want it over with.

I stand before him, eyes cast down, praying he

will direct me on exactly what he wants me to do next, because there is no way I will be able to even guess.

"Lift your nightgown and bare yourself. I want to see," he commands so easily.

Does he not find his words, and what he's asking me to do out of the ordinary? He seems so cool and casual, and acts as if this is just an everyday occurrence for us. Maybe for many lovers, but definitely not for us.

Attempting to drum up the nerve to pull up my nightgown, I peek up and make eye contact. With our eyes connected, I feel the thundering beat of my heart, a tingle between my legs, and a bizarre nervous desire rocking my body. With one powerful expression that tells me he is losing his patience and I better act fast, he gives me the courage to surrender to his request. When I pull up the hem to my belly, I shudder as the warm air from the roaring fire in the room touches my ass that my lack of panties doesn't prevent.

I'm bare. Exposed.

He stares at my nightgown. His eyes seem to darken as he takes in every lacy inch. "Remove it completely."

I pause, not sure I have the inner strength to do as he asks. He hasn't seen my body exposed fully in bright light since...well, I don't know when the last time was. Insecurity of my body takes over, and I'm not sure I'm willing to be nude completely.

"Apollo," I begin.

"I'm your husband. You're my wife. I want you naked." He glances at my bare pussy. "I want to appreciate all of you."

The way he says the words has jolts of electricity sizzling through my veins. The sane and reasonable part of me wants to scream no and storm out of the room. Yes, we are married, but we're estranged. And even if we weren't, why is Apollo acting so out of character? I should leave, but the sinful and wicked part of me wants to do exactly what he commands without hesitation.

My mind and body are at war, and I'm not sure which one I want to win, and which one will be defeated.

"If I have to do it for you," he says, breaking my internal dialogue, "I might just have to spank that naughty ass of yours before I lick every inch of that body."

Spank? Lick? Is this man for real? Oh my God, this is for real.

My mind might scream no, but my body does exactly as he asks, and I remove the nightgown, standing nude before him.

CHAPTER
SIX

Daphne

"I like that your pussy is bare," he says as his eyes seem to darken right before me. Even though he's staring at the most intimate part of my body, I don't feel threatened or afraid.

Humiliated, yes.

Ashamed, most definitely.

Nervous, without a doubt.

But never do I truly fear this man.

"You know I do. I haven't changed that." Has it really been that long since he's last touched me, that he doesn't remember that I remove any trace of hair almost obsessively?

I can feel the heat of his stare on my bare pussy, but I don't conceal myself. I stand and await his next command.

"Good." His eyes look back into mine. "Sit down and spread your legs," he directs, his voice husky.

Suffocated by the fear of the unknown, I do exactly as he asks with no hesitation, though missing the way he hungrily gazes at my body. Spreading my legs, I lower my head to see his face now that he's kneeling between my thighs. The strong features, the firm air, the sensitive but unyielding eyes.

He places his palms on my legs and spreads me even wider as heat ripples over my body in waves, leaving me breathless. "Apollo," I whisper. "I—"

Further words are lost as he lowers his mouth and kisses the top of my mound. The unexpected intimacy makes me want to beg him to stop, yet also leaves me oddly craving more. Every time he exhales on my bare skin, it reminds me of how foreign this sensation is, and yet I can't help but like the fact that Apollo is actually touching me. His hands are on my nude skin, and the thrill of that knowledge almost makes the embarrassment of being in this vulnerable position in the fire's light disappear.

Almost.

I'm not sure if it's the fact he spreads my thighs even further apart as he licks from the top of my pussy all the way to my ass, but my face feels as if it's boiling beneath the surface.

Apollo continues to lick and kiss every inch of my heated sex. My face roasts even more when he uses his fingers to spread my pussy lips so he can lick that neglected skin as well. The man is being thorough.

The hardest part of this situation is the unknown. I don't know how long this will last and if I should really allow the orgasm to come or if I should fake it like I've done before. I don't know what I am supposed to be doing, and I don't know what's going through Apollo's mind. Does he like what he's doing to me? Does he like what he sees... my bare pussy writhing against his face as I purse my lips together to try not to cry out?

It feels good. Too good. I'm not sure if I should make my feelings known, but I'm not sure I can hide them either.

After a few more licks and kisses to an area of flesh where my thighs meet my pussy, he asks, "New rule in our marriage. If you want to come, then I'm the one to make it happen."

I shake my head, not liking the fact that he's trying to set a rule in a marriage that is nothing but a long list of Godwin rules. But when I get a finger shoved in my pussy in response, I practically howl, "Okay! I won't try to make myself come again by myself."

"You will ask for my help."

"Yes." Though I still am not sure I actually mean the words. But I don't want to risk him getting angry and stopping. Not when I'm so close. So close...

Apollo continues finger fucking me as his tongue swirls around my clit. My skin burns in want, and sweat beads on my upper lip as my body continues to gyrate on his steady and perfect mouth. Moaning, gasping, whimpering, I close my eyes and give myself up to the moment...to Apollo and his perfect dominance. He's demanding to please me, and I love it. I have no other choice but to release all my thoughts, my worries, and my resistance. My body submits to his tantalizing control over me.

"You're fucking beautiful," he whispers. "This is the sexiest pussy I've ever seen."

Yes, this is what I need. After all this time, this is what I crave without even knowing it. Not just an orgasm, but an orgasm given by Apollo. Somehow, this all seems right. So right, when I had given up hope I'd ever feel this way again.

He pauses a moment, rubbing his hand along my heated flesh. Dipping his finger down the crease of my butt, he presses past the cheeks of my ass and rests his finger on the entrance of my tight hole, teasing me with the mystery of what's coming.

Maybe I should stop him, or at the very least tense up, but I don't. I don't scream no, though I should. I don't shoot up off the couch, though the woman even a day ago would have. I don't curse him out in outrage, though I'd never allow this before. By licking my pussy, had he sucked all the resistance out of my body? Has he fingered me into complete submission? Or am I so desperate for any touch by this man that even his finger in my ass is welcome?

Slight pressure is added, but not enough to break past the puckered flesh and enter me fully. Slowly, he returns his finger to my silky folds, pulsing with desire. I can't hide the fact that I'm dripping wet, and there is no hiding my hunger from Apollo, who now spreads the signs around my bare skin.

A deep moan rumbles in his chest and escapes as he thrusts his finger, followed by a second, into my hungry sex. I buck against his hand, mewling in pleasure. Lightheaded and panting with the need for more, I do everything I can not to beg to be fucked right then and there. The fingers aren't enough. I need his cock buried inside of me. I need it thick, long, and hard, and I have no shame in admitting that fact.

"You have such a tight pussy," he praises.

His two fingers are soon followed by a third, as he pumps in and out of me, demanding my passion. Crying out as he stretches me wide, I know it's required so I can comfortably take the size of his dick. It's his silent way of warning me of what's coming. It's as if I can read his sinful and dirty thoughts.

It's been so long since we've last had sex that he's preparing my born-again virgin pussy to accept him.

With my thighs spread wide, I can do nothing more than allow the climax to build. And when he removes his slick fingers and presses one into my anus without warning, the orgasm rocks my body at an intensity that has me screaming out. Submission explodes through my body like the crack of a leather whip. Moaning, I press against his hand, driving his finger deeper into my forbidden channel, his touch entrenched within me as I melt against him. I like his finger inside of my ass and have no shame in admitting that I do.

Why have we never done this before?

It's so fucking good.

We should have done this before.

With one hand buried in the taboo place, he places the palm of his other hand on my still needy pussy, continuing on with the finger fucking. One, two, three. I finally free my mind and allow another orgasm to build. My breath catches in my throat as I hold back a cry of erotic yearning and years of need. I can't focus, lost in a haze of ecstasy. Pleasure and a biting pain from the stretch weave themselves together, escalating until I cry out my husband's name.

"Apollo, Apollo..."

He cups his hand over my pussy, using it to adjust my body until I am tucked snugly into his arms. Unconsciously, I nuzzle my face against the warmth of his neck, and my body melts against him. The feelings, the emotions... Nothing can describe them other than being safe and cherished.

He has handled me his way, and I have allowed it. What I didn't expect is this aftermath. I didn't expect to enjoy his warm and soothing touch after the orgasm. We've never been the cuddle type. But that's exactly what we're doing now.

He slips his hand around my waist, lowering me to the rug-covered floor below. Fingers laced, thighs rubbing against thighs, my breasts mold into his torso, the clothing between us begging to be ripped off. Not wasting another moment, Apollo frees his hard cock from its restraints. He kneels before my face and places his thick shaft to my lips. I look up and into his eyes.

No words needed to be said.

I open up my mouth and allow his cock to lie against my tongue. My instinct is to pleasure him. Nothing impedes how badly I want to make him groan out my name. Watching bliss blanket his face fills me with a purpose I did not know existed, and I wonder why this is the first time I experienced this sensation in my lifetime.

As I hungrily suck his ready dick, I fully submit to a man who demands it. Up and down, I move my mouth until I am rewarded by my name escaping his lips in the most passionate of ways. My name never sounded as good as it does the moment it slips from his mouth.

I add my hand and pump his cock while licking all around it. His body shakes and tenses, and he pulls me away as he takes a deep breath.

"We didn't kiss before we went to bed. A husband and wife should kiss every day. Every night," he says, his gaze dipping to my mouth. "It's another new rule. I don't want it broken."

Reflexively, I moisten my lips, slipping my tongue

across my mouth, waiting for his to make contact. Slowly, we kiss, soft, romantic, and pure. He slides his hand to my pussy, driving my thirst for sex to a whole new level. I'm driven to the edge, wanting desperately to beg him for more.

"Please, Apollo. I need you."

I guide my hands up under his shirt, releasing a long sigh when they run along the defined muscles of his body. The mature years of his life have been good to him, very, very good. He's always had the most amazing body. Knowing he's still bruised and battered from the accident, I'm careful as I softly caress him, avoiding the bandages that remain.

While my fingers go to work releasing the buttons of his nightshirt, he nibbles on my ear, my neck, driving my need even higher. In a hungered blur, I pull off clothing that gets in the way, followed by him doing the same.

Apollo cups my face and plants a slow, deep kiss on my lips. His mouth blazes a path from my mouth back to the side of my neck. I let a sensual moan escape my lips, hoping to encourage him to keep going.

Skimming my fingers down his rippled stomach, I touch the head of his hard cock. "I want this. Now," I command.

He pauses for a moment, gazing over my nude body as he does. "My God, Daphne. You're more beautiful than I imagined a woman could ever be."

Simply looking at his hard, thick erection brings

on the beginning of an orgasm again by sight alone as I continue to stroke the tip with my fingertips. The mere thought of what's coming almost drives me over the edge.

He leans forward, takes hold of my hips, and pulls me closer to him. Kiss by kiss, he lowers himself down until his face is inches from my sex.

"I could feast off this pussy all night." He doesn't wait for permission, but kisses my pussy, followed by licking my throbbing clit.

I tense at the intimate and tantalizing touch. Part of me wants to stop so we can just skip ahead to the fucking part of the night, and the other part wants the feeling to never end. He swirls his tongue in circles, lapping up every sign of my arousal. I moan with complete abandon. My body seems possessed by Satan himself. I have absolutely no power against him. Lick after lick, Apollo brings my body to another level. Just when I believe I can take no more, he thrusts his finger past the lips of my pussy. In and out he plunges, pulling gasps and moans from me.

I need more. So much more, and luckily Apollo doesn't make me wait long. I gasp at the sensation of his cock finally pressing against me.

Closing my eyes in ecstasy, I dig my fingers into his shoulders as he presses beyond the tightness, entering me completely. The delicious sting is quickly replaced with an erotic pleasure that captures my breath.

He continues to place gentle kisses all over my

neck and face while his thick shaft probes deeper within. The contrast of soft and hard pushes me toward that familiar edge. Sparks, electricity, pure animalistic need washes over me, drowning me in pleasure as we both rock each other into completion.

CHAPTER
SEVEN

Apollo

Daphne's breathing hard as she whispers, "That was different. So different."

"How so?" Warning bells are going off in my head. I don't want her to catch on that I'm Ares, and getting this close and this intimate is a sure way of making that happen.

"You've never been so...demanding. So... determined." She moves her face away from my neck so she can look me in the eye. "We've been so cold lately. Distant. I'm surprised by what happened. I didn't think you and I were...compatible."

Fuck.

What the hell just happened? Clearly, I crossed a line. I acted in a way very unlike Apollo.

I don't know how to be a husband. Husbands and

wives sleep in the same bed, so I made that happen even though it almost gave me away. Husbands and wives fuck, but now I'm second guessing that. I even put on pajamas when no self-respecting man would wear satin pjs and still have his own balls attached. My father's idea, and his demand for me to make this happen, was starting to seem an impossibility. Me trying to be a husband is not working, and I'm not sure I can pull this off. I've never even been in a long-term relationship before. I haven't lived with a woman, and I sure as fuck haven't gone to bed with one unless we had fucked ourselves into oblivion.

I still lay on top of Daphne as we both regain our normal breathing, the bulk of my body crushing her tiny frame as the weight of the world crushes against me. This wasn't planned. This wasn't what's supposed to happen. She's my brother's wife. Not mine.

Was my brother's wife.

Was.

Yes, we have to remain married. I need to be a husband when I don't even know what the fuck that means. I know I need her in my life to keep this ruse alive, but boundaries have to be set. I owe it to my brother. I do. I had no intentions of fucking her and actually enjoying it. That muddies the waters. That turns them pitch fucking black.

Did I just betray my brother while he's not even in his grave yet?

Rolling off of her, I stand up and quickly dress in these ridiculous pajamas again. I don't want to look at Daphne lying on my brother's living room floor, no doubt looking sexier than she ever has to me before. So. Fucking. Hot. And she tasted so damn good. I'd be lying if I tried to deny the worst, fucking filthiest truth...

The woman does something to me, and as my cock twitches again for round two, I reach for her nightgown and toss it to her, still avoiding looking at her again.

There is a hard truth about what just happened.

I took Daphne against her will.

She did not consent.

She did not willingly and consensually have sex with me...Ares.

She called out my brother's name as we fucked. Not mine.

I've killed, tortured, lied, and stolen in my lifetime. I've never claimed to be a good man. But nothing has ever been worse than what I've done to her just now, and what I'm most likely going to do again. Because one thing is for sure...there's something about this woman that makes me want to sin.

"I'm sorry if things got carried away," I say, though there is a sick truth I'm struggling with. I loved every damn moment of what just happened. Wrong or not, I took her, and I want to take her again, and again, and again.

But for now, I need to resist. I need to allow the obsession to ease so I can think clearly.

"Don't apologize. I liked it," she says as she holds the nightgown against her chest, not getting dressed yet. "I didn't mean to make you think otherwise when I said 'demanding' or whatever."

I decide to take a risk by bringing up the past, when I know nothing for sure. "I'm aware we've been distant. I know we've both needed space." I hope these are words that Apollo would say.

In the corner of my eye, I see her fiddling with her nightgown with a facial expression I can't read. I'm sure there are a million things running through her head. They sure as hell are running through mine. Deciding to man up and stop being such a fucking coward by not looking at her and not giving her the respect of my full attention, I put out my hand to help her stand. Still clutching her gown to cover her breasts—her delicious and luscious breasts —she takes my hand and allows me to assist her off the floor.

Her big brown eyes meet mine. So wide. So innocent. So full of questions. Questions I don't have answers for. It isn't hard to see that Daphne is not the type to just casually have sex. It's also clear she and my brother were not actively having sex. I know she isn't that type of girl to simply fuck without a thought, and therefore, what just happened between us is most likely fucking her up as much as it is me.

"We should probably get to bed," she says softly,

being the first to break our stare. "We have a long and hard day tomorrow."

Releasing the breath I didn't realize I had been holding, I say, "Yes, sleep sounds good."

I should hold her, whisper sweet nothings. Give her praise. Isn't that what good husbands do? I do none of those, however.

Without saying another word, she rushes out of the room, her nightgown still not on, her bare ass still on display, and her dignity leaving in tatters.

I'm an asshole.

I know this much. But was my brother an asshole?

Does she expect a kind man or a jerk?

How do I do this? How do I become my brother without betraying his memory and without breaking his wife?

Apollo

How do you walk into a funeral—*your funeral*—and act like everything is fine? I'm a dead man, and yet, I'm alive. I'm laying in that coffin, and yet, I'm walking up to it to say goodbye to a body that looks like me.

Who am I saying goodbye to?

The pictures on display everywhere are of Ares—me. But the body laying in the coffin in an expensive Armani suit with his hands crossed at his chest is my brother—Apollo.

Who is he? Who am I?

I'm not sure I even know anymore.

"Father wanted an open casket. It's fucking twisted, if you ask me," Athena says as she approaches and stands by my side, looking down at my brother's dead body in a coffin lined with white satin. "No way would Ares want everyone walking up and towering over him. It's putting him in a position of weakness. Dead or not, he'd hate this."

I smirk. My sister knows me so well. How fucking right she is.

I can see a line of makeup at his hairline and grimace. "Is he wearing foundation? Fucking lipstick?"

Athena leans closer to the body to examine. "I suppose they have to. Otherwise he'd be white, or blue, or gray. Something." She shrugs. "Another thing Ares is going to haunt our asses over." She tilts her head and scrutinizes some more. "I've heard that they sew the eyelids shut so the eyes can't suddenly pop open and stare back at you. Do you think that's true?"

I wouldn't put it past my sister to actually reach down and open Apollo's eyes to see for herself. "Makes sense," I say, realizing that my sister and I are sick motherfuckers. Who stands and truly examines the body of their dead brother?

She looks around the room and shakes her head. "He'd hate how many people are here. There are so many fucking people. I doubt Ares even knows all these people coming in to pay their respects. Respect to who? Ares or our father?"

"Did you pick the church?" I ask.

We're standing in the largest Catholic Church in Seattle. A church that rarely hosts services anymore because it acts as more of a museum and tourist attraction than anything else. But leave it to the Godwins to have their family event here. We aren't even practicing Catholics.

"What do you think?" Athena asks. "Father has to have the biggest and the showiest. Promise me that when I die, you burn me and throw my ashes off that cliff by the tree of forgiveness. I don't want anyone staring at my dead body wearing cheap foundation." She glances back at my brother. "And when they burn me, make sure my eyes are open. I want to see my way to Hades."

Not wanting to discuss another sibling dying, I turn away from the coffin and look at the room of black. She's right. I don't know a majority of the people wearing their expensive funeral outfits and acting like they're mourning over a man they barely know, if at all. I see some board members, some business acquaintances, employees of Medusa, and some other random people who I know are there only because they feel they have to be. Optics and all. I also see the extended Godwin family members milling around and having small chat.

They are part of the Godwin family tree. Although on a weaker branch that could snap any minute if the mighty Troy Godwin deems it so.

My uncle Leander and his wife Stella are standing near their daughters. Calypso, Leto, and Electra, cousins I haven't seen in person in years. Not since my father and his brother had a falling out over

Poseidon Shipping and the running of it. My other uncle Hector and his daughter Selene are present. They both seem uneasy, no doubt hating to be at a funeral so closely after losing their wife and mother, Willow. The last time I saw either of them was at Willow's funeral.

Yes, they are all here. But like Athena said, is it for me or for my father? Or are they here simply because we share the same last name, and they feel they have to?

"Well, that's shocking," Athena says, pointing to the door. "I'm surprised he came out of his cave to say goodbye to his brother."

For the first time in years, I see Phoenix—my younger brother—enter the church. Athena is right. It is shocking. I'm just as surprised to see my brother. He doesn't do family gatherings. Phoenix does nothing that involves people. At least not Godwins. And by the looks of how uncomfortable he appears, it's clear it took all his might to be here. I appreciate it since my agoraphobic brother rarely leaves his domain. But I suppose the death of a brother is a good enough excuse to man the fuck up and walk out the front door.

"Ares was everyone's favorite," Athena says. "Makes sense everyone would turn out."

I give her a side eye and struggle not to huff. Everyone's favorite? Hardly.

Noticing the priest is working on getting

everyone to take their seats, I decide it's time to find Daphne and take the seat next to my father.

Growing up a Godwin, there were a lot of things I got to do in life that no one in my class, or any of my friends got to do. Money, power, and our family name allowed me to experience places, events, and live in an almost fantasy world. But nothing will top this.

I get to sit in a church and watch my own funeral.

Athena begins the funeral by standing before the room and demanding their silence and attention with ease. When she's satisfied that all eyes are on her, she begins. "Thank you all for coming to pay respects to my brother... Ares Oedipus Godwin. I'm not going to stand here and tell you things about him you already know. Yes, he was a good man. Yes, he died too early. Yes, it's a shame he died while lesser men still live." She pauses as she stares at the audience, making eye contact with many. "I loved him. I never told him that. Godwins don't say words that reveal emotion. We don't express our feelings. But I fucking loved him."

Her voice doesn't crack. A tear isn't shed. But I can see my sister's pain. She's lost weight, and the dark circles under her eyes tell a story of a woman grieving. I don't know why my father hasn't told her the truth about me. Athena is the keeper of Godwin secrets. There isn't anything too dark or too sinister for her. So it doesn't make sense, other than maybe losing Apollo would be too much for her to bear.

Losing Ares causes her to lose weight and sleep. Maybe losing Apollo would destroy her, and my father knows it.

I don't know how to process her words. I feel warmth and love, but I also feel as if I'm betraying her. She's up there giving her truth while I sit here and hide in my lie.

Daphne, who hasn't said anything to me since we entered the church, reaches for my hand and holds it. Apollo was never a touchy-feely man, and I wonder if he'd allow the comfort given. I then remember how he had reached out for my hand in our last hours. Correction—*his* last hours. So I allow Daphne's hand to remain in mine.

"If there is anyone who'd like to come up here and say something, now is your chance," Athena continues. "But remember one thing. Ares was not a man to accept weakness. He was made of stone, just as the rest of the Godwins are. So don't come up here with the waterworks and the hearts and flowers. Respect Ares, and don't shed a single tear. That's how he would have wanted today to go."

Sitting and watching cousins speak of childhood memories, business acquaintances speaking of good and even hard memories, and random people just speaking to get their moment in the light was like an out-of-body experience. They were all talking about me. Me. And yet, I was watching them. Hearing them. I was a goddamn ghost in the room, and they had no idea.

Fortunately, Phoenix didn't approach the front of the room and speak, so it wasn't out of the ordinary for me not to as well. I sure as fuck wasn't going to stand up there and talk about myself.

My father was the last to speak. As he took the podium, he paused as he looked around the room, taking in each and every person who attended. He was taking notes of who came, and most certainly, who didn't. Though everyone in the family had his brown eyes, and brown hair—though his is graying—not one of us yet possess the level of authority he has. We all can wear the expensive suits, the priceless watches and jewelry, but we can't be him. We don't have what he does and doubtful we ever will. He has the ability to strike down his enemies with a single look. If he told you to jump off of a cliff, the only question someone would ask is...*when?*

His eyes lock with mine as he begins. "Ares represented loyalty. There wasn't anything he wouldn't do for this family." He breaks the stare and continues on. "And if we had a chance to get Ares back, there isn't anything this family wouldn't do for him."

My father has never told me he loves me. He has never told me he's proud of me. This right here is his version. And for the first time since my brother died, tears burn the back of my eyes as a single tear falls. I swipe at it as quickly as it came, but the squeeze of my hand tells me that Daphne saw.

"Ares showed us what family is. And we all

should take a page from his book and learn. We are Godwins." His eyes now lock on his brother, Leander, and then his other brother, Hector. "It's time we act like Godwins. I only hope the last tragedy in this family for a long time is losing Ares."

As we all make our way to the front of the church, I feel as if I've been beaten to shit. We still have to go bury the body in the family plot, but only immediate family are invited for that. I wish I could opt out of going because the last thing I want to see is Apollo lowered into the ground while I get to live the life that was stolen from him.

Daphne is still holding my hand, a support I hadn't expected would be so needed and welcomed. "I'm going to go get our coats," she says, leaning into me.

I lean down and kiss her forehead. I don't know why. It's not something I had ever done before with anyone, but it just felt right.

Just as I pull my lips away, I notice Phoenix staring... Actually, glaring at Daphne and the way her hand is locked in mine. There's disgust in his eyes. There's no reason he shouldn't like Daphne. Even though we all knew Daphne and Apollo were having marital issues, I don't think anyone held it against the woman. And why wouldn't he be happy to see a marriage maybe reconnecting, or a wife giving her husband support on the day his twin brother is being buried? The daggers shooting out of his eyes make little sense. As Daphne leaves to get our coats, I walk toward him to see what's going on. But before I have a chance, he's marched over to our father and starts whispering something in his ear. Whatever he's telling my father has his eyes narrowing, his jaw tightening, and then his eyes searching the room before they land on mine.

Daphne

I know something is wrong when I see Troy storming in my direction. I know something is *really* wrong, when I notice Apollo is crossing the room just as fast to intercept whatever it is Troy is about to do.

Without saying a single word, Troy takes me by the arm and forcibly pulls me into the coatroom. No one is in the room until Apollo's brother, Phoenix enters, followed closely by Apollo.

"What's going on?" Apollo demands He clears the distance to where Troy is bruising my arm with his grip. He snatches me away from his father and adds, "What are you doing?"

I've never seen Apollo stand up to his father, speak in any tone that isn't respectful, nor ever defend me. But at the same time, I've never seen his father so angry with me. There's fury in his eyes, and as I glance over at Phoenix, I notice the same rage is in his. I cower behind Apollo, not sure what I've done to deserve this animosity, but also not sure I have the strength to stand up to them. I'm outnumbered.

"Ask your wife," Troy says between clenched teeth.

Apollo turns to look down at me. I can see he's as confused as I am.

When Apollo doesn't do as Troy demands, he takes a step toward me, but Apollo only pushes me further back behind him in protection. "How rude of me, Daphne. You've never met my other son, Phoenix. He oversees the security at Medusa Enterprises. He's the son who likes to watch all. And when I say *all*... I mean *all*."

My heart drops. Oh fuck. Oh fuck. Oh fuck.

Apollo must notice the fear I'm feeling in my facial expression, because he takes a step away from me so he can get a better look at me. He's still says nothing, but I see question in his eyes.

"Phoenix just informed me of some information. He reviewed the security footage of the night Apollo killed Jenson in the boardroom. It's shadowed, and it's very hard to see. So hard that we had given up hope of ever being able to make out who was the one who ratted out Apollo to the authorities by giving them video that they recorded. We saw a body. But we couldn't put it together." He pauses to make sure that Apollo is paying attention. "We had watched all the footage of the elevator, other areas of the tenth floor. Every person was accounted for. And we had noticed that Apollo's darling wife was also on that floor. There was no reason for Phoenix to believe that was out of the ordinary. Why wouldn't she be on the floor where her husband's office was?"

I can't breathe. I can't swallow. I can't move.

"Except Phoenix could finally work the video through programs to ultimately make out the shadowed figure. And guess what he saw, Daphne? Guess."

I say nothing. Do I need to?

"He saw Apollo's darling wife, with her phone out, videoing the boardroom." Troy crosses his arms against his chest. "Funny. Don't you think?"

Apollo takes another step away from me as I see him processing the words his father just spoke.

"And," Troy adds, "Phoenix was able to get hold of the actual footage of what the authorities had. And guess what? That footage was taken at the exact angle you stood at. Weird right? Weird, because no way in hell would a Godwin, a wife of Apollo, dare betray this family. No way would anyone be so foolish."

"I'm going to fucking kill you," I hear Athena say as she emerges from the shadows of the room, clearly hearing everything. "I'm going to cut off your legs, throw you on top of Ares's coffin, and bury you alive."

She doesn't charge me, but I expect her to. I

expect them all to. I back up until I'm up against the wall of the coatroom. I look at Apollo and tears begin to fall. "I'm sorry. I wasn't thinking. I..."

"It was you?" Apollo asks. "You went to the cops?"

The way he looks at me...

Oh God...the way he looks at me. The pain in my heart is as if he's already stabbed me.

"I acted out in desperation." I look at Troy, Athena, Phoenix, and then back to Apollo. "I wanted out of the marriage, and I thought this was the way. But if I could take it all back—"

"Ares was going to go to jail for the rest of his life because of you," Athena hisses.

"Do you know what the punishment is for betraying a Godwin?" Troy asks with a devilish grin. He doesn't look angry. He actually appears amused. Like this is all fun and games for him.

"I'm sorry," I say again, noticing that all four of them block the only way out of the room. I consider screaming for help, but by now, most of the guests will have left, and even if they heard me, would they even dare go against Troy Godwin? Plus, making a scene could just make this situation worse.

"We're leaving," Apollo announces, surprising me by grabbing my hand and tugging me to him.

"*Apollo*, she did this to *you*!" Troy booms. "She videoed *you* and then it snowballed to the point where your brother was going to go to jail forever. All because of what your wife did to you."

It's clear that Troy, Phoenix, and Athena aren't going to get out of the way of the door. But I hold on to Apollo's hand as if it's my lifeline, and truthfully, it is. The fact I'm still alive and he hasn't killed me says a lot. But then again, it was Ares who was the killer in the family. I suppose I should be grateful he's in the coffin right now.

"She needs to die," Athena says as Phoenix nods. "Either you kill your wife, Apollo, or I will."

Apollo takes a deep breath and then says. "We aren't going to do anything right now in a coatroom. In a *church*. I'm going to handle this my way. *My way.* She's my wife, this is *my situation*, and I need you all to back the fuck off."

I've never heard Apollo speak so firmly before. Never. And clearly, by the way that Troy, Phoenix, and Athena stare back with mouths open, they've never heard it either.

"She needs to be punished," Troy says, his eyes narrowing in on me as he no doubt is thinking of all the ways to make that happen.

"And she will," Apollo says. He then glares at me and orders, "You go home. Now. You wait for me there." He then turns toward his family and says, "We are going to go bury my brother. He deserves to be put to rest before we do anything else. The priest is ready, and we aren't going to keep him waiting." He pulls me through the sea of hate until I'm outside the coatroom. "Go home, Daphne."

Fury. I can hear it, feel it, taste it in every syllable

of his words. But I also see...reason. Apollo has always been the reasonable one.

I've never been so relieved but also terrified in my life. What happens now? What do I do? Where do I go? Do I listen to my husband? Or is he the one who's going to kill me?

CHAPTER

TEN

Daphne

It's dark outside, really dark, but I can still make out the shapes of the cars below. I don't see him.

Not yet.

Being in the heart of downtown Seattle means outside is loud and active, but the walls of the hotel snuff most of the city sounds. The ringing of my ears and the pounding of my heart are all that remain.

Hiding in the hotel is temporary. I know this. You can't hide from Gods. And Zeus himself confronted me tonight. I can't walk away from this unscathed because Troy Godwin knows what I did. They all know what I did. But I need time. I need to think. I need to plan; or maybe I need to hide.

Looking down on the street below, I wonder if Apollo will come for me or if It will be Troy. Maybe neither. Now that Ares is dead, they can't send the family hitman, so they have to handle me themselves. Maybe I'm not worth their time and they will simply hire someone to take care of me. A nameless and faceless employee to take out the trash.

My eyes flutter closed, then open, then closed again as I try to wash away the memories of the funeral. The way Apollo looked at me as his father informed him of what I did...

I've never seen what a man betrayed looks like. Now that I have...

Fuck. I wish I could take it all back. I wish I could go back in time and talk down the hurt woman on a mission for revenge. It isn't worth it. The pain won't go away. It won't take away the demons. Don't do it. Don't do it!

Why did I do it? Why?

My phone rings, interrupting my desire to turn back the pages in this dark, macabre book. Walking over to the table, I utter a groan when I see it's my sister. I'm half tempted to not pick up—fearful that she'll notice the fear in my voice and want to help—but I also know Ani's relentless and will keep trying all night until I take her call.

"Hi, sis," I say as I sit down on the couch. I try to even my voice to disguise just how terrified I am, but my sister knows me better than anyone. My best option is to say as little as possible in this conversation.

"How was the funeral?" she asks.

"Hard," I reply, not wanting to lie to her ever.

"I wish I could have been there for you. I wish I—"

"I understand why you weren't," I cut in. Although I hated the reason why. Her asshole husband would never allow her to leave Heathens Hollow. Not even to support her sister and help with a family death. There is never a reason to leave him. Ani is to forever be by his side unless he wants to go off and drink and do drugs with his buddies.

"How's Apollo doing?" she asks.

Should I tell her that he may want to kill me. He may want me dead. The rest of the Godwins do. "I think he'll have a full recovery," I say instead.

"I have news."

Please tell me you're leaving your husband. Tell me he's finally done something that went too far and you're asking for a divorce. Please let this be the call where you ask for help and allow me to get you out of that awful situation. Let it be a call of sanity. Of reason.

"I'm pregnant," she announces.

I swallow down a deep sigh that struggles not to erupt from my body. "Are you sure this is what you want? Are you sure—"

"Of course I want the baby!" she interrupts.

"I'm not talking about the baby. That's amazing news," I quickly clarify. "Of course it is. I just mean... Are you planning on raising the baby with him?"

"He's the father, Daphne." I hear her sigh, but I'm

not sure it's directed at me or the fact that my question is only reminding her of the turmoil she's had inside her since finding out she's going to have his child.

"You could come here. With me. We can raise the baby together. Ani, you don't need him."

"You and I both know it's not that simple."

"But it could be."

There's a long pause and then she asks, "What do you mean when you say we could raise the baby? What about Apollo?"

I don't answer right away. I don't know how to respond or what the answer even is. Ever since the accident, I feel like I'm a blind woman feeling my way through a maze. Things aren't so black and white as they were before. Nothing makes sense anymore. Nothing is clear.

"Are you finally divorcing him?" Ani asks.

"You and I both know it's not that simple," I parrot her earlier statement. "Besides, it's not about Apollo or Mark. This is about the baby. You and I could do this. We don't need anyone but us."

There's a long pause. Silence on the other end. But silence is good. Silence means that Ani is thinking about the offer. She's considering what her future would look like if she broke away from her abuser.

"He'd never let me go."

"We won't ask," I say, not wanting to lose the

conversation but already feeling her slipping away to her life of acceptance.

I hear Mark's voice in the background. "I need to go," she says in a low tone. "But I wanted to share the good news. I'll try to call in the next day or two." She hangs up the phone before I can say another word, but it's not something I'm unfamiliar with.

This is how our conversations go. She uses the hidden cell phone I gave her when her husband's not around. Our conversations are quick, secretive, and always end with me wanting to rush to her far away tower and save her from the monster.

There's a knock at my door. "Housekeeping."

It seems I'll never get used to the fact that high-end hotels like this turn down the bed for you. Not wanting the nightly service, I open the door to send them on their way.

"Thank you, but I won't be needing your service tonight," I say with a welcoming smile, but pause when I sense something is off.

The housekeeper appears afraid. She looks at me with wide eyes and a pale face. My heart stops for a split second, unsure what can make the woman look the way she does.

"Is everything okay?" I ask.

My question is answered when the housekeeper is pushed aside, and Apollo stands in her place. Dark hair, piercing eyes, and the same look of betrayal on his face from when I left him at the funeral.

Apollo hands the woman a wad of cash and gives

a warning look that sends a shiver down my spine. "Nothing out of the ordinary happened tonight. It would be a shame to find you tomorrow."

"Yes, sir," the woman says and turns to hurry away. She doesn't even look at me, but I don't blame her. Who would stand up against Apollo Godwin? I don't think the money had anything to do with her leaving and no doubt keeping her mouth shut. The poor housekeeper feared for not only her job but even her life.

No one messes with a Godwin.

Then I realize I should fear for my life as well.

I try to slam the door shut, but Apollo has already placed his black leather shoe on the threshold and uses his arm to open the door even wider.

His eyes snake down my body. "Now, love, this isn't how you treat your husband. On the day we bury my brother, I expect better from you."

My breath hitches as Apollo forces his way into the hotel room, shutting the door behind him. I glance over my shoulder at the couch where I had left my cell phone. I also consider screaming but feel I should be very careful in how I handle this situation with Apollo. Screaming, running, or even fighting could get me killed. I have learned one thing since becoming a Godwin and that is that they don't like messes. And they are very, very good at cleaning them up.

"I don't know why you're here," I say, taking a few steps backward toward the couch.

"Oh, I think you do," Apollo counters as he walks toward me slowly. He reminds me of a mountain lion stalking his prey—calculated, stealth-like, deadly. He stops when he stands directly in front of me. "I told you to go home."

"I...I felt getting a hotel room would be better... Considering."

A feral flash of his teeth nearly buckles my knees. "Considering."

Blood courses chaotically through my veins. "You should be with your family. Grieving."

He chuckles, which isn't exactly the reaction that I expect. "You sure know how to change the mood of a funeral." A small smirk lights up his face. "I prefer rage over sadness any day, so I guess I should thank you."

"I didn't know your father," I begin, swallowing back the large lump in the back of my throat. "I didn't expect for him to confront me like that at the funeral."

"Did you think you could get away with it? Not get caught? You had to know we have cameras everywhere at Medusa Enterprises."

"I expected you'd eventually find out," I admit. Except every day that passed in which I didn't get confronted was a day that built my confidence that I had indeed gotten away with it after all.

"And did you know there would be consequences? You had to know my father would demand consequences. That I would as well."

Images of death flash before my eyes. "If I scream," I begin.

"If you scream, then innocent people die. I have men in the hallways prepared to clean up any mess that should arise." His eyes lock with mine, and for a moment I see...sadness. But then the look vanishes as quickly as it came, and his arms cross against his chest. "I hope to keep this as clean as possible. But that's entirely up to you."

I can hear the rapid beating of my heart in my ears. "I want you to leave right now." My voice cracks as I issue the demand.

"Yes, well... We all want things in life, now don't we?"

I steal another peek at my phone, wondering if it's even possible to reach it and dial 911 before Apollo can stop me.

"You could try for the phone," he says, never taking his eyes off me and somehow reading my mind, "but then things would get dirty." He glances at me from head to toe with a devilish grin. "But maybe you like to get...dirty?"

"What are you going to do?" Asking the words seems to take whatever breath I have left in my body. I feel faint as I try to play out every scenario of what might happen to me in my head. The likelihood of me getting out of this situation alive seems less and less likely with every gruesome thought playing in my mind.

But this is my husband. My husband. Apollo

wouldn't kill me. Maybe his brother would, but he's dead. His father would, but he's not here. Even Athena would gladly slit my throat. But not Apollo. Not my husband.

Not answering my question, Apollo asks his own. "Why did you do it? Why go to the police with the video?"

"You know why." I swallow hard.

"No. I don't. Tell me."

"I thought it would be my life raft. I wanted off the Godwin boat. You know this. You and your family wouldn't allow me to leave. I simply wanted to leave," I say softly, repositioning my weight from one bare foot to the other.

"I took—my brother took the fall for what you did."

"*You* were supposed to take the fall," I counter, my voice coming out screechy. "I turned you in. Not your brother. It's not my fault you let Ares take the blame for killing that man."

He doesn't respond but seems to study every inch of my face. I feel as if he's trying to read me, dive into my thoughts. His proximity and the way his eyes seem to devour every inch of my skin have me taking a few steps away from him.

Closer to the door.

Closer to my chance of making a run for it.

"Do you think I came here to kill you?" he growls as he takes slow, calculated steps toward me, closing the distance I just created between us.

He's toying with me. He's toying with me like a cat does with a mouse right before the kill.

"I don't know why you're here," I say as I spin on my heels and bolt toward the door.

A sharp pain erupts in the back of my head.

Darkness.

ELEVEN

Apollo

Never hit a woman. If my mother was still alive, she'd be livid with me for knocking Daphne out the way I did. Men do not abuse women. Not a pop to the face or anything that could mar a beautiful smile with bruises or blood. That's not to say the men in my family didn't discipline and punish when deserved, and we all have wicked ways of doing such acts. But we do not physically harm an innocent female in an act of uncontrolled violence. I don't know all the ins and outs of the relationship my brother had with Daphne, but I can safely say he never beat her. The Godwin family has rules, and not beating a woman is one of them. My father has always been a ruthless son of a bitch. He goddamn tortured my mother at times...mentally. Not to mention what he did to his children. But never did he beat my mother. Never would he slap her face or punch her in a fit of rage. And yes... He was a man who raged.

I will have to ask for forgiveness later to the Godwin ancestors who still haunt us to this day. But I didn't have a choice. I know Daphne would not go quietly. I saw her cagey eyes darting around as she tried to come up with an escape plan, and now was not the time to quiet her screams or deal with her nails clawing at my face. Though the Godwins are connected deep in the hotel world, we don't own this one, and the less of a scene, the better. There is plenty of time for Daphne's fear and acting out in the privacy of Olympus Manor.

Catching Daphne's limp body in my arms, I cradle her close to my chest, trying to ignore the wafting aroma of lavender coming from her long chestnut hair. I also try not to pay attention to the smoothness of her bare legs I have scooped over my arm—flesh to flesh.

I want to be mad. I want to stay mad.

Anger will keep me focused. Remembering this woman laying in my arms tried to destroy my brother, and pulled me into it, and our family... Yes, I need to remain angry. I was going to spend the rest of my life behind bars because of her. She betrayed our family, and she nearly destroyed any chance I had of freedom. She wanted to bring Apollo down, and for that she must be punished.

Her small frame makes it easy for me to walk toward the door. As I exit the hotel room, my men are waiting outside in the hallway. I can hand Daphne off to any of them, but I like the warmth of her body against mine. I should never admit this, but I will not give up this small pleasure. I will handle my brother's wife—now my wife—myself. Plus, it makes sense I would carry my wife and not want another man to touch her.

"Is the helicopter ready?" I ask as I walk down the emergency stairs, paying close attention that Daphne's head or feet don't hit the railing or wall.

"Yeah," Johnny—a man who's loyally worked for my family for over a decade—says as he follows close behind with his gun ready just in case. "We're good. The car's in the alley waiting to take you there."

I pick up my pace when Daphne stirs. A soft groan escapes her pouty lips, and her long eyelashes flutter. I have a sleeping beauty in my arms who is about to become a screaming banshee if I don't act quickly. I don't want to knock her out again, but I also don't want to deal with a hysterical woman fighting for her life. She needs to be in the car before she awakens.

When I reach the town car, I position Daphne's lifeless body into the backseat as gently as I can. She's already going to wake up with a nice size goose egg on the back of her head, and I have no intention of adding anymore bruises and cuts to her body if I can help it. I rush to the other side of the car and crawl into the backseat next to her. Without giving much thought, I lift her head and position it on my lap. Banging on the soundproof glass that separates me from the driver, I signal it's time to leave.

Daphne groans again and moves her head from side to side. I instantly regret the placement of her head as the side of her face brushes up against the tip of my cock. I don't want her to have any control over my mind or body. The last thing I need is to muddy the waters—

But fuck!

Her face touches it again, and my cock has a mind of its own as it hardens and tents my slacks like I'm some horny teenager.

I stare out the window and think of the task at hand. *Focus, focus.* I will not look down at her angelic face, her luscious lips, or the way her silken hair cascades around my thigh. I will not look at her black, lace panties that are on full display since her dress bunched up when I placed her in the back seat. I will not picture my cock plunged into that pussy of hers which only hides behind a thin piece of fabric.

Fuck it...

Yes, I will.

I can't help but imagine how tight her tiny little hole will feel milking my—

Like a bolt of lightning, Daphne opens her eyes and sits up. Cowering to the door with wild eyes, she puts out her hands to block an attack that isn't coming.

"Stay away from me!" she screams. "Don't hurt me."

Yes, this is the reaction I'm expecting. Luckily, we are already in the car heading to Heathens Hollow, and there is no one to hear her cries.

"Calm down," I say as I reposition my throbbing cock so it isn't so obvious how hard it still is.

Her eyes dart around the car and at the passing scenery. "Where are you taking me? What are you doing?" The high-pitch sound of her voice and the way her chest heaves with every syllable, I can see that she isn't following my command and is anything but calm.

"Panicking right now will not help your situation."

She reaches for the door handle and quickly finds it to be locked from the outside. I can't help but grin, imagining the woman jumping out of a moving vehicle in nothing but a black dress, panties, and running barefoot on the rain-soaked streets of Seattle. I'm seeing just how much of a spitfire my brother married, and I can't say I blame him for it. There's a lot of courage and spunk in that tiny frame of hers. Hell, she had the guts to try to decimate a Godwin by betraying him. Not even our bravest opponents would be so bold.

Like a caged animal, she presses her body further against the door—if that's even possible as she stares at me with wide eyes and a trembling lip. She reaches for the back of her head and rubs. "You knocked me out. You hit me," she says.

"If there was another way, I would have. The last thing we need is a scene in the hotel lobby. I knew you wouldn't leave with me quietly."

"Do you blame me?" She glances outside again. "Are you taking me home?"

I don't answer her. I know she's afraid, but that is exactly what I need right now. Fear gives me power, and Daphne Godwin needs to truly understand how powerful I am. If I could truly be me—Ares Godwin—she would piss herself and beg for mercy, knowing just how terrifying I am. But right now, I'm Apollo in her eyes, and because it was so easy for her to betray my brother... she clearly isn't afraid of Apollo. At least not yet. Yet...

"Are you taking me to your father?"

She'll learn she should fear me rather than my father.

"Please," she says as her body shivers. She doesn't cry, which I admire. I figured she wouldn't break easily, and she isn't letting me down on my assumption. I knew she would be a worthy opponent. "You don't have to do this. It's not too late to let me go. I'll just leave. I'll go be with my sister. I won't ask for anything in the divorce. Just let me go and we can act like this marriage never happened. That's all I ever wanted. I just wanted out."

I still don't say a thing but stare out the window instead. My brother wouldn't marry a woman who lacked intelligence. From the little I know, Daphne is not a woman to underestimate. I know if I'm not careful, it's likely she will read my face. She may pick up on the turmoil of thoughts and emotions raging inside of me. I will not give her any weapon to use against me if I can help it. She may have been a fierce opponent with my brother, but she's not a match for me, and by the time I'm done with her tonight she'll know it.

"Listen, motherfucker!" she shouts as she pummels me with her fists. "Stop this car immediately!"

And there it is.

The reaction I had truly expected.

Daphne Godwin is no wilting flower. This is the spunk I've prepared for, and I already have a plan for just how I am going to handle this pistol.

It doesn't take much effort to snatch both of her hands together while glaring directly into her eyes.

"No," I state sternly.

"Fuck you," she spits.

Her eyes dilate and flare with rage as she glares back, but I can still see a twinkle of fear in them. I have tortured and killed enough to know exactly what the look of fear is, and Daphne possesses it even though she's doing a hell of a job attempting to conceal it from me by her aggressive bravado.

"I don't know what you're planning on doing. Or what your father wants, but I'm your wife. It might mean nothing now, but I still believe it did at one time. I'm your wife, Apollo. *Your wife.*" She struggles to free her hands from my hold.

"Exactly. You are my wife. My *wife.* So explain to me why there is footage of you filming me kill that man. And tell me why you would go to the authorities. And tell me why you wanted to see me spend the rest of my life behind bars. Are those the actions of a wife?"

My question is accusatory. I already know the answer. I already know Daphne's goal was to bring down my brother in the most vindictive of ways. It backfired on her when I took the blame for him, but she had no way of knowing just how strong our brotherly connection was and that there wasn't anything I'd do for Apollo and the Godwin family.

"And tell me how you could live with yourself knowing they were going to lock Ares in jail for the rest of his life for what you did. They could have even asked for the death penalty."

"I told you. I didn't know Ares would get pulled into it. I was only lashing out at you. Just you."

I nod. "Yes... The actions of my *wife.*"

It was hard talking about my brother, and it was even harder talking about me in the past tense and saying my name as if it wasn't me. I need to regain control. I need to feel anger rather than turmoil. The upper hand needs to be taken back by me, and I know how to do it.

I faintly remember her sister at Apollo and her wedding. I'm pretty sure Daphne's close to her, so I take a risk by using the most effective weapon of all —family.

"So maybe I should make your sister pay like you tried to do to my brother," I say. "Maybe your sister should be the sacrifice for your crimes."

She freezes.

I know mentioning her sister is playing dirty, but the truth of the matter is I can annihilate everything important to her if I choose. She needs to realize this and tread lightly. Woman or not, wife of my brother or not, my mercy only goes so far.

I release her wrists and turn my head to stare out the window again. I gave her enough to stew on to keep her behaved. Bringing up the demise of the family is usually enough to shut up—

"You son of a bitch," she screams as she punches me square in the jaw.

I didn't see that coming.

"You leave my sister out of this! Do you hear me?" Daphne continues to punch me as I shake off the blinding stars from a powerful right hook. "Torture me. Kill me. Rape me. Dump my body in some shallow grave, but leave her the fuck out of your sick madness!"

Snatching her wrists again, I struggle with her attacking body. "I'm giving you to the count of three to stop. One," I snarl. "Two," I continue as her body yanks and gyrates around in a futile combat. "Three," I say as I flip her body over my lap, pinning her down with the weight of my legs on top of hers to prevent her from kicking. I've never tortured or killed a woman. But that doesn't mean I haven't tormented them in other ways. Ways that may make Daphne wish I treated her like I treat the men who cross me instead.

"Let me go!" she screams over and over as I make sure there is no way she can break free from my hold. Daphne's balled up fists are pinned behind her back with one of my hands, and her body lays rigidly over my knee.

"Bad, bad choice, my wife. Bad."

Her dress is already halfway up her torso, exposing most of her stomach and all of her bottom half. Her panty-clad bottom is on full display, upturned on my knee as I press her down. She continues to demand her release, but I ignore her futile dictates.

"I'm about to show you what happens if you're bad."

CHAPTER
TWELVE

Daphne

I have no idea what's going on. I don't know if I should be afraid for my life, or livid toward my attacker. Fury sizzles through me, but so does terror as I'm held pinned down on my husband's lap.

Should I demand my release?

Should I beg for mercy?

Should I just accept my fate and...

What is my fate?

Death?

Rape... Can you even be raped by a man you vowed to honor and obey?

Yes, no... The uncertainty of what's coming nearly sends me into a full-blown panic attack.

What's next?

Agonizing torture I have only seen pictures of or heard horror stories of?

And what about my sister? Is she in danger as well? I've learned you never underestimate a Godwin.

"The quicker you learn to obey me, the better, princess," Apollo says as he applies pressure to my trapped hands at my lower back. He's never called me princess before. There's a sinister seduction to it.

One of his hands engulfs both of mine, and no matter how hard I try to free myself from his grip, I make zero progress. I know the man is strong. How can he not be, considering he's a Godwin and part of one of the most feared families in not only Seattle, but possibly the world? But I never considered myself to be a weak woman either.

I try to kick my legs, but they are also restrained with the weight of his. There is absolutely nothing I can do. And that fact becomes even more clear when Apollo reaches for the waistband of my panties and yanks them down to my knees.

"Stop this!" I squeal, but already know my demands are being ignored. "Stop!"

Is he going to rape me? I wouldn't have profiled my husband as a rapist, but I'm doubting every single thing that has led up to this moment. But I've never told Apollo no before. I've never had to. He was the one who created the distance. He was the one who put up the wall. Not me.

"You clearly don't know who I am," he says. "I take commands from no one. Especially you."

My ass is completely bare. My pussy rubs up against the fabric of his pants with every move I make as I attempt to escape his hold. I have never been so vulnerable, nor humiliated, in my life. Or so I think...

Nothing could prepare me for what comes next.

I hear the sound before I register the pain. The palm of his large hand comes crashing down upon my ass—over and over again, in rapid fire. I remain completely inaudible as the man I vowed to spend the rest of my life with spanks me like an errant child in the back of a car while another man, I have yet to see through the tinted glass, drives on as if this is a common occurrence.

My silence is not because of submission, but out of utter shock.

Is this really happening?

Is my husband seriously *spanking me* over his knee instead of fucking me against my will as I had expected?

As each slap of his hand grows in intensity, so does the burn. A deep fire blazes not only on my ass but also throughout every inch of me. So much shame and embarrassment floods within me I can barely inhale. Blood rushes to my face, which adds to the lightheaded feeling caused by hanging over his lap.

"Stop," I say again, though this time with much less conviction.

Apollo volleys several more spanks on my bare flesh with growing force. "Tell me to stop again," he nearly growls. "Dare to *tell* me what to do."

I should heed his taunt and say nothing more, but as I am finding out, I'm not exactly making the wisest decisions of late, or I wouldn't be here in this car with Apollo at his complete mercy.

"You can't do this to me."

"I can." He continues on with the spanking, one painful swat after another. "And I will. You think you know me because you and I are married?" The stinging blows never cease as he speaks. "But you have no idea. Not really. You'll soon get a very intimate glimpse into the kind of man I truly am. And your first lesson's right now. If you don't follow my orders, there'll be consequences." He spanks even harder on the sensitive flesh where my ass meets my thighs. "This little spanking will be nothing compared to what I'll do to you. So, I advise you to tread lightly and do exactly as you're told. This is a warning. A small and easy warning."

This was far from *easy*, and I can't imagine how much harder this could get.

I bite my tongue and don't say another word, hoping the punishment will soon end. But I can't hold back the gasps and whimpers that escape through my lips with every searing swat to my flesh. It hurts! It fucking hurts more than I thought a spanking could. Apollo's hand feels as if it suddenly has morphed into a solid piece of wood.

Apollo positions my legs so they are spread as far apart as possible in the position I am in. He then spanks my inner thighs, dangerously close to my exposed pussy. I hold my breath each time his fingertips graze the delicate, intimate flesh. His slaps on my inner leg aren't as hard as he has been spanking on my ass, but the sting is far worse.

The cool air on my moistened sex heats my face. I want to scream, cry, shout out in disgust, but the shame and humiliation is so much that all I can do is muffle every noise that wants to come from within.

Maybe if I lay perfectly still and remain completely quiet, Apollo will stop the assault.

But Apollo has other plans than a simple cease and desist.

I should have known he wouldn't avoid my spread and susceptible pussy.

The slap to my silky folds forces a sound from my lips that resonates between a moan and a whimper —both erotic and painful.

You can hear the wetness of my flesh against the fingertips of his hand. The sound fills me with the ultimate mortification, and I know there is no way Apollo will miss my body's reaction to his force.

He doesn't say anything—which I didn't expect —but instead spanks me a few more times on the lips of my pussy.

Jesus. Can the driver hear the sound of hand smacking wet skin?

If Apollo doesn't kill me and put me out of my misery, the embarrassment surely will.

Finally, the pussy spanking stops, but it's replaced with Apollo shoving a finger inside of me.

"Don't," I moan, though anyone listening wouldn't believe I want it to stop.

"Have you not learned?" Apollo asks. "You don't *tell me* what to do."

I expect the punishment to continue because of my verbal outburst, but instead, he pumps his finger in and out of my pussy. I buck and writhe against his hand, unsure if I want his finger fucking to continue or for it to end.

Sadly, my body decides for me as intense arousal forms with every press of his finger deep inside of me.

No. No. No.

But my body won't listen.

Yanking out his finger just as I drift away in euphoric bliss, Apollo brings his finger coated with my juices to my face. "Lick it off."

I stare at his wet finger, musky with my scent, uncertain I heard him correctly.

He places his finger on my lips and presses past them. "Clean my finger."

Not really having a choice, since his finger already rests on my tongue and I can taste the saltiness of my desire, I do as he commands. I suckle on his finger as my pussy throbs for more.

"That's right. Swirl your tongue around," he says. "Next time I'm forced to shove something inside your mouth—or your pussy—it won't be my finger."

A shiver runs down my spine at his threat, but I compliantly lick as I continue to suck, hoping to please him.

Clearly satisfied with the cleanliness, he pulls out his finger from my mouth. "Punch me again, or even strike out at me, and I'll not use my hand. I'll take my belt to this tight ass of yours." He swats each cheek harder than he has done before, causing me to cry out with each one. "Are we clear?"

When I don't respond right away, he swats me again even harder. "Are. We. Clear?"

"Yes," I answer. Who the fuck is this man? Apollo has never...never... "Yes."

The spanking stops, and Apollo positions my body back to upright. The blood rushes back to my head, making me dizzier than I was before. He frees my hands, but after what he just did to me, he might as well have placed handcuffs on them. I wouldn't dare try to hit the man again. He's stronger than me obviously, but he also has no scruples. I know he will do exactly as he threatens and whip me with his belt if I do so.

Godwins don't bluff. I know this.

I reach down to pull up my panties but freeze when Apollo grips my wrist firmly.

"No. Leave them exactly where they are."

I almost tell him to go fuck himself and pull up my underwear regardless of what he says, but my throbbing ass—and pussy—keeps my mouth shut. I have no choice but to sit back and ignore the fact that my naked and heated flesh pulsates against the leather of the seat as my panties bunch up right above my bare feet. Chills run across every inch of my skin, contrasting with the beads of sweat that have formed on my upper lip. My heart beats so loudly I can hear it in my ears. I don't know what is going to happen to me, but I can also see that demanding answers is not the way to go. I have to out think the man. I have to remind this man he married me. He chose to make me his wife. And there must be something in his heart holding him back from what his other family members would do.

Ares would have already killed me.

If Apollo wants me dead, he would have done that the minute he forced himself through my door. He clearly wants me alive for something.

Is it love? Doubtful. Not Apollo. I realized shortly after our vows the man was incapable of loving anyone.

I just have to figure out what it is and give it to him. I will not play hero or martyr. There is nothing I can say that justifies what I did. I can't deny it, nor would I. But I will do whatever he wants to get out of this marriage alive and hopefully with some dignity intact.

I squirm in my seat, trying to ease the pressure. I wouldn't dare look Apollo in the face right now, but I swear that in the corner of my eye, I see a smirk.

Bastard.

If I get out of this alive I'll run as far away as I can from the name Godwin. Nothing is worth this, and living in poverty on the Eastside of Heathens Hollow sounds heavenly right about now.

I stare out the window to get my bearings. It makes sense that he's taking me out of the city somewhere, but it appears we're heading toward the helicopter.

A flash of panic hits me.

He's taking me to Heathens Hollow.

Olympus Manor. Where we will be alone. Isolated. No one will hear my screams. The manor sits on a cliff overlooking the sea. It's a perfect place to toss my body over the edge and no one will be the wiser. And even if they did, it could be considered an accident. A suicide. Hell... The Godwins can make it anything they want.

There were many rumors that surround the Godwin family manor. But even more rumors about the island of Heathens Hollow. The island is known for tales of Satanic rituals, sex parties that take kink to the next level, and even that it was the location for sex auctions. Torrid tales swirl around this place, even though very few people know for sure.

"Olympus is calling," Apollo says as the car pulls up in front of the helicopter.

I don't know what he means, but there is no way heading to Heathens Hollow is a good idea. He's taking me there for something yet unknown, and then to rid of my body with the rest of the Godwin's victims.

Apollo gets out of the car and walks around to my side.

I can't get out of the car. If I do, I have no chance at all. Once I leave Seattle, I know it's the beginning of the end.

CHAPTER

THIRTEEN

Apollo

Never stick your hand inside the cage of a wild animal.

I know better than this, and yet, as I reach into the car to pull Daphne out, the heel of her foot kicks me square in the nose, reminds me of that painful fact.

"Don't touch me," she screams, though her voice sounds hoarse and ragged.

Blinking back tears and tasting the blood gushing out of my nose into my mouth, I shout through clenched teeth, "Are you fucking kidding me?" Wiping away the blood, though more keeps coming, I call out for my driver. "Johnny, give me a hand, will ya?"

This little vixen clearly needs more of a lesson on what acting out gets you.

Wide-eyed and half naked, Daphne most certainly puts up a fight. She kicks, she punches, she even bites poor Johnny on the forearm. She isn't going down without a fight, but a fight I will give her right back.

"Motherfucker!" she screams, kicking and slapping away at us as we both crouch into the car, attempting to pull her out.

I should have tied her up, and I'm sure Johnny agrees. But then again, are those the actions of a *husband*?

I try not to laugh when sweat pours down Johnny's forehead as the tough guy struggles against a wee little lass. Her panties are long gone, and she has not a care in the world that all her naughty bits are on full display as she attempts to fight us off. No one would believe this story if they weren't seeing it firsthand.

Once we have her out of the car, I order, "Bend her over the hood of the car."

Johnny does as I ask with very little effort. Now that Daphne isn't in the backseat and at an odd angle for us to get a hold of, we once again have the upper hand with strength, and my six foot five inches tall driver who is nothing but a solid mass of muscle doesn't have to even try hard to hold her over the hood and keep her in place.

Because her panties have been completely shed

during her struggle, she is totally bare from the waist down. Johnny has already raised her dress when he bent her over. Her white ass still has blotches of pink from my earlier spanking with my hand. A spanking that clearly didn't teach her a thing.

I unbuckle my belt and yank it through the loops in one big swoosh. The fact that Daphne looks over her shoulder at me tells me she knows what's coming. Her eyes widen even more as her mouth falls open.

"Let me go," she says as she tries to break free from Johnny's hold. The brute of a man simply moves to the side but keeps her pinned down onto the hood and takes a hold of her hands in his.

"You better not hit me with that belt," Johnny says with a chuckle. "I don't get paid enough for this shit."

I laugh even though blood still runs from my nose. "Don't worry. I have the perfect target in front of me."

I'm speaking of Daphne's perfect ass. I had no intention of fucking her when this all began, but after seeing her ass bent over, spanking her wet pussy, and feeling her inner walls tighten around my finger as she mewled in want and in protest I seriously rethink that plan.

I glance around, making sure no approaching cars are coming or people in the distance. The pilot is inside the helicopter but at the angle it's at, I doubt he can see us. I need to get her inside and take off for

Heathens Hollow as quickly as possible, but I am also a man of my word and act immediately. I told her what I would do if she struck out at me, and she sure as fuck did that, so it's time for her to pay for her crime.

I fold over the leather of the belt in my hand and approach.

"I warned you, princess."

She remains silent, though I can see how hard she's breathing and can almost hear the inaudible curses going on in her head. Part of me wants to listen to each and every one. I find her strength and fire damn sexy, even though my fucking nose throbs and could very well be broken.

The sound of leather on her backside is truly a beautiful sound. Lash after lash, I bring the belt down upon her naked ass.

Primal, raw, forbidden and yet so old-fashioned and pure.

Her body tenses with every whip of my belt, and she raises up on her toes, but she doesn't plead for mercy. I think stronger men twice her size would have already cried out for me to stop.

But not Daphne.

I can hear her gasps with every blow of my leather, and I can see her flinching, but she never begs. She can't move because of Johnny's hold, but a part of me believes she would have submitted to my belting regardless of if I held her in place or not.

As welts are forming on her white cheeks, I

decide I will cut this discipline short. We still have a lot to accomplish, and I don't trust being out in the open for long. That, and my cock is raging hard, and if I don't stop now, I'll have to plunge it deep inside of her right here on the hood of the car. I'm a dirty, kinky bastard, but I'm not up for fucking in front of one of my men.

"If I stop, are you going to behave?" I ask, ready to bring the belt down again if I have to.

She nods.

"I can't hear you."

"Yes," she says with a sound of defeat in her voice and also visible with how she lies on the hood fully with all her weight.

"Take off her dress," I order Johnny as I place my belt back through the hoops of my pants.

Johnny does so with zero fight from Daphne. I have whipped her into submission...for now. I know that submission only lasts for so long, and I will need to force it upon her again soon enough.

I stand before her, locking my eyes with hers even though the sight of Daphne standing here completely nude nearly takes my breath away.

Is it necessary to have Daphne completely naked in order for her to obey me?

No.

But it sure as hell doesn't hurt.

"I'm not a man you can fuck with," I warn. "Clearly, I've never taught you this lesson."

I see her bite her lip, and I can see the "fuck you" blaze in her eyes, but she remains poised.

"Are you going to kill me?" she asks quietly. "I know it's what your family wants. Your father expects it."

"Death is not always the worst thing that can be done to someone," I answer.

Noticing she doesn't have any shoes on, I scoop her up and cradle her in my arms without hesitation.

She doesn't resist or fight me. She simply turns her head to stare out ahead as I walk toward the chopper. Yes, she is submissive for now... Or she's putting on one hell of a show that she is.

"Bring the car back to the house," I call over my shoulder to Johnny. "I'll let you know if I need anything while at Heathens Hollow."

FOURTEEN

Daphne

I hear the whispers of death as we enter the manor.

I have always felt this way every time we came here for an event, but this time is different. This time the whispers are coming for me.

Forget the fact I am naked, I have no shoes on, and I have just been humiliated by my husband, I am now walking into my coffin of my own free will. I've given up the fight, and I'm ashamed that I have. I'd like to say it's because I'm calculating. Or I'm scheming a way out of this, and all that may be true deep down in my soul. But right now, as Apollo ushers me up the large winding staircase, I'm fucking scared.

I know it's his bedroom, even though I've actually never spent the night in Olympus Manor.

We always left right after a family affair. I always got the feeling Apollo wanted to leave the property as soon as we could. We never made ourselves at home in the family estate. I always got the same feeling from his siblings as well. They arrived because Troy ordered them to, but none of them appeared happy to be present.

A large king-size bed, mahogany dressers, full-length mirror, an oriental rug, and a brown leather chair by a small table and lamp are in this room. It's the kind of room that belongs inside a mansion or some rich-person's penthouse. It doesn't have the haunted, gothic elegance of the main part of the manor.

My eyes dart to the bed, and my breath hitches when I realize why he's taking me to the room. He's going to want sex. I'm naked, vulnerable, and completely at his mercy. We had sex last night, but that was different. Maybe it was because I felt sorry for him that he had lost his twin. Or maybe it was wishful thinking that we could repair our marriage. Or maybe I was simply horny and hadn't been touched in ages.

But this time... This time things have changed. This man isn't my husband any longer. This man is a monster.

Who knows what he has planned for me, and I'm too scared to demand answers.

I can't make my feet move even if I want to. There is no way my inner soul will allow me to step across the threshold of my own free will. There is no way at all. So, I stand in place and will my knees not to buckle.

"I'm not going to fuck you, if that's what you're worried about," he says, pulling me into the room with a hard tug. "I have something else in mind for you."

I stumble inside and would have fallen if it wasn't for Apollo reaching out and steadying me.

"But if you truly don't want your sister or you to die, then I expect you to obey me completely. Piss me off, and I won't play so nice. I'll make your sister pay the same way you stood back and watched my brother pay."

My head spins, and I don't know if I want to scream, curse him out, cry, plead for mercy, or simply break into a million pieces, never to recover again.

"What do you plan on doing with us then? If I obey?" I somehow ask.

"Well..." he begins as he leads me to the far side of the room. There is no moonlight coming from the window because of the heavy velvet curtains that are drawn, but there is a very large skylight on the ceiling of the room that allows a moon beam from the full moon to cast in. "You worked really hard to put me in a cage for the rest of my life, and had no issue when Ares was going to be in a cage for the rest of his."

I freeze when I see what is before me now that I've fully entered the room.

"And since you want to put me in a cage so badly…" He walks over to the large, gilded cage on the other side of his bed against the wall. "It seems fitting that I put you in a cage instead."

I wouldn't have been able to speak even if I had anything other than futilely begging for mercy to say. The gold bars of the cage are intricately woven in a beautiful design of ivy and flowers. It's the type of cage that would house a flock of parakeets or exotic birds. It's meant to be a decorative item in a sunroom, or a conservatory. It doesn't belong in a bedroom next to where you'd sleep. The cage door also has a padlock on it, and nothing else inside.

"Get in," Apollo demands.

"You can't be serious," I say as the reality of my situation knocks the air out of me.

"Now," Apollo says. He stresses the "now" with a severe slap to my bare ass, which has me squealing out in surprise rather than pain.

I remain frozen. Not out of defiance, but out of paralyzing shock. Apollo, however, must read my lack of movement as the former. Without warning, Apollo picks me up under the arms and walks the couple of feet to the edge of his bed. He then folds my body over and presses my upper torso against the mattress. I can hear the swish of his belt again being removed from his pants.

"No," I say. "No."

I try to stand up, but he holds me firmly with one hand. I then try to reach back to protect my backside from another whipping, but Apollo snatches both my wrists and pins them at my lower back. Sadly for me, it only takes one of his hands for him to do this, so the other one is free to yield the belt again.

I press my face into the mattress, which muffles my howl when he brings the leather down on my still-sensitive flesh. The fiery lick is enough for me to break any of my pride that's still present.

So I will beg.

"Please. I'm sorry! You don't have to do this! I'll get in the cage. I'll get in!"

"I don't repeat myself, princess. It's best you learn this now," he says as he continues to lash me with the belt.

It doesn't seem like he is bringing the leather down on my ass as severely as he had done outside on the hood of the car, but my skin still aches from the earlier discipline, so every crack of the belt on my upturned bare flesh has me crying out. Thankfully, the punishment doesn't last long. As I lay on the bed —not daring to do a thing without his permission—I can hear him place his belt back on and buckle it. It terrifies me he will spank my pussy again and then fuck me with his finger. I don't want the shame of that again, and almost prefer a true beating with his fists rather than the humiliation of Apollo knowing once again my body reacts to his heavy hand. My ass stings, but I feel the wetness between my thighs.

"Now get up and get in the cage," he commands again, sparing me of that shame.

Not having a choice—not unless I want this situation to get worse—I get up quickly, walk over to the cage, duck my head so I can walk inside, and stand awaiting his next order. At least being behind bars, I won't be touched by Apollo any longer, and I can sit and pull my knees up to my breasts and try to conceal my stolen modesty to some level.

Once inside, Apollo walks over to his bed, pulls off a white fur blanket, and tosses it inside.

"I'm sure you're cold," he says as he then closes the cage and latches the lock.

There is a small part of me that wants to tell him to go fuck himself and take his fucking blanket with him, but he's correct. I am cold. And the blanket not only looks warm, but it will cover me fully for the first time since being stripped by a stranger. I yank the fur up to my neck and completely drown myself in the blanket. I'd cover my head too if it wasn't because my curiosity is winning out. I can't take my eyes off Apollo, wondering what he will do next.

"It's late. We'll start again tomorrow," he says. "It's best you get some sleep."

Sleep? How does he expect me to sleep? Though I can see outside via the skylight, and I can see it is still night, but I am sure dawn will be near soon.

And what does he mean by "we'll start again tomorrow"?

There are so many questions running through my head—all with no answers. This is nothing but complete madness, and there is no way I can come up with a reasonable way to conquer this. But I have to try. I have to think...

So, he locked me in a cage.

Was this his plan from the beginning?

Now what?

Just as I am drumming up the courage to ask, Apollo turns and leaves the room. It isn't until his bedroom door shuts, it hits me I am truly inside an animal cage. I can move around a little. I also can completely lie down and stretch my legs out between the bars if I need to. Putting my hands on the bars, I shake as hard as I can, but nothing happens other than the cage moving slightly. I also shake the door to see if it's possible to open, which it isn't with the lock in place.

I am kidnapped.

Trapped.

At his mercy.

Inside a gilded cage.

But I refuse to cry.

I will not break.

I will not allow this beast to tear me down.

He is the animal. Not me.

He belongs where I am.

He should be in this cage.

He is the damn creature who needs to be confined.

I gasp for air as my heart beats so hard against my chest, I feel actual pain.

I can't breathe.

I can't breathe!

Closing my eyes, hoping this nightmare will somehow end, I do everything to steady my breathing. In and out, I chant internally. I need to remain calm. If Apollo wanted me dead...

No, he doesn't want me dead. He wants me in a cage.

CHAPTER

FIFTEEN

Daphne

I must have fallen asleep, because as I wake, sunlight is shining through the skylight window above my prison bars. Cocooned in the fur blanket, I surprisingly slept well considering I was locked in a cage inside a madman's bedroom. Even though I had been on a metal cage floor, the blanket provided enough cushion that I don't wake up feeling achy or stiff. My sore ass from yesterday has also dissipated, and it's almost as if the entire nightmare of being kidnapped by my husband hasn't happened, except when I turn my head and see Apollo sleeping soundly in his bed, the Band-Aid the good night's sleep provided rips off in a flesh-tearing way.

He doesn't snore.

He always used to snore.

All dragons in their lair snored.

I sit up and run my fingers through my hair. Not that it matters what I look like now, but it gives me a small piece of humanity. Especially since I'm covered in fur, huddled in a cage like a scared animal.

I watch Apollo sleep. He doesn't look like a kidnapper, a killer, a creature of the night who steals innocent people from the safety of the life they know. He doesn't look evil or vile. In fact, the man is handsome. He always has been from the moment I first laid eyes on him. Gorgeous. The man could make me weak-kneed with just one glance in my direction. A part of me had forgotten just how handsome my husband is, but seeing his face laying peacefully against his pillow, and glancing at his newly wounded and still bandaged arm that peeks out from the blanket and hangs over the side of the bed, he has a sexy appearance I have never seen before. This is what the man would look like waking up to him after a night of him fucking my brains out. And it hasn't been so long that I don't remember that Apollo knows exactly how to fuck a woman's brains out. The other night, he took it to a new level, and just the memory of us laying on the floor in front of the fire leaves me...

Apollo must sense me staring at him. He always slept on edge and was ready to pounce at any moment. Insomnia was his best friend, and I remember how he never stayed in bed with me.

Never. He paced the house like a lion in a too-small cage.

"Good morning, wife," he says with a husky voice and a glimmer of mischief in his eyes. He sits up and stretches, revealing his bare chest as he does so.

I try not to look but justify my gawking by saying it's merely out of habit.

A bad habit.

I need fucking rehab from this man.

"When I came back into the room last night," he says, "I found you sleeping all wrapped in white fur like a little bunny. I liked it. My little bunny."

Calling me a damn bunny, and the fuck that I'm in a cage like an animal, any thoughts that the man is handsome wash away and are replaced with rage.

"I need to use the restroom," I snarl as I try to not picture myself clawing his eyes out like a caged tiger would do. If I focus too much on causing this man pain, then I will act out the minute I can, and I know that wouldn't be a wise move. I have to out think this man.

Apollo gets out of bed in nothing but a pair of underwear and walks over to the cage with disheveled hair and sleepy eyes. He grabs a set of keys that rests on a dresser nearby—but not close enough for me to reach while I'm in the cage—and opens my prison.

"Come on," he says.

I climb out of the cage, dragging the fur blanket behind me.

"Leave the blanket," he says firmly.

I freeze, considering telling him to go fuck himself, but do as he asks instead. I need to use the restroom now and don't have the time or energy to fight the man... Yet.

Once I cross over the entrance of the cage, Apollo helps me the rest of the way. He then takes my upper arm and leads me out of his room, down the hallway that looks upon the foyer below us, and into a bathroom.

"There're towels, shampoo, soap and stuff in there if you'd like to take a shower. There's also a drawer with spare toothbrushes and toothpaste. Everything you should need to get yourself cleaned up is in there. If there isn't, let me know. I'll send for someone to deliver it," Apollo says, surprising me with his hospitality.

Am I a guest in his house or a kidnapped victim locked in an animal's cage?

"Can I have my clothes back?" I ask.

"No."

"You just said if I needed anything to ask."

"You'll remain naked while here," he informs.

"Which is for how long? You still haven't told me—"

"Go into the bathroom," he interrupts.

Part of me wants to continue to press and find out exactly what Apollo has in store for me, but I don't wait for him to change his mind while he's being hospitable, even though he's forcing me to remain nude.

When I close the door behind me, it's the first time I feel somewhat human since being kidnapped. I have privacy. No one is staring at me. No one is holding my arm. There is no cage.

There is also not a window big enough to crawl out and to escape from. There is one way in and one way out.

CHAPTER

SIXTEEN

Daphne

I consider walking out of the bathroom with a towel wrapped around me but think better of it. I'm pretty sure Apollo will have me remove it and will most likely punish me for trying. It was nice to take a shower, brush my teeth, and I even blew my hair dry. I expected Apollo to bang on the door telling me I was taking too long and to come out immediately, or even charge in himself since there isn't a lock on the door, but he never did. He allowed me to take my time, which I did.

Plus, I'm not exactly looking forward to going back inside that cage.

I have to remain calm, obedient, and act like the submissive wife who clearly Apollo wants.

I know my time will come where I can figure out

a way out of this mess... if I can just stay level-headed.

And patient.

Caged or not, I have to remain steadfast and not try to kill the asshole with my bare hands. Even if I did, he has a ruthless family who would seek revenge. Getting rid of one Godwin would just unleash the wrath of more gods.

Mustering up the courage to walk outside and face Apollo—naked—I open the door with a shaky hand.

"Did you enjoy your shower?" Apollo asks as soon as the door opens.

Apollo clearly has taken a shower of his own. He's fully clothed in black slacks and a black button-down shirt. His hair is brushed to perfection like it always is. Just like the first day I met him, the man appears dapper. He even smells good. His cologne wafts around his body.

"Yes, thank you," I say softly.

I don't know why I'm feeling an overwhelming sense of bashfulness, but I cross my arms against my chest to conceal some of my nudity.

Apollo places his hand on my back and leads me toward his room.

Toward the cage.

I can't just walk and act like nothing is happening. We continue on up above the foyer. Apollo is on the outer edge of the hallway near the banister. I am on the inner side.

It would be a long fall down...

A neck-breaking fall down if one were to tumble over the railing...

If one were to be *pushed* over the railing...

Not taking the time to think the idea through and not taking the time for fear to set in... I turn my body and attack.

I push Apollo with all my weight and with every ounce of strength I can. "You son of a bitch!" I shout as I claw at his face hoping I can also stun him.

Apollo stumbles toward the edge but takes a hold of the railing, preventing his fall. His wide eyes and awkward stance proves the man underestimated me. He did not expect this to happen. I take his moment of shock as my advantage and charge at him with my body again as a football player would tackle a quarterback.

I'm going in for the kill, still swiping my hands at his face. Because he has to hold on to the railing, Apollo can't block my hands, and I'm able to get some gashes across that handsome face of his.

Blood trickles down his cheek, flesh under my nails, but nothing distracts me as I lunge into him, hoping he will flip over the wooden rail to his death.

Right now I'm a goddamn psychopath, bloodthirsty, determined to destroy.

But Gods are immortal. They can't be defeated. I should know this. Shit... I should know this.

"What the fuck are you doing?" he snarls as he counters my beating on him by restraining my body with his muscled arms. His strength overpowers mine as his senses and balance return. Not only does the man not fall to his death, but he doesn't even come close. The only thing I did is bloody his face a bit with scratches and piss him the fuck off.

I have to fight.

I have to run.

I have to save myself because no one else will.

But I'm helpless, restrained, vulnerable to the villain holding me close.

"What the fuck were you thinking?" Apollo growls. I have never heard such sharpness in his tone before. Even when I had punched him in the nose. "I tried to be fucking nice to you, and you repay my civility by trying to kill me? You were smarter than that, at least I thought you were. I had expected a far better opponent than what I just saw here."

"Fuck you." I struggle against his hold, but the only thing I succeed at is rubbing my naked ass all over the front of his pants. "You're sick. All you Godwins are! You can't just keep me here like this."

With what appears to be very little effort, Apollo picks me up and carries me back to his room with long, fast strides. I hardly have time to process what is happening at the speed of his walk. As we cross the threshold to his room again, I do everything within my strength to break free. My arms and legs flay, I butt my head back and forth, I hiss with every aggressive move I make.

I have truly become the beast.

A beast trying to survive.

Apollo tosses me to the ground and then takes hold of my hair with one of his enormous fists. Forcing my head back so that I look up into his face of fury, he hisses, "I'm done playing nice."

CHAPTER

SEVENTEEN

Daphne

I remember once when I was really young, I had watched a huge storm brewing in the west. The dark clouds swirled around and came at me faster than I could take shelter. I had run as fast as I could while the wind howled around me, slapping at my face. Rain, lightning, hail. A torrential downpour of chaos all around. I remember that storm clearly and the fear that I had felt.

It was nothing compared to the storm standing before me.

My bravado has dissipated completely.

"You think you can try to kill me and get away with it?" he bellows out.

"You can't expect me to go back in that cage and

not do a thing," I stammer, terrified at the fury I see in Apollo's eyes.

I hate myself for it, but my words come out as a sob as the tears follow. I don't want him to see my weakness. It makes me hate him even more.

He reaches out, grabbing a handful of my hair, pulling me mere inches from his face. "Do you think tears will work? Should I have mercy on you *now*? Now that you show fear in your eyes and remorse in the quiver in your voice?"

"I'm sorry," I squeak. The sting from my hair being yanked by the man causes tears to well in my eyes even more. "What do you expect from me? Do you want me to just give up? I have to fight to the death. You know this."

He tugs my hair harder, forcing my head to go back so I have to stare into his demon eyes. My throat stretches—so exposed. I wonder if he'll bite down and suck from my blood like an ancient monster that tales are told of.

"I was fucking kind to you this morning, and you repay me by trying to throw me down to the foyer of my family manor? Did you actually think that would work?"

"I hate you. I always have." The words shoot past my lips like a bullet before I have time to think them through. Before I have time to really ponder the consequences that will come from such a defiant utterance.

Apollo's eyes darken. Fury is visible. Wrath is inevitable.

"You don't know me."

"I do. You pretended to be the nice guy. The hero to save me. But you're the villain in the story."

He smirks. "Yes, well... Villains are made. And you just created the worst villain of all."

"All I wanted was out. To forget you and the Godwin name forever. But you refused."

"No one forgets the Godwin name. Never. And right now... You'll remember right now forever," he snarls.

I want to apologize. I want to plead for compassion. I want to reach into the depths of his evil and pull out even an ounce of humanity.

And yet, I want to kill.

I want to decimate. To destroy. To rip his flesh from his bones with my teeth. Beg or kill. Plead or destroy. Fuck him. The powerful woman in me won this battle. The courageous queen in me takes full control.

I spit in his face, smiling when I can see the shock caused by my rebellion twinkle in his eye.

"Fuck you," I say as my eyes lock with his, daring him to unleash the true villain inside.

Show me.

Show me the villain I created.

"Right now," he repeats. "Right now, you will remember for the rest of your life."

Without wasting another second, Apollo takes hold of my body and lifts me off the ground.

I try to fight him off, even though I know it's pointless. He's bigger. Stronger. Apollo will win this battle regardless of how hard I struggle.

But that doesn't mean I won't try.

"Don't you dare fucking touch me!" I scream as I try to scratch out his eyes.

Gripping my hands above my head, he flings me back hard against the bed, only giving me a second to realize I'm completely nude at this point—and on a bed—with a man raging.

"I will do more than touch you." Gripping both my wrists with one of his beefy hands, he pauses long enough to stare into my eyes. I can feel his breath against my face. His cologne poisons my nose and nearly seduces me with its toxic fragrance. My body reacts to the close proximity, no matter how much I internally curse it for doing so.

I take a deep breath and cease in my struggles.

Still clasping my hands above my head, he reaches for his belt buckle and releases it from his waist.

His eyes tell me what he's going to do even before his actions do. The fury pulses all around the darkness of his demanding eyes. I know this very moment that I have no choice but to succumb to his vexation.

"When you went to war with Godwins, did you think you'd win? Surely, you know the kind of people we are and what we do to people who cross us. Are you a fool?" he asks as he wraps the leather around my neck, pulling it through the clasp.

I shake my head. "Please," I beg.

"No!" he bellows as he tightens the belt. "You are Mrs. Godwin. Mrs. Apollo Godwin. Do not show weakness! Do not beg! You are the all mighty who can take down someone in this family. Right?"

He tightens the belt even more as he straddles my body. He releases my hands, so I'm able to pull at the leather to no avail. The more I struggle, the tighter he pulls.

"Can you breathe?" he asks with a seductive evil lining his question.

I can't speak and can only shake my head. Blackness threatens to take over as my ears ring. I really can't inhale as the leather gets tighter and tighter.

"Look at me," he demands. "Eyes on me, princess."

I open my eyes and stare into his, silently begging for my life. My trachea feels the pressure of the belt, so much so that I can't even swallow the saliva building up in my mouth.

"I want you to remember this. Whenever you think something I do, or something I dictate is so awful, I want you to remember that it can always get worse. Stop acting out against me. Stop thinking you are a match." He tightens the belt, causing blackness to edge around my vision. "If you doubt me, if you disobey me, if you ever question my actions, just know that it will be much worse for you."

I buck my hips in an attempt to throw Apollo from my body before the inevitable darkness completely takes hold.

He looks over his shoulder and down at my writhing legs and then back into my eyes. Without saying another word, he loosens the belt just enough that I can take in a shallow breath of air. It isn't enough to fully fill my lungs, but enough to keep me alive. Just when I hoped Apollo had finally felt it had taught me my lesson enough and he would remove the belt, he surprises me by getting off my body and flipping me over onto my stomach.

A familiar feeling of fear takes over as the memory of the belt spankings from before.

He loosens the belt a little more, this time allowing me to wheeze and gasp. The burn of my lungs ease with every inhale, and the shadows on my vision disappear. I can breathe—though uncomfortably.

He crashes the palm of his hand against my bare behind. "I have expectations for tonight. Expectations that will be met." He continues to spank my ass. The loud sound of flesh hitting flesh echoes against the walls of the room.

The continued humiliation of this awful act that Apollo seems to favor threatens to take back the little air I have just got. Why does the man feel the need to constantly punish me this way when he never placed a finger on me before?

The belt is still tight around my neck, but I can no longer focus on the struggle to breathe. The searing swats of his hand on my ass are the only thing my mind can address. Desperation crackles from my core, all the way to the tips of my toes. I can't cry out, I can't plead, I can't demand. I can do nothing but gasp for air against firm leather and allow the assault of *another* spanking to continue.

And oh how it continued.

Over and over, Apollo rains down slap after slap against the entire surface of my exposed skin. I try to wiggle away to no avail, and am only rewarded for such an action by a harder spank to my ass. The palm of his hand feels the same as if he were using a solid piece of wood or metal. Such strength. Such sting. Such mortifying pain.

Silently, I beg him to stop. Hoping somewhere deep inside he can read my mind and know how terribly sorry I am. I should have never tried to kill the man. My life is in his hands, and I should never forget that. I am a prisoner, not his match.

Spank after spank, fire erupts from the depths of my ass and sizzles its way to the surface. Tears fall freely from my eyes and my wheezing grows louder against the choking belt that Apollo still holds firmly against my neck.

"Would you like me to remove the belt?" he asks while still continuing to spank with fury.

I nod my head, as it is the only thing I can do.

"Very well. But I'm not done with it yet." He pauses in the blistering punishment and removes it from my neck. The rush of air that enters my body the moment the pressure releases makes my head spin with the intensity of oxygen my body so desperately hungered for.

I remain on my belly, absolutely still. I don't want to give him any reason to continue on and just pray that he views my lack of movement as complete defeat. He is the victor in this battle. I am merely a fallen soldier hanging on by a thread. My prayers are not answered, however, when I feel the lash of leather crack against my already punished ass.

I scream out in pain, but more out of shock than agony. "No," I rasp, barely having a voice. "No more."

"Yes."

Apollo whips me with the belt again, and although I want to turn around and fight him from doing so, I know I have no choice but to lie there and take it. I reach for a pillow with both of my hands and squeeze tightly as the next blow comes down harder than the one before.

"Do you understand I expect complete submission tonight?" he asks as he licks me with the harsh sting of leather again.

"Yes," I answer between clenched teeth, though I have no idea what is going to happen tonight, and why it seems so important to him.

"Do you value your life?" he asks as he whips me again.

"Yes!" I cry. "Please!"

"Then never strike out at me again. I've lost all patience for your feisty acts." He cracks the belt against me again, this time to the awfully sensitive spot where my ass meets my thighs.

"I won't do it again," I say as I struggle for air. Between a still sore throat, and the belt lashing, I can barely squeak the words out.

"Good girl." He tosses the belt to the side of the bed. He replaces the belt with the palm of his hand and begins caressing my burning flesh with the gentlest of touch.

I hiss in response, yet my body hungers for more. Self-hatred suffocates me from how my body reacts to this assault. Everything deep within me knows the sizzling electricity coursing through me is wrong and yet, I want more. What exactly that "more" is, I'm not sure. I just know I need more.

"Remember that, princess. Your survival will depend on you understanding you're not in the position to fight me. You've entered *my* world. And frankly, I'm tiring of spanking this ass of yours."

I nod between ragged breaths.

He dips his finger between the juncture of my thighs, collecting the juices of my heated sex on his fingertips, and brings them to my nose. "Do you smell how turned on you are?" He raises them to my eyes. "You can cry and plead all you want, but it's all for show. A part of you likes this." He brings his fingers to my mouth and presses them past my lips. "You can't deny how wet this makes you."

He forcibly swirls his fingers along my tongue, giving me no choice but to suck his fingers into my mouth, tasting my own musky essence. I have never been this aroused, let alone known what it smells like, looks like, or tastes like. I stare into his eyes and lick his fingers clean.

The way he looks at me. The way he studies my every move...

Am I pleasing him? I want to please him...

Wait, no!

What the fuck has gotten into me?

Who am I?

Has my time in the cage actually turned me into an animal?

I should be screaming. I should be in agonizing torment, praying for death over his touch on my body any longer, and yet...

"You like discipline, you like pain."

I shake my head with his fingers still invading my mouth. "No," I mumble against his fingers.

"Yes," he argues with a slight smile. "My beast likes the claws."

Fuck. How can this be? I hate him. I hate everything about what he's done to me...and yet I want his finger to return to my pussy and rub my clit. I want his touch. I want it more than anything. I hunger. I crave. I need. My ass burns, my neck throbs, but my soul ignites for more. I want it again.

Choke me, beat me, and please, oh please fuck me.

Harder.

Forceful.

Apollo Godwin.

He is pulling his pants down. I know. I can hear him, sense him, feel his sexual presence without even having to look over my shoulder. He will fuck me...and God help me—I will allow him to. Actually, I am two seconds from begging him to.

It isn't a cry for help that escapes my lips when his cock penetrates my wet pussy. It isn't a curse, or a demand for him to stop. It is a gasp of delight, followed by a moan of pleasure. My mind screams to resist, yet my body demands me to yield. He is inside me, balls deep.

I am one with my villain.

Malevolence has merged with my soul, and all light that held on by a thread becomes conquered by the darkness of my husband's claiming.

Over and over, his cock thrusts. It doesn't feel like any other fucking of my life. No, this is animalistic.

Animalistic fucking. Yes, this is nothing but a fucking of the beasts. In, out, in, out. There is a rhythm. There is a cadence. My body marches in tempo to his control. His cock conquers my pussy.

Possession.

There is no way to describe it other than Apollo's

possession of his captive. This is not a husband and a wife making love. This is not how we've done it before. This is different. So very different.

His hard cock enters my wet pussy, and it stings because it's been so long since we last had sex. It burns from the inside out. It scorches my core. It annihilates all that is good left inside. All that is left is fucking broken, as I'm sure he intended to do. All that is left is sex, conquer, demand, hate, and beauty.

A dark, awful, alluring beauty. Fucking beauty. That is what there is. Nothing but dark, fucking beauty.

He says I will remember right now forever. Forever I will remember.

Pulling his cock out of my body, Apollo puts his face right up to mine. So close that I can feel his breath against my lips. "You are my wife. My *obedient* wife. Remember that."

He presses his mouth to mine in what I think will be a kiss, but instead, he pulls my bottom lip in between his teeth and bites hard.

"Do not make me teach you another lesson," he warns, leaving me with the taste of blood in my mouth.

Apollo pulls me to the cage by the hair, although he isn't being as aggressive as before. With his cum dripping down my leg, I enter the cage like the animal I am, not knowing what's coming.

EIGHTEEN

Apollo

I march from one side of the hallway to the other in a frustrated fury. The woman is reckless, borderline insane, and refuses to back down.

Daphne. My *brother's* wife.

A woman who has betrayed my family and should never be trusted. Taking her to Olympus to fix the problem shouldn't be an issue. It's black and white. Easy. At least that's what it's supposed to be before feelings got involved. Before we changed our dynamic of brother and sister-in-law. Why the fuck did I have sex with her? I fucked it all up because my cock got in the way. Now...well, now...she is just plain infuriating. She is a seductive, sensual, and stubborn woman. Not just a woman who I can throw over the cliff outside the manor. She's not a nameless, soulless person. She isn't someone I can just dispose of. I can't define the emotions I have but they are there. Fucked up and chaotic emotions. Relationship-type emotions.

I stop pacing at the memory of spanking and fucking her, and grind my teeth, a futile attempt to fight back the craving, the desire, the need... the confusing connection.

I pace the hall again, fighting the urge to hit something. Why did she go and fuck up so badly? Why in the hell would she make such a deadly decision—knowing who this family is and what we have the power to do? She has no idea how much effort it would take to fix this and save her life—if it's even possible with the kind of vengeance my father and sister want. No doubt Phoenix wants her dead as well, but I'm sure he's back in his cave and none of us will hear from him for another decade or so. Athena and my father are a different story, however. They expect me to handle it. They have deadly expectations.

And yet... I haven't killed her yet. Why? Out of everyone, I should be the one who wants revenge the most. I've killed for far less, and I didn't give it a second thought if someone wronged my family. And what am I doing now rather than killing her? I'm having sex with my brother's wife.

But then again, if I truly want to live my life as Apollo, then she is *my* wife. Daphne is the woman to be by *my* side. Sleeping in *my* bed.

But I don't do relationships.

Fucked, yes.

Possessed, hell yes.

Dominated, without a doubt.

But I don't do relationships.

So this should be another reason to just end her life and make Apollo a widower.

Drawing my hands through my hair, I suddenly realize what it is that has me so upset.

My cock wants her again. *I* want her again.

Fuck.

Fuck.

I storm to the kitchen and grab a cup of cold coffee from earlier. Staring out the window, I sip the sludge, wondering what the fuck I'm going to do. I'm losing my damn mind, and I need to get my shit together.

Enough is enough. I'm getting too lost in my own demons. Once I cool down and get control again, I'll prove my demons will not control me.

But for now, I'm still fucking pissed.

Pissed at myself.

I head back to the room, determined to not let her see just how much her actions and her very presence sends me on a spiral of destruction.

I've never been one to lose my temper. Though I'm known—or was before I died—for being ruthless and deadly, I always acted with a level head and steady emotion. My father is known for his rage and fury. The staff of Medusa Enterprises often operate under fear rather than respect. My grandfather, on the other hand, rarely lost his control. When it came to Cronus Godwin—the true patriarch of our family —every action was meticulously thought out, and no act was out of anger. I often considered myself much like my grandfather until this very moment. Nothing could break my stone exterior. Nothing—until her.

Daphne almost got herself killed.

By my hand.

I had wanted to kill her, punish her, and then fuck her all in a span of a few minutes. The woman had made me completely lose control, and I hated myself for it.

I am not a man to lose control.

Staring into the mirror over my dresser and dabbing at the claw marks on my face with a tissue, I try not to look at Daphne crouched in the furthest corner of the cage. I need to calm down, and her very presence causes my blood to boil.

This is not how I do business. I have a plan and need to follow it to a tee. This little vixen will not change that.

Blood trickles down my cheek.

Fuck. It looks like I got my ass kicked. A grown man wouldn't even have the guts to attempt what Daphne just did.

"There will be consequences for this," I say, more to myself than to Daphne as I continue to stare into the mirror and not her as she watches me from the cage.

"How long do you plan on keeping me here? Like this?" Her voice is softer than before. Her rage has clearly simmered, which helps soothe my inferno.

"I warned you to behave." I nearly hiss in pain when the tissue touches a deeper scrape, but I won't give her the satisfaction of knowing she caused me discomfort.

"I know. I wasn't thinking. I acted on impulse."

She's attempting to tell me what I want to hear, but I'm not a fool; I recognize her lies. She's smart. Very smart. And the fact she literally tried to kill me, or at the very least seriously hurt me tells me she's as ruthless as I am. I may have truly met someone who has the same level of darkness that runs through her veins.

"Actions speak louder than words," I say.

"I...yes, I know. I'll *act* better."

Though my homicidal thoughts are leaving my body, I'm still furious with Daphne for what she tried to do to my brother. Yes, I took the fall, but her intentions were to destroy him. She went after my twin, who I'd throw myself on a sword for. Why would she do something like that in the first place? Surely not just for a divorce. I don't buy her bullshit excuse.

I knew Daphne was a smart and savvy woman when she entered the family. My father would have never allowed the union if she hadn't been. Before she walked down the aisle, I had watched her. Studied her every move. I had to make sure she was good enough for my brother. Though she came from the Eastside of Heathens Hollow, she didn't act like some backwood hillbilly. Though not formally educated, she was street smart and extremely sharp. Landing Apollo Godwin as her husband was a score, and she knew it. I didn't see her as a gold-digger, however. I saw her as a true survivor. A woman who wasn't going to just live in a shack forever but would fix her situation however she had to do so. I admired that. I think everyone in our family admired that.

Though I hadn't seen even a glimpse of the woman I believed her to be since stealing her from the hotel. All I see now is a woman acting out without thought, and if she was any other person, and if I was still acting like Ares—the man I once was —she would have already had her neck snapped.

"I don't have time or the patience for your antics." Swiping at the last bit of blood, I wonder how I'm going to explain the condition of my face to people tonight. Between my swollen and bruised nose from yesterday, and now that my face looks like a mountain lion attacked, it will certainly give the partygoers something interesting to discuss when I'm not within earshot.

"I'm sorry," she says. She is holding onto the bars of the cage with a look of desperation in her eyes. "I'll do whatever you say if you will let me out of this cage. I won't act out. I swear it."

I turn to face her head on. "You'll do exactly what I say, regardless of whether I let you out or not." I'm not messing around anymore, and it's damn time she understands that fact.

She nods as tears fall down her face. I freeze. I feel this overwhelming need to comfort her, and it fucking pisses me off more than anything. I'm literally tending to my wounds, but I'm itching to wrap my arms around her and kiss away her tears.

I'm a goddamn sadist... to myself!

"I don't understand what you have planned," she says slowly and calmly. "I also don't believe you want me dead, or you would have done that already. So please," she swallows hard, "I didn't mean to try to kill you. It won't happen again."

She sits on top of the fur and doesn't cover up her nudity. I'm not sure if she's doing it to show her obedience to me since I have made it clear she will remain nude, or if the thought of using the fur to hide her body hasn't even crossed her mind. But it's hard for my eyes to not travel to her hardened nipples from the coolness of the room.

But I need to focus. She is right. I have a plan.

"Fine," I say, ignoring the sting on my face. "I'll give you one last chance. But if you even so much as come close to pulling a stunt like before, I'll kidnap your sister and put her inside that cage with you."

She doesn't flinch at my words or even grimace in the slightest as I had expected her to do. Instead, she surprises me when she smiles enthusiastically and says, "Yes. I understand. Just tell me what you want. Anything."

I'm not so stupid to think it will be as easy as that. Not with this woman. And frankly, I don't mind a bit of defiance. It'll make it fun to discipline and break the bad right out of her. But I do like seeing that I have at least regained some control over the woman without having to beat the shit out of her which isn't, and never will be, an option. She doesn't have to know that little secret, of course.

I need fear on my side.

Especially for tonight to come off without incident.

"I'll be back," I say, as I know I still have a lot to do to get ready for the evening. "You sit there and think about how when I return, you are going to be a good little wife."

CHAPTER
NINETEEN

Apollo

The sound of the family helicopter landing has me rushing down the stairs and out the front door to cut off the impending storm. I know it's one of two people, or possibly both, and I have to meet my opponent outside to shield Daphne from the wrath as best I can. This isn't their fight. This isn't their mess. This isn't their wife.

"It's a good sign to see you standing outside by yourself," Athena says as she approaches.

The helicopter turns off its engines, which tells me that Athena doesn't plan on staying long and plans to still fly out today. Otherwise, it would just return to Seattle and wait to be beckoned again.

"Cliff or shallow grave?"

"Neither," I answer as she kisses me on the cheek.

She pulls away and narrows her eyes. "Please tell me that bitch still isn't alive."

"She's not your concern."

"The fuck she isn't. She betrayed our family."

"No," I say calmly. "She betrayed *me*."

Athena releases a heavy breath and rolls her eyes. "I should have expected you couldn't handle this. You've never been the killer in the family. That was Ares, and I guess now that he's dead," she looks up at the house behind me as if she can see Daphne, "I'm going to have to step in and fill that role."

"I have it under control."

"Clearly you don't if her brains aren't splattered on the rocks below that cliff."

"Sometimes there is punishment far worse than death," I say, wrapping my arm around her shoulder and guiding her a few steps away from the front door just to make sure she won't suddenly charge inside and get to Daphne before I can stop her.

"You know Father will not allow her to live," she says. "Even if you can convince me, there is no way he will let that happen."

"I have this under control." I lead her back to the helicopter. "You can go back to Seattle. I'm sure you have a lot of work to do."

She stops walking. "I'm actually not here to kill Daphne. Although I can fit it into my schedule if need be." She reaches into her purse to pull out her phone to look at it before adding, "I'm here to meet with dear old Uncle Leander. Apparently, Poseidon

Shipping needs a little reminder that Medusa Enterprises is the head of the beast."

"Is he stepping out of line again?"

My uncle has always resented his older brother, and even us, for the way we run Medusa. Although he runs a division—a very powerful division—he'll always have to answer to the heir of the empire, Troy. To say the two brothers don't get along is an understatement. Somewhere along the line, they agreed to a truce to some degree. Leander runs Poseidon from Heathens Hollow. Troy stays in Seattle except for a vacation. They have their territories. Troy has the land. Leander has the sea. Usually, the two can agree, but there is always the occasional clash of the titans, and it seems Athena's job today is to stop an impending battle.

"Arms deals with Russia is the rumor," she says, texting someone as she does. "Our cargo may not be on the up and up. I'm here to remind him we don't do criminal." She looks up at me and smiles. "At least not on the surface."

"Yes, the Godwins are known for our squeaky-clean reputation." I chuckle and shake my head.

Someone once asked me what Medusa does. It was easier to actually tell them what we don't do. We thrive on hostile takeovers. We love to conquer, destroy, and then rebuild. There isn't a business we won't touch, claim, and then run even better.

Medusa is the modern-day Viking.

"He's getting messy," Athena says. "Father sent

me here to make sure our uncle knows he better clean it up or his brother will." Athena finishes her text and then looks back at the house. "So where is Daphne?"

"In a cage," I answer.

Athena laughs. "If only." She laughs again, clearly not taking my answer seriously. "Although a cage is exactly where she belongs. It's a shame, really. Daphne had a lot of potential. I appreciated her ability to be a scrapper, but she also could act like a chameleon and fit into any situation with grace and elegance. She really could have been an asset to our family."

A black sedan pulls up to the drive, and a man in a suit steps out and rushes to the other side to open the back door for Athena.

She looks at me, pats her hand on my arm, and says, "I'll let you handle Daphne. But if it's too hard, or you feel you can't do it...let me know. I understand that she's your wife, and though you may be a Godwin, your heart may not be made of stone."

"I just need some time. I'll handle this my way and make sure Daphne can't hurt this family ever again." I look at Olympus and then back at her. "But I appreciate the offer. If you really want to help me, keep Father away. I'll try to work from home, but I need a few days off. I need time to just remember my brother, get a grip on what this new life looks like without him."

I see a flicker of pain in her eyes, and only I'd be

able to see it as I know my sister so well. She quickly recovers but says, "I miss him."

"I do too."

"He was the heartbeat to this family." Her eyes cast to the tree of forgiveness. "Do you think it's our family's penance for all the wrong we do? Do you think Ares was taken from us as a punishment?"

"I don't know. I ask myself every day why it was him and not me."

Her eyes remain on the tree for several more moments, but then Athena seems to shake off the trance she was in and says, "I'll cover for you," she says as she walks to the car. "But don't take long. Medusa is a shitshow with all the scandal. At least the press is concentrating on the death more than the murder and trial. So I guess that's good. But our stocks are plummeting, and I sure as fuck don't know how to do numbers. That's your department."

"Do you want me to go with you?" I ask as she climbs into the car. I know Athena can handle herself with anyone, but I still want to offer.

"You just worry about the numbers and that Jezebel inside. I'll worry about operations."

CHAPTER

TWENTY

Daphne

Apollo's been away for hours. My emotions have gone from claustrophobia, fear, rage, sorrow, impatience, and a million others during the isolated period. Time seems to trickle by as I sit in my prison behind the bars. This *teaching me a lesson* of his is successfully driving me mad. I can barely focus, definitely can't come up with a plan, and because of my good nights' rest, I can't sleep the time in this cage away. When he left, I had no choice but to follow his orders. I have to think of how I will behave and not act out again. I can't risk Apollo getting my sister involved in this mess because of my outbursts.

Oddly enough, I'm happy when Apollo returns. Anything but this agonizing wait in the cage with nothing but my thoughts of what has happened and what is still to come.

"Have you had some time to cool down?" Apollo asks as he walks straight toward the cage. He has a large box with a red ribbon tied nicely in a bow on top of it. "I've brought you a present."

He unlocks the cage and then walks over to the bed and places the package on the bed. I remain still, unsure of what he wants me to say or do.

"You can come out," he says over his shoulder.

Wanting Apollo to see how serious I am on "behaving", I climb out of the cage as quickly as I can and stand with my arms at my side, awaiting his next command.

"Come open the present," he says.

I walk over toward the bed, unsure why he feels the need to buy me a present. I'm his captive. Nothing but a woman in a cage. A gift doesn't fit this picture at all.

With shaky hands, I take hold of the ribbon and untie it. I feel Apollo's eyes on me watching my every move. Once the ribbon is undone, I lift the lid of the box and look inside, confused.

Really confused.

I'm not exactly sure what I'm staring at, though I have a pretty good idea that this gift of his is anything but.

"It's time we get ready for a party we're attending this evening." He takes me by the arm and leads me to the door. "I'm going to allow you to go to the restroom one last time before we get you dressed." He pauses and turns me so I can stare directly into his eyes filled with intense warning. "If you even so much as flinch against my touch or act out, you won't be happy with the consequences. Are we clear?"

I nod.

"I asked a direct question. I expect a direct answer. An answer of respect."

I nod again. "Yes...sir."

My mind is blank. There isn't the slightest act of defiance inside of me. Not after having hours to think through every action I can make, only to realize it will end with me pissing off Apollo and getting my sister involved. Hours of plotting and strategizing only to have the result always come back to the word "behave".

Once we return to the bedroom, I'm still unclear of what the items in the box are for. I have a pretty good idea, but surely my thoughts are far too wicked and filthy for what Apollo really has in store. I seriously doubt he would go to the extreme thoughts my abused and battered mind goes to.

"Let's get you dressed." He leads me back to the box.

"Where are my clothes?"

"Gone."

"How am I to get dressed then?"

He points to the box. "We have everything we'll need in there."

I don't need to look inside the box again because Apollo pulls out the first item for me to see. It's a furry, white bunny tail attached to a metal butt plug. I have seen pictures of sex toys, but never had any experience with them. I led a pretty vanilla life until now and really can't process what Apollo plans to do with the tail.

Or maybe I'm in denial. Maybe I don't want to comprehend.

Or maybe... I do.

"We're attending a special event tonight at The Vault. Tonight, we get to bring our pets," Apollo says.

The word "pets" has my eyes go wide and mouth open. I've heard stories of The Vault on Heathens Hollow but have never been. An old nineteenth century bank in the town's center is rumored to be the place that hosts sex parties of all kinds. Not just anyone can get in the door. It's believed in order to enter, every guest must reveal a deep secret to The Vault Keeper to be used as collateral. No one is allowed to speak of what truly happens in The Vault, and if you do, well... The Vault Keeper has your secrets that could be used to destroy you.

Apollo and I have only attended charity events, boring art shows, or mundane social gatherings that I always struggle not to yawn through. Going to a place like The Vault is not what we'd ever do. We are Godwins... Godwins attend fancy balls and expensive dinners. We don't go to secret, dark, sex parties that torrid tales are whispered about.

How could my betrayal have changed this man so much? I feel like I'm staring at a stranger right now.

My heart speeds up at the thoughts of what Apollo will say next—of what he will *do* next. I keep expecting him to say he's just kidding, or maybe that he's only pretending we're going to a place like The Vault as another threat to continue teaching me the lesson. Surely, he doesn't expect us—Mr. and Mrs. Godwin—to lower ourselves to such debauchery.

Apollo chuckles with a mischievous smirk. His brown eyes twinkle with little lines around them. He has an almost boyish charm. If I didn't know what a ruthless man he is behind that charismatic face. "You look surprised." He pauses and studies my expression. All I can do is stand and focus on breathing enough so I won't pass out. "I'll be bringing you as *my* pet, so we need to make sure you're the prettiest one there. I'm a Godwin, so my pet needs to be the best one at the party."

He reaches in the box, pulls out a small bottle of lubrication, and opens it. Without pause, he squeezes some liquid onto the silver plug and coats every inch.

Oh Jesus. What is he doing? Why?

"This one's large. Much larger than I'm sure your tight ass can take comfortably." He pauses and looks at me with questioning eyes. "I'm assuming you have a virgin ass. Am I right? My memory is shot, but I'm sure I'd remember if I had fucked you in the ass during our marriage before the accident."

I nod at his vulgar question. Of course we never had anal sex. It's not like he ever showed an interest in it anyway.

"I figured as much," he says. "But that's about to change."

"What are you going to do?" I swallow hard and feel stupid for asking. Clearly, I know what he plans on doing with that tail. Or at least I think I do. Though the size of that plug looks far too big. There is no way it will fit inside of me. Virgin ass or not.

Is he doing this to scare me? Maybe he wants me to beg and plead. Maybe this is a form of punishment —to make me think he's going to shove that tail into my ass and take me to a public place. A sick mind game.

"As I was saying. I can't give you a small or simple tail. You have to be the most impressive. In our world, bigger is better, princess." He motions for me to lie down on the bed. "And after your actions this morning, I'm not really going to feel sorry for you. Consider it a consequence."

I don't move. This is not a bluff or a threat. This is really going to happen, but I freeze rather than doing what I know he wants me to do. Not out of defiance, but because the shock of what is happening paralyzes me.

"Lay down on your stomach. I'll be gentle unless you test my patience."

Imagining Apollo being anything but gentle with that tail, has me quickly complying as he asked. I position my body just as I had the night before when he took his belt to me.

"Every pet tonight will have a tail of some sort. Though all the pets are different, which makes it even more interesting. You'll be the most elegant of them all by the time we're done."

I hear the lube squeeze out again and then feel Apollo's finger touch the seam of my ass. He doesn't stop there but continues on until his finger presses against my anus. I tighten up and try to squeeze my ass cheeks closed.

"Trust me. You're going to thank me for this when the tail gets inserted. I advise you to allow me to lube you up."

Is this man fucking serious? I'll *thank* him?

"Spread your legs wider," he says as he nudges them apart with his legs. The action makes it easier for his slick fingertip to reach my anus.

I gasp at the invasive touch and close my eyes tightly. I need for this to just get over with, and I make a mental decision not to fight it.

He applies some pressure on my hole, which sends an electric shiver up and then back down my spine. I expect to hate every second of this, and yet my throbbing pussy once again betrays me. I hate that my legs are spread wide because I'm almost positive that Apollo has a full view of my sex that is getting wetter with every swirl of his finger on my anus.

"It's a shame this ass of yours hasn't been fucked

before. You're truly missing out," Apollo says as he presses his finger a little harder on my puckered flesh.

"Last time I checked, you weren't interested in fucking my ass," I counter back, trying hard not to focus on my growing desire. "I can't exactly fuck it by myself."

Apollo laughs loudly. "That's the worst shame of all. We need to rectify that, wife."

I'm rewarded for my snarky retort by having the metal plug placed on my asshole and pressed in without giving me enough time to prepare. It slides in but spreads me the entire way.

"Oh my God," I moan as I cling to the bedding on the mattress. "It's too big. I can't. I can't." Sweat beads on my skin and my breath hitches as the tail burrows deeper inside of me.

"You're doing just fine," Apollo says as he places one of his large hands on my lower back to ensure I stay in place.

I mewl like an animal as I writhe on the bed.

I have truly become his pet.

The plug is deep inside of me, and I can feel the fur of the tail against my still sensitive ass from the earlier punishment.

Apollo reaches for my upper arm and takes hold. It doesn't hurt, but his grasp is tight. He forces me to sit on the edge of the bed even though the tail is now being pressed inside of me even deeper. He kneels down and reaches inside the box, pulling a long chain and metal choker from it. The metal is adorned with diamonds all around it. I have no doubt it is by far the most expensive torture device ever made.

"You don't need to chain me," I say as panic sets in. "I have no intention of trying to escape."

He doesn't reply but grabs me by the back of the neck, pulls my head into him, and clasps the collar around my neck, securely locking it into place. It's tight enough that when I swallow, I feel my flesh connect with the cool restraint.

Tugging on the collar to make sure it's locked, Apollo says, "You'll remain collared and in this tail until I say otherwise."

I caress the collar with my fingertips as I squeeze my asshole around the plug. "Please tell me you will not make me wear all this in front of other people."

"Yes." He stands up, not caring in the slightest. "It's the theme of the night."

"Apollo. I know you're angry with me. Furious. But I'm still your wife. We still have a reputation to uphold. We can't just arrive at a sex party with me dressed like this." I take a deep breath, feeling hysteria knocking on my mental stability. "The Godwins own the land of Heathens Hollow. Imagine what people will say if it gets out that we were—"

"Enough," he interrupts.

My heart beats so hard against my chest that I'm positive I could die from the hysteria overwhelming me. I can't believe Apollo is even considering this. He's always been focused on reputation and the family name until this time. He wouldn't dare soil our standing in high society. Regardless of how he feels about me, parading his wife in nothing but a bunny tail and a diamond collar is the type of scandal we can't come back from.

I get up and walk to the mirror to see if my image is as bad as I think it is. The heavy chain of the leash drags behind me, only pulling at the collar more. When I see my reflection in the mirror, the contrast of the dark metal with sparkling diamonds to my skin makes my awful situation even more of a reality. Staring back at me is nothing but a pet, collared, chained, captive.

Spinning to glare at Apollo, I say, "You can't be serious! I can't go anywhere dressed like this. If you want to punish me, do it in private. Not for all to see."

No response.

"Please! I swear to you I'll be good. I'll be good and never give you an issue again. I wouldn't dare betray you or any of the Godwins again. I think you know that or you'd have killed me. But Apollo..." I point to the bunny tail and then the collar. "Please think about what people will say. I'll never be able to show my face on this island again." He still says nothing. "I don't need to be in a collar and tail to be your pet. Can't we do this... Whatever you have planned in the privacy of Olympus? I'll fucking crawl on hands and knees all night if that helps. Just keep this...punishment...our secret."

No response.

My chest constricts, and I wheeze with all my might to take in some air. I'll die of embarrassment, mortification, and... No punishment could be worse than this. All eyes will be on me.

Daphne Godwin dressed as a sex bunny. Naked. Vulnerable. Being walked in The Vault by a collar.

This is Apollo's way of destroying me. Not killing me... destroying me.

Crumpling down to the ground, I pull my knees to my chest and allow the tears to fall. If Apollo's goal was to break me, then he succeeded. I now know he will not kill me. That was never the plan. His plan was to bring me to my knees and have me submit to his every command. His plan was to break me, not kill me. But maybe I want to die. Maybe I want to die so I don't have to endure this humiliation any longer.

I'm so lost in my misery that I don't hear Apollo approach me. For a moment, I actually forgot he's even in the room.

Looking up at him with tears streaming down my face, I beg, "Please, Apollo. You, out of all people, know. You know how hard I've worked to change people's view of me. It was so hard to be the respected, distinguished, admired Mrs. Godwin that you wanted in a wife. Don't take that all away by forcing me to attend an event like this."

"Did you worry about the Godwin name when you tried to have me arrested for murder?" he asks.

"Did you care about the Godwin name when my brother was crucified by the media even before his trial began? Did you care about what people were saying about us or thinking about us then? Why care now?"

"It was a mistake," I choke out. "An awful mistake I wish I could take back. But Apollo… I beg you." I pull at the collar to emphasize my appeal.

He kneels down beside me and looks me straight in the eyes. "Look at me and know that I'll never let your name get soiled. I may dirty up this body of yours, but I'd let no one say or think anything negative about you. Not as long as you are my wife." He places his fingertip on my cheek and strokes softly. "It's called The Vault for a reason. What happens in that bank will never breech the walls. Never. What happens tonight is just as private as what we've done in the cloak of this manor."

I shake my head. "People talk. You and I both know how toxic the talk of Heathens Hollow can be. I don't want to go back to being that girl from the Eastside of the island. You saved me from that. Please don't make me go back to being that person."

He moves his fingertip and gently runs it along the collar where it meets my neck. He dips his finger between the metal and flesh and says, "Tonight, we can be anyone we want. I don't have to be Apollo, and you don't have to be Daphne. You are simply my bunny and I your master."

"No," I wheeze, continuing to cry. "Please." I

should be in a gown. I should be in expensive heels. Jewels should drip off my ears and hang heavy around my neck. I'm Daphne Godwin and that means something...or at least it did. He's stripping me down to nothing, and if his intent is to break me by doing this, well then, he wins.

He removes his hand from the collar and places it on my head. Slowly, he strokes his fingers through my hair, never taking his eyes away from mine. "Shhh...just calm down. No more tears."

"Then don't make us go to this. Please!" He shakes his head. "We're expected at The Vault. I can't arrive without my pet. So dry up those tears and trust that though your *dignity* may not be protected tonight, your reputation and the privacy of your name will be."

His gentle touch and petting of my hair eases some of my distress. Apollo has always been a man of his word. If he says my reputation is safe, then I'm leaning toward believing him. Besides, do I really have an option? And the one thing about Apollo and his family is they protect what's theirs with ferocity. Their name and reputation are everything. If Apollo destroys my reputation by attending this party, he does the same to his.

"That's a good pet," he praises when he sees I'm no longer trying to plead my way out of this situation. "Tonight will be a night to remember." He continues to stroke my hair. "You're going to handle yourself just fine."

Would I be? How could I be *just fine* ever again?

"I hate this," I cry. "Why are you so cruel? How can you be so cruel to another human being? I may have fucked up, but I'm still your wife. I'm still the woman you married."

He gives a crisp tilt of his chin. "I know."

"So, why are you doing this to me?" I point to the cage. "Why?"

"Consequences, princess. You had to know there'd be some."

"Do I deserve to be treated like an animal?" I ask. My words seem to make a difference, but I also get the sense that there is no use trying to convince Apollo to go against whatever twisted and dark plan he has.

Apollo places both palms on each side of my face and forces me to stare directly into his eyes. "You need to behave. Tonight's event will start soon. You don't want to know what happens to pets who disobey, and I promise you that this collar, cage, and butt plug will be minor in comparison. Behave. Do you understand me? You have nothing to prove. You'll lose."

"I've already lost," I point out. "I'm wearing a collar and a tail while being held captive. There's nothing more for me to lose."

"But there is. I have ways of making my enemies lose so much more. Don't push me. Just don't." He leans in and kisses me gently on the forehead before standing. He extends his hand to assist me up now that I'm no longer crying and having a meltdown. "We're going to be late."

Standing, I take a moment to allow the slight dizziness to dissipate. Apollo places his arm around my body to hold me steady while the room swirls around me. It doesn't take long to feel back to my old self. My old self with an addition of a bunny tail and a collar, that is.

"Are you hungry?" he asks.

I nod, wondering if he's going to make me eat out of a bowl on the floor of the cage or some other humiliating act.

"Good. There will be food at The Vault." He stands back a few inches so he can take in my entire appearance. "You look absolutely perfect, my pet. Perfection."

Apollo picks up the chain, and the removal of the weight hanging helps ease the pressure on the collar a little. He then leads me out of the room.

CHAPTER

TWENTY-ONE

Daphne

I'm naked.

I'm naked with a collar around my neck and a butt plug attached to a tail up my ass.

I am naked, being escorted by a leash into an old historic bank to what is secretly known as The Vault, full of men who watch our every move as we enter.

There is a man wearing a dark suit, a black cloak with a hood, and a mask standing behind the counter as a bank teller would. The mask is demonic and conceals who the man is behind it.

"That's The Vault Keeper," Apollo says as he guides us in his direction. "Get your secret ready."

Secret? I've heard that giving a secret is the only way in, but I hadn't really planned on doing it, and I have no idea what to even write down. How truthful does Apollo want me to be? I was told that once I marry a Godwin, I never reveal a single secret. Never.

We approach the window, and The Vault Keeper pushes two pieces of heavy card stock and two Mont Blanc pens in our direction. I see dark eyes behind the mask but can't see anything that humanizes this person at all beyond that. Even his hands are covered in black leather gloves.

Apollo quickly takes the paper and pen and starts writing something down. I don't dare try to peek even though I want to. What secret is he writing? What is he willing to tell a complete stranger? Godwins are known for their ability to keep secrets. It's one of the main reasons that they don't believe in divorce. Once you marry into the family, you are privy to the secrets that live inside their walls. Never would they allow someone to have access and then leave with the knowledge. That would be them willingly giving power away. Godwins don't give power away.

Before I even start writing my secret down, Apollo folds his paper and hands it to The Vault Keeper. The masked person takes a minute to read it, folds it again, puts it into a safety deposit box, and nods his or *her* approval. I assume The Vault Keeper is a man, but there is no real way of knowing. They both then look at me, waiting for me to write something down.

I quickly write down that I was the one who turned Apollo in for killing a man. I assume that it's a secret worthy enough of getting into The Vault, and if it upsets Apollo I gave such a secret, well that's on him. It's his fault for taking me here to begin with. The Vault Keeper reads it, glances at Apollo, and then nods his head in approval as he puts my secret into the locked box as well. The Vault Keeper then nods his head again and points to a staircase that leads beneath the bank. It appears as if we earned our key into the secret club.

As we walk down the stairs, the only thing that my mind can focus on is the smell of food. I'm famished. A huge table is lined up with dishes of pasta and meats. No Italian restaurant could compare to the spread that I gaze upon as I take the last few steps, entering the room just a few inches behind Apollo. The fragrance is like a kick to my empty gut, and I'd do just about anything—include walk naked—to eat the food.

"Gentlemen," Apollo says with a nod to a few of the guests who stand nearby.

Luckily, I don't recognize any of the men in the room, and I count my blessings for how long it's been since I've lived on Heathens Hollow. None of those men were friends with my dad, but then again, the Godwins never would lower themselves to interacting with men like him. I don't think any of them recognize me as the shoeless, dirty, Eastsider I once was.

"Where are your pets?" Apollo asks.

"We have them all in a room together," one man

replies. "There's some business to discuss before we begin the party, and we didn't feel it was a conversation that our..." the man pauses and looks at me, then back at Apollo, "that our pets need to hear."

Apollo nods and hands the leash to a man who appears to be staff rather than a guest standing on his right. "Bring my pet to join the others," he commands, never once looking at me. I don't know why the fact Apollo doesn't look at me bothers me more than the fact I'm naked and being treated like an animal.

I'm being cast off to someone else, and I hate it. I hate leaving Apollo's side.

Why?

Why the fuck should I care?

My stomach gurgles as I'm led away from the table of food. I wonder how long it will be until I'm allowed to shove a forkful of pasta into my mouth.

I must walk too slowly by the display because the man now holding my leash tugs me a little harder to silently command me to keep up. As I pad barefoot behind him, and am led to a closed door, I look over my shoulder and see Apollo sit down at the table with about ten other men, and there are looks of concern and anger on all of their faces. Jaws are locked, eyes dark and narrow, and tension thickens the air.

I can't help wonder if it has something to do with the Godwin family and that is why Apollo felt the need to pay a visit to The Vault when we've never attended before.

The door is opened, and I'm shoved inside. I take a moment to adjust my eyes to the dimly lit room. I already know there will be other women in the room since I'm going to join the other pets, but I'm not prepared for what I see.

Sitting on the floor are ten women. One pet for each man outside.

There are several kitties, puppies, another bunny, and even a unicorn. Each of them are collared and tailed just as I am, and some even have wrist and ankle restraints with far more chains attached. I suppose I'm lucky to only have my leash as the only heavy metal chain. Their eyes are wide and curious as they examine me quietly as the man pushes me the rest of the way in, presses me on my shoulders until I kneel on the ground, then silently closes the door and leaves to join the male guests in the other room.

Being on all fours, I'm not sure what to do. Should I crawl closer to where they all sit? Should I say something? Each woman is naked, vulnerable; but they don't seem frightened or upset to be in the situation they are in. And I'm once again relieved I don't recognize any of the women, which means they may not know who I am.

"We have a new pet tonight," one woman—with a kitten tail—says with a smile. Her lips are red, her makeup dark, and her hair is up in two ponytails to appear more catlike.

"Pretty," another woman who has bunny ears besides her collar and tail says. Her voice is soft and seductive.

I remain still. Silent.

"Why are you acting like you just saw a ghost?" the red-lipped woman asks. "We don't bite."

The women in the room giggle, and I easily see that everyone is... comfortable.

"What's your name?" she asks, cutting off the laughter.

They don't recognize me...yet. I consider giving a fake name but trying to keep my true identity is going to be impossible once we join the men. Apollo Godwin and his family own Heathens Hollow. Even if the women don't recognize me, they will soon recognize him.

"Daphne," I answer as I reposition myself to sit on my thigh. The large tail makes it impossible to fully sit on my butt, so I have no choice but to find a position that seems to enhance my sensuality when, in fact, that is the last thing I am meaning to do.

"Daphne Godwin? Apollo's wife?"

I nod and swallow the lump that forms in the back of my throat.

"We are sitting with royalty," a girl, who leans against a wall, says. She is dressed in a black puppy tail and has a black leather mask covering her face. Her costume is far more extensive and involves leather jewelry with a thicker collar than others. "Godwins rarely attend The Vault." Her eyes glance at my tail. "He even gave you a white tail and a diamond collar. Very... Godwin-like."

I struggle to process the women before me. It's clear they are all here by choice. Every single one of them, and they assume I am as well. And for some bizarre reason, I don't want to let on that my husband has taken me to Heathens Hollow, and everything about this situation is forced. It's like I'm in a high school locker room trying to fit in with the cool cheerleaders or something. I also have been so groomed to protect the Godwin name at all cost, that I don't want to mar Apollo's reputation at all. Ironic, since trying to destroy him is what landed me in this situation.

Regardless, I remain silent.

It isn't like they can help me anyway if I told them the truth. They won't cross a Godwin and help me escape. Not if they value the land they live on. They only lease the land. Not own. A Godwin can evict without cause, and most certainly will if given a reason. If anything, they may make the situation worse if they told their men about me and then the men told Apollo. I don't think Apollo would appreciate a scene at The Vault.

Awkward silence is soon replaced by the women going about whatever conversations they were having before I entered the room. I've never been one to really like cocktail parties or social gatherings. But

I married into that life, however, so I have attended countless numbers of boring, pointless nights. I'm not good at small talk just for the sake of it. I'm not good at laying on the charm to complete strangers.

But at least at those parties, I had a fucking dress on.

Here I sit. With a tail in my ass that's growing more uncomfortable by the minute and a collar that still feels humiliating regardless if it's made of diamonds. And the other women just sit around in their own tails and collars, but they don't seem the slightest bit uncomfortable. This is ordinary for them. They all smile and chat on as if they are at their very own cocktail party...minus the dresses and pretentious designer purses and heels.

And the craziest thing about it all is that I'm the odd one in the room. I don't know how to just sit comfortably. I don't know what to look at or what to do. I don't want to stare at their nudity or how some have ears or fake eyelashes. One woman even has contact lenses in that look like the iris of an actual cat. I don't want to stare, but I can't help it.

I can't get comfortable no matter what position I try to sit in. It must be obvious because the red-lipped woman looks at me again and says, "Not used to the tail?"

"It's...big," I answer, not really sure what to say but regret how whiney my response sounds.

"It's best to not move so much," she advises. "The weight of the plug is shifting around and stretching you with every move. It's best to relax and stay as still as you can. Don't clench."

Before I can ask exactly how you don't clench when your body wants the invasion out, the door opens and the staff member who brought me here stands in the doorway.

"Come, pets. It's dinnertime. Your masters are waiting for you to join them."

Praise the fucking lord. I could eat a bowl of cat food at this stage.

Every woman moves toward the door on hands and knees, crawling with their leashes dragging behind them. I take this as my cue and do exactly the same. The heavy weight of my tail becomes even more obvious as I crawl like an animal in single file to the main room.

All the men are seated at the dining room table, including Apollo at the head. They all watch us enter the room with smiles and hungry eyes as we interrupt their meeting. I make eye contact with Apollo, and I see he seems pleased. Whether that is with me crawling like a good pet, or that he sits in a room full of women on hands and knees. Regardless, I never break my stare as I follow the other women under the table. Each woman rests at the feet of their "masters", and I pick up quickly that I'm about to do the same at Apollo's feet. I don't have time to process or even protest that we are under a table. Slacked pants and black leather shoes are all we can see of the powerful men.

And the most twisted question of all runs through my head...

Are we going to eat under the table at the men's feet?

And why do all the surrounding women seem happy? They're smiling. Some are rubbing their faces on their man's leg like an obedient pet would do. Others crouch and patiently await whatever will come next. No one is blushing. No one is crying. No one is pissed or holding back fury. Not one single woman is in distress of any kind.

Apollo reaches under the table and places his palm on the top of my head. He gently runs his fingers between my hair...petting me.

Petting his bunny.

And fuck me... My pussy throbs.

"Let the pets eat first," I hear Apollo's voice say from above. "Since they're behaving so well."

Shortly after, I see bowls of penne pasta with red sauce and thick pieces of sausage pushed under the table. Each woman grabs a bowl and positions it in front of them. The red-lipped woman is the first to place her face into the bowl and begin eating it as a cat would. No hands. Just her mouth.

Every other woman quickly follows. It isn't savage, as one would expect, having ten women under a table eating out of bowls with their mouths. In fact, the women have a certain elegance and grace about them. They clearly have had practice at it.

Me, however, not so much. Even getting my

face to the bowl feels odd. It forces my ass out and high, causing my asshole to tighten against the plug. I have to spread my thighs to help me in lowering my face enough, and the cool air against my damp pussy embarrasses me. What if the other women see the signs of arousal? What if they see how wet I am getting as my breasts and hardened nipples caress the cold floor as I take bites of the pasta?

By the sound up above, it's clear dinnertime has begun for the men as well. They laugh and speak as people would do at any normal party. As if there are not ten of their pets eating out of bowls at their feet.

Apollo's hand reaches down and touches my spine as I'm hunched over my food eating. Softly, he runs his fingertips up and down, soothing me. Comforting me. Looking up from my bowl and at the other women, I see that other men are doing the same to their pets, and every woman has a look of pride and contentment on their faces. And I understand... I feel warm and safe under Apollo's touch. I have no idea why, and I have no idea why I press my body up against his leg so that I feel his warmth against me. But I do.

After we are all done eating, each woman pushes their bowls out from underneath the table, and I see the feet of someone coming along to collect them. I watch everything all the women do and copy the best I can. I even lick my hand and wipe it against my face as an animal would bathe. We all have red sauce on our faces, but I see it is our duty to clean ourselves while the men continue to talk up above.

For the most part, I can't really make out what is being said. It seems like idle chatter, but then I hear Apollo say "Poseidon," and I struggle to listen the best I can. Captive or not, I am still a Godwin and know that though Poseidon is part of Medusa Enterprises, it's always been a thorn in Apollo's side. I had heard my husband use the words "shady," "illegal," and "cowardly" to describe the division often.

"Poseidon is bringing the danger to Heathens Hollow. It's right on our docks now," a man speaks.

"Athena is working on it," Apollo says. "I don't think I have to remind any of you just how *convincing* my sister can be. You have nothing to worry about."

"They've been slowly doing this for years," another voice says. "I don't think your family is truly aware of how deep this vein runs. Poseidon isn't some small business on the island you can easily muffle."

"My uncle runs Poseidon, but my father runs Medusa, and that trumps everything. Poseidon is simply a branch of the family tree. A tiny twig compared to Medusa," Apollo says. "Athena is having a little *chat* with dear ol' uncle. I can assure you."

"We don't have to tell you this, but we value the privacy of Heathens Hollow. The last thing we want is attention directed our way," another voice says.

"Our local sheriff can only deflect the authorities for so long."

"Understood. We've had enough legal shit as of late," Apollo says. "My family is determined to leave that shit in Ares' coffin. We have no desire to get involved with any of Poseidon's side hustle, nor will we allow it."

"We appreciate you coming here and telling us this in person," someone says.

"Of course. But enough of this talk for now. We have some beautiful pets at our feet that need some attention. Pets," Apollo calls out. "Come out and sit on your master's lap."

TWENTY-TWO

Apollo

I've seen nothing so beautiful in my entire life. Daphne stands before me with a drop of marinara on her nose, flushed skin, wide eyes, and an aura of complete submission around her. I enjoy her feistiness but love this look of complete surrender even more. I feel her body tremble beneath my petting, and my cock hardens as she presses up against my leg.

My pet. My perfect and obedient pet

I motion for her to come sit on my lap as the other pets are doing. Some straddle their master's laps, some curl up, others want to be cradled like a baby. I'm curious what Daphne will do.

She takes a few tentative steps toward me with heavy lids and pouty lips. I want to fuck her right then and there, but it would be rude to leave The Vault this early, and I'm not sure I want to push her too far by forcing public sex... yet. I pat my lap and wait, though anything but patient. I want her nude body on me immediately.

She glances around as if taking her cue from the others and then sits on my lap as if I'm a chair. I think I'd prefer a straddle with her pussy lips spread wide, but I enjoy the delicate nature of how she perches herself on my knees. I pull her back against me and position her so she's cradled in my arms. Swiping with my thumb at the marinara on her nose, I chuckle as her face reddens even more.

"Being a pet suits you," I say.

She doesn't respond but looks down to avoid my stare.

I cup her breast. "Look at me, Daphne."

She obeys immediately which has my cock twitching against her tailed ass.

"Did you get enough to eat?" I ask.

She nods.

"Are you sure? I know it must have been hard eating that way."

"I did okay with it," she says softly, breaking my stare by looking down again.

I reach for my glass of wine and bring it to her lips. "Drink."

She does so, allowing me to hold the glass for her. The simple act of providing wine makes me want to provide much more. My protective instincts and the need to pamper and nurture the woman is taking over the need for revenge and punishment. Whether or not I like it, seeing Daphne soft and compliant does the same to me.

I take a second to look around and see some men standing up from the table with their pets leashed at their feet. I'm pretty sure they're all thinking what I am and want to partake in some fun pet play, but I still want to talk to them about Poseidon and what's been happening behind our backs on Heathens Hollow before I lose their full attention. Now that I've had some time to gather my senses and not feel completely blind-sided because Poseidon has been operating in dealings we'd never agree to, and that Athena wasn't overreacting when she arrived today, I wanted to make sure I had every detail.

"Gentlemen, before we go off and enjoy this party in our individual ways, I would like us to go out and enjoy a nice cigar under the full moon tonight. It won't take long, and I think our pets will be fine here without us for a short time."

I stand up and place Daphne on a fluffy black rug nearby. She takes my cue instantly and sits on the floor as a good pet would. Her white tail contrasted with the black, and all I can do is picture myself fucking her on it, but business first. Picking up the cedar box of cigars, I motion for the rest of the men to join me.

Daphne

I don't want Apollo to leave. Maybe it's because I still felt awkward sitting with the rest of the women who chat among themselves, or maybe it is some other reason, but I don't want to be left here without him.

As I sit on the rug looking around, I realize that the entire time I ate, I was petted, was caressed, and held, I didn't think about my current situation. I wasn't a captive. I didn't feel a prisoner. I was not scared for my life or afraid of Apollo seeking vengeance.

I didn't want to run and hide.

What I wanted was more of his touch.

Tears well in my eyes. What the fuck is wrong with me? Why am I feeling this way? Or better yet, why aren't I trying to escape now that no one is around to make sure I stay in the room? The other women pay no attention to me, and even if they did, they don't know I am held here against my will. So, if I get up and walk out of this room, they won't give it a second thought.

So, on shaky legs, I do just that.

"I need to use the restroom," I say loud enough that if anyone is paying attention to me, they can hear.

One step at a time, I walk toward the bathroom on the ground floor. Once I close the door behind me, I release a deep breath. This is not being the good little bunny. This is not behaving. What would Apollo do when he finds out?

Trying not to picture his face, or think of how a belt will feel spanked on my ass again, I reach behind myself and pull out the bunny tail, rinse it off, and place it on the bathroom counter. It's the ultimate act of defiance, but I can't exactly make a run for it with a large butt plug up my ass either. Looking at myself in the mirror, I see the diamond collar and decide to keep it on. I have no doubt it's worth a fortune and it may come in useful if I need access to more funds while on the run. Not knowing how to remove the chained leash without risk of breaking the diamonds, I decide to leave it and carry it as I run.

Taking another deep breath, I open the bathroom door and hope none of the women will notice I removed the tail, or that I'm heading toward the exit.

Me leaving, will unleash the wrath of the Gods the minute Apollo finds me missing.

Heading toward the door leading to the lobby of the bank, I glance over my shoulder and see that no one is paying attention. I know I'm naked, but it doesn't matter. I rush toward the exit as fast as I can.

I freeze when the front door opens and heavy footsteps storm my direction.

"What the hell are you doing in the lobby?" Apollo asks, with the other men close behind.

I wonder if my trembling legs will even hold me

up. What can I even say? There are no words. No excuse. No way out of this situation.

Apollo glares as he marches past me. The smell of cigar and fury blend. He points to the door. "Back in The Vault, now."

I don't hesitate and do exactly as he asks. I can't play the hero. I tried and failed miserably, and I fear that if I anger him or push Apollo in the slightest, he will demand my sister be brought to him then and there as a punishment for my defiance.

I walk right past Apollo but pause just enough to look into his eyes, silently pleading for mercy.

"Now," he says between clenched teeth.

I nod and scurry downstairs, praying that my sister won't pay the price for what I tried to do. I hold my breath and pray that I didn't just embarrass Apollo. I know that betraying the man is one thing, but embarrassing him and publicly showing disrespect is another.

As I enter the main room of The Vault, the pets are still lounging about and talking, completely unaware of what occurred, or that there is even a private *issue* between husband and wife.

The sound of the men walking down the stairs send chills down my spine. Each one passes me and walks toward their pet. It's as if nothing happened.

Apollo walks up beside me and takes my hand. "You're in trouble, my pet. Deep trouble."

TWENTY-THREE

Apollo

I'm not angry. It's only human nature for Daphne to do what she did. But regardless, penance has to be paid. The men know what she did, and the other pets can see that she has removed her tail. If I let her off with just a verbal warning, there will be chatter from everyone behind my back that I'm nothing but a pussy-whipped husband. The weak Godwin brother, which sadly, my brother often had the reputation of being. But from now on, the name Apollo Godwin will not come across as weak or out of control.

A public discipline session is the only answer.

She jumps the moment my hand smacks her ass.

"Oww!" she squeals, her toes rising on the floor and her hands moving to cover her rear, protecting herself from further punishment.

I will not allow her discipline to be over that easy. If I do, how will it make me appear to the other men? I take hold of her body and bend her over the table where we just had our meal.

"Put your hands above your head." My lips nearly at her neck as I lean down, moving her hands, placing them on the table before us. "Don't move," I warn, bringing my hand back down to the curve of her ass before swatting her bare behind again.

Her hips jump and her toes push up, moving her backside slightly higher. I've never spanked anyone with an audience before, and though I would prefer to have this little spitfire back in my room in private, I have no choice but to show all the men—and their pets—how I treat my bunny when defiant.

This embarrassing and shameful act is on her. I warned her to behave.

It's high time she takes my threats seriously.

Her firm ass on display for all to see turns me the fuck on. I know it's obvious my cock tents my pants, but no doubt Daphne's curves and smoothness of her skin are doing the same thing to every man watching. I want to not only spank her ass, but touch and taste the sweet cream that drips from her pussy.

She is wet. I can see it glistening back at me. Begging for me to lick it off of her.

My hand comes down repeatedly, smacking her bottom from the crease all the way down to where she sits. I don't want to bruise or blister her rear by spanking her too hard since the shame of a bare bottom spanking in front of others should be punishment enough. But with every searing swat, Daphne grows wetter and wetter. The harder I spank, the more she seems to enjoy it, which only makes me want to crash my palm against her flesh even harder.

She whimpers and gasps, moaning with pleasure. I watch the swelling of her pussy as I spread her legs further apart to swat the sensitive flesh of her inner thigh.

I smack up against her pussy, hearing her sharp gasp as her legs slam shut, capturing my hand as her hips thrust.

Oh yes. I can see...

My little pet wants me to finger fuck her with all to see. No shame. No bashfulness. Lust has taken over.

"You want to come, my bunny?" I ask, leaning closer as her legs unclench and my fingers dive into her wetness, stroking her folds and the fire between her thighs.

She nods as an erotic mewl escapes her lips. Her body tightens and eyes squeeze shut as her passion seems to grow right before my eyes. She keeps her hands above her head, her fingers splayed out before her like an animal clawing, gripping and tugging at the wood under her grasp. Daphne's lips part and her breathing rushes out deeper and heavier as my fingers caress the folds of her wet pussy, teasing her clit, circling her toward orgasm.

Eyes are all on us. I know it. Daphne has to know it.

Being at The Vault has taught me one thing...

My wife appears to be an exhibitionist and a masochist. I fucking love it.

Let's show you off, my love. Let's show you off.

I pet my wife's wetness, feeling her swell under my ministrations as her insides clamp down, clenching onto my finger as I add a second. I thrust my fingers in a curved motion, as her hip grinds into my palm. My other hand comes up to smack her reddened ass repeatedly. Daphne cries out with each searing swat as she trembles against my palm, gasping and moaning.

"Do you want to come, my pet?"

She nods in response.

"Answer me with respect," I command as I pump my fingers in deeper and harder.

She moans and thrusts her hips to meet the motion of my hand. "Yes, please," she barely whispers.

"*Yes, please*, what?" I stop moving my fingers and slowly pull out as a punishment for not answering properly. Respect is everything in my world, in this room, at The Vault in front of these men. If she doesn't give me the respect required, I will steal it from her.

Thrusting her hips back to force my fingers in deeper, she cries, "Please, *sir*. Please make me come."

Relieved that I don't have to take the punishment

to an even harsher level, I praise, "That's my good pet."

I can see, hear, and feel the orgasm travel through her body as I watch her toes curl, her hands clench, and feel her juices coat my fingers.

"Feel free to scream loudly, princess. Let everyone hear just what a kinky pain slut you can be."

She cries loudly as her entire body stiffens and then quivers on the table.

As her body calms, I slowly withdraw and lean down, pushing her hair to the side, kissing a soft path against the pale skin of her neck. "I expect you to behave from now on. Are we clear?"

I slap her ass harder than all the times before combined.

She doesn't even flinch as her euphoric bliss seems to take over her body.

"Yes, sir," she murmurs, still panting from release. "I'll behave."

Daphne

"Are you wet for me?" Apollo asks.

My voice shakes as I nod. "Yes, sir."

"Good. I want you to tell me why you're wet. I

want everyone in this room to hear your words. Speak loudly."

My pussy throbs at his question, the warmth spreading through me as his finger swirls over my puckered hole, forcing a whimper to slip from my throat.

"I want to please you."

"Good answer," he says and pushes into my bottom hole, the wetness from my pussy having soaked the wood of the table as he uses my juices to thrust his fingers in past my dark entrance.

The throbbing grows with intensity as he pumps his single digit in and out of my hole. "I want to stretch you, make you ready for when I claim you, my pet. Have you been picturing my cock inside of your ass instead of the tail? Is that why you removed the tail?"

I don't know the right way to answer. Does he want the truth? What is it he wants to hear? I don't want to humiliate myself anymore since I know all eyes are on Apollo and what he's doing to me, and yet I also know not answering can make things a hell of a lot worse.

"No."

"Wrong answer," he says.

I hear giggles from the other pets as one finger turns swiftly to two as he pushes inside of my ass, stretching and giving me both pain and pleasure as he surely can smell my scent of arousal.

"Once you have my cock buried deep in your ass,

you'll change your mind." His breath tickles my spine, and as he withdraws his fingers, he plants soft kisses over my lower back, forcing my hips to grind against the edge of the table.

I desire more than just his kisses over my skin. I want to feel his breath on my pussy and his tongue lapping at the juices that flow freely from me because of him. "I want your tongue on my clit," I admit, the words blurting out in an instant. My sexual desire is taking over all reason and control.

Apollo chuckles. "Will someone please hand me her tail?"

A moment passes, feeling as though it goes on forever. I know the dreaded tail will be returned to its "home" but the worst part is that the entire party will see it stretch me to impossible lengths as Apollo inserts it back inside of me.

I feel the hint of lubricant as he slides the bulbous head of the metal plug in past my tight hole. I squirm and shift my hips, finding the strain of the flesh of my anus uncomfortable as it fills my bottom.

Apollo continues to push the implement fully inside until there is no further for it to reach, as the plug's girth feels heavy and wide inside of me.

"Stand up," Apollo commands.

Careful not to push the tail out, I keep my ass clenched. Doing as he instructs, I stand naked in front of him.

"It's time for us to head home," Apollo announces. The thick undertones of his voice and the warning in his eyes tell me I am not to hesitate in the slightest.

I stand by his side so he can take my hand in his. I'm too ashamed to look over my shoulders at the other men and their pets. I had wanted to please Apollo, and yet, I didn't.

Apollo says his goodbyes and we exit The Vault. Olympus is waiting, and hopefully a husband who isn't too upset with my behavior.

One step.

Two.

I walk toward the unknown.

TWENTY-FOUR

Apollo

"Naughty, naughty wife," I say as I walk in the room and close the door behind me. Daphne scurries to her cage as if she thinks it will protect her. "And to think you were doing so good."

"I tried," Daphne says, as I can see her inch her way back to the furthest corner of the cage. "Are you," her voice cracks and her bottom lip trembles, "going to punish me again?"

I smile. "Oh, I plan to punish but in the most wicked of ways," I say as my cock hardens immediately at the thought.

I motion for her to come out of the cage, and she does immediately, submission still evident. I walk over to her and assist her beyond the bars and guide her over toward the bed. She doesn't hesitate in the slightest. She gasps when I lower her onto the bed face down and ass up, but she still doesn't put up a fight.

I tap on the base of the plug deeply rooted in her ass. "You were a good bunny until you attempted an escape."

She remains silent, but I can hear a soft moan as I tap the plug again.

"It's time we take this plug out and replace it with something else," I nearly growl.

I bring my lips down to her neck, sucking and nipping at the sensitive flesh as my fingers move from her pussy back toward the plug and I pull it out. She squeals as it pops free, but still remains in position. I tease her back entrance with my finger and listen to her breaths and moans, discovering what she likes and what she loves.

"I'll make you mine, my pet, and claim you here," I say, my fingertip swirling over her asshole, pushing gently past her tight flesh as I hear her gasp. I withdraw my finger as quick as it entered her. "Do you want me in this ass of yours?"

"No."

"Don't lie, princess. I know when you're lying, and there are even more consequences for lying. So I'm going to ask you again. Do you want me in this ass of yours?"

"Yes..." She barely whispers the answer.

"I can't hear you. What?"

"Yes, I do. God help me, I do."

I work my pants loose, springing my cock free, stroking the length from tip to base, wanting to satisfy this woman who damn near consumes every sensation in my entire body. With one hand, I stroke myself and with the other, I slide my fingers over her slick pussy and into her warmth and wetness, bringing her juices back to her ass, pushing my finger inside, stretching her rim as I thrust in and out. I can't wait to feel her tighten around my cock.

"More," she hisses.

I push two fingers past her tight little hole, slow at first to stretch her and then pump my fingers in and out, listening to her breaths and moans. Her hips don't seem capable of holding still, not that I mind them gyrating in front of me.

"I want you to fill me with your cock," Daphne confesses fully, her voice practically tinkering on the edge, begging for release.

With pre-cum on the head of my cock, lube from the tail, and her slick juices glistening over her ass, I push my cock in past her anus. Placing my hand on her lower back, I steady her as my hands move to her hips, caressing the skin at her sides with each slow thrust, in and nearly out, as I guide my cock inside of her tight hole.

She cries out in undoubtedly both pleasure and pain as I inch my way in.

My hips move, thrusting against her ass, one hand sliding down between her thighs, stroking and flicking her clit with my finger as I feel her tighten and clench against my dick.

Her insides spasm all around me as she grits her teeth, muttering my name under her breath.

She appears to keep her sounds down. At least that is how it seems. I can see that she doesn't want me to know just how much she's loving it.

I thrust into her harder. Aggressive. Cold. Or so I try.

But my hands caress her flesh, my heat merges with hers. Any ice around my heart melts as Daphne orgasms from the ass fucking that I had originally intended to cause her pain.

I give this woman pleasure.

She gives me even more.

"I'm never letting you go," I say, my breath coming out with a heavy pant as I spill myself into her.

No.

No.

This is not the plan.

I pull out of her as quickly as I entered and resist the urge to kiss her, to hold her, to cuddle her into my arms. "Get on your hands and knees and crawl back to your cage to sleep," I order.

I am an asshole.

A fucking prick.

Yes.

Yes.

That is the plan.

I have to remember that I'm not truly Apollo Godwin. I'm the villain. The bad guy. I'm the bad twin. The killer twin. The dark side of the duo.

And Daphne is not my wife.

Daphne

I wake up in the middle of the night, with the sharp chill in the air and dread pumping through my veins. I don't want to hear his heavy breathing as he sleeps or feel amiss for not being in that bed with him. I want to escape. Leave him and his family forever. And God help me... I want to fuck him. Fuck him hard over and over again.

Is it possible to want both at the same time?

A moment of peace as he sleeps. A moment of safety as his arm lays draped over the edge of the bed which is never how he used to sleep. He used to be a back sleeper. Clearly Olympus Manor has changed him.

It's changed him so much.

The full moon casts a powerful beam of light into

the room—bouncing off the metal of the bars of my cage—only illuminating my harsh reality. I am a captive in a family manor with my captor who is also my husband. I have only myself to hold on to, even though my strength is fading. A strength turning into a pool of thick dark weakness, threatening to strangle me in despair.

Fuck Apollo. Fuck him and the rest of the Godwins straight to hell. And yet, as he sleeps, I remember small glimpses of his humanity. There are many. He's given me small peeks, as of late, into his soul that shows he isn't all black inside. There's something in his eyes I've never noticed before.

"Apollo?" I whisper, breaking the silence of the room. I look through the bars at his face as he sleeps. He looks so peaceful, gentle, and even kind. This is not the rough man who punished me repeatedly then took me without so much as an ask. This sleeping man is not a monster. Or is he? Maybe he's just a beast in slumber. "Apollo," I say again a little louder.

His eyes flutter open. "You should be asleep," he says in a scratchy voice.

"Am I going to die?" My question is direct, blunt, but it can't be held back any longer. I have to know the truth.

"Go to sleep."

"Are you planning on killing me?"

"No."

"Then keeping me in a cage as your pet forever instead?"

"Would you rather I kill you?" He takes a calming breath. "Did my discipline earlier not teach you anything? You should be afraid of me, not poking the bear. Go back to sleep. The sun's not up yet." He says the words, but his eyes linger on me hungrily. I see how he looks at my bare pussy and my exposed nipples. I can sense the intensity in his stare, almost feel the heat of his body even from afar.

"But your family still wants me dead, right?" I ask. "I seriously doubt any of them have changed their mind. You've never stood up to them before."

"There's a lot you don't know," he says.

"I know that when it comes to Troy Godwin, no one, not even you or your siblings, go against his wishes." I pause and then add, "And I know I made an awful mistake. One that your father, your sister, your brother, and maybe even you, will never forgive."

He sighs deeply and repositions his body where I see the last bits of moon light highlighting every curve of every muscle. "Did you really want to see me in jail forever?"

I shake my head. "I gave little thought before I acted. I was just so hurt. I wanted to make you hurt. And I felt so trapped and weak. And I didn't want to be weak any longer. So I asked myself what Athena would do, and well...that's how I decided to betray you and Medusa." I grab hold of the bars and press my face closer. "And when your brother took the fall for it, I really wanted to step in and confess, but the tidal wave had already hit. I didn't see a way to fix it. I froze. I became immobile to do or say anything. I took the cowardly way out and just remained quiet. I thought if anyone could get out of this mess, it was Ares Godwin, and I needed to step back and allow him and the Godwins to do what they did best, which is fix anything. I feared I'd only mess it up further. Your brother was a powerful man. I respected him. Feared him. But more than anything, I had grown to love him as a family member. He was always kind to me. To be honest, he was the only Godwin who even tried to make an effort. I'm sorry he's gone. I'd love to apologize to him and beg for his forgiveness, as I'm doing to you."

"Is that what you're doing?" Apollo asks. He seems to soften right before my eyes. "Begging for my forgiveness?"

"Yes, and not just because I'm in a cage."

He chuckles. "But I'm sure you hope to not be in there any longer."

"Do you blame me?"

He remains silent for a bit. He finally lets out a deep breath and asks, "You said you were hurt. Why?"

"You know why."

"I don't. Tell me."

I try to not let the familiar bite of anger take hold every time he acts like my request isn't, and never has been, important. "My sister. I asked you over and over. I begged you. And yet, you always shut it down."

"Shut what down?"

Tilting my head, I study his face. Did the accident make him black out this part of our life? The doctor said his memory would have holes because of his head injury, but he's been doing so well remembering most everything else. I occasionally can see an emptiness in his eyes when I mention something about our past, like there is no recollection of what I'm saying, but then he seems to remember quickly. But not this time. This time, he really appears to have no clue what I'm talking about.

"You don't remember?"

He runs his fingers through his hair and glances out the window before saying, "I don't remember. I wish I did."

His words are like a punch to the gut. He doesn't remember the reason our marriage shattered to a million pieces. He doesn't remember why I wanted out of our marriage so badly that I'd go to the authorities with information that would destroy him. He doesn't remember *why* we are the way we are.

"I can see that me not remembering this is hurting you. Why?"

"Because it's the catalyst for our destruction. If only you—"

"If only I did what?" he interrupts.

For some reason, I don't want to say it again. I don't want to ask again. I begged constantly. I offered everything, anything, if only he'd do as I ask, and yet right now, I don't want to repeat what had become a broken record. "Do you remember the kind of relationship my sister and her husband are in?"

He slowly nods, but I'm not sure if he really does or if he's just nodding for my sake.

"He's an abusive asshole," I say, just to clarify for him if by chance he doesn't remember that fact. "He beats my sister over and over. Punches, makes her bloody. He's even broken her arm." My voice cracks. I swallow the bile forming in the back of my throat. "I fear he's going to kill her someday."

I see his jaw lock, and his eyes narrow.

I continue on. "She won't leave him. She told me that if she ever did, he'd hunt her down and kill her and kill me too, as payback."

Apollo sits up quickly. Rage washed over his face. "The fuck he will. The fact that he even threatened your life is reason enough for me to kill him with my bare hands. How dare he threaten you."

"He's threatened me multiple times. But..." I don't understand why the sudden change of heart. A complete about face. "That's just it, Apollo. I asked you to kill him. I begged you to. And when you refused, I even asked if I could have your brother do it. You refused that too. I know your brother was the family hitman, and for some reason I didn't understand, you forbid it. I wanted her husband dead and came to you for help. You turned me down, over and over again." I stop speaking as I try to process the clear anger I see on Apollo's face.

"Did I ever give you a reason?"

"You said that the Godwins don't get in the mud with pigs. You said that you and your brother are busy with genuine problems. You said that my sister made her bed and can easily get out of it. You said—"

"I was a fucking asshole," Apollo interrupts, clearly pissed. "That fucker deserves to die. The only reason I haven't gotten out of this bed to hunt him down right now is because for the life of me, I can't remember this shit."

"I just want my sister to be safe," I say, more to myself than to Apollo.

I sit back and pull my legs to my chest, feeling the overwhelming need to cry.

"I'm assuming they live on Heathens Hollow?"

"The Eastside."

"I'll take care of it today."

My heart skips. "Wait... Just like that?" I move closer to the door of the cage.

"Yes. Just like that. Give me the address."

An odd sense of panic mixed with excitement sizzles through my veins. "No plan, no— you can't just walk into the house and kill him."

"Why not?"

"Apollo, you act like it's no big deal to kill a man."

"I think we both know this isn't going to be my

first rodeo." He smirks, but I can see he's uncomfortable with this discussion. His body is tense, and his face even more so.

"You make it seem so...simple," I say softly.

"I shouldn't have refused you when you first asked. And if I didn't want to do it, then I should have asked Ares. Because he wouldn't have hesitated for a second. Not only would he have killed him, but he would also have made him suffer."

I'm confused by the change of heart. Why now? Why, after all this time?

"I hated you for saying no. I hated you for not helping me. Not helping the only family I have," I confess.

"You should have," he says. "It's warranted."

"I hated you so much, but I couldn't just divorce you. I knew when I married a Godwin that divorce was out of the question. Troy, Ares, Athena... Everyone truly believes the vow *until death do you part*. And I knew death was inevitable for breaking the vow. But I was miserable. I couldn't look at you. I had lost all respect for a man who I had thought would save me and keep me safe. So, when I walked in on you killing that man in the boardroom, I recorded it. I saw it as my chance to destroy you. I wanted out and knew this was a chance to be free of you forever. It was the pain in my heart that made me do what I did. You were willing to kill a man for business in the Medusa boardroom, just not willing to kill for me."

"And your sister?" he asks. "Is she okay right now?"

"For now," I answer.

"Does she want him dead?"

I shake my head. "No. I'm sure she doesn't. But it's either him or her. I know this in my gut. I have to protect her. I have to." I release a deep breath. "She's pregnant. Which means that now a baby is in danger too."

"Then we will. I'll take care of it." He lays down on his back and stares at the ceiling. "I should have done this before, but I will handle it. I promise."

"You'll kill him?" I'm not sure I'm hearing him correctly. What does taking care of it mean?

He turns his head. "Yes. I'll do whatever you ask. Besides, he fucked with the wrong Godwin by threatening your life."

"You'll do it *yourself?* Not hire someone?" Now that Ares is dead, I'm not sure who would be the person to handle this. Yes, Apollo killed someone in the boardroom of Medusa, but I didn't peg him as a ruthless killer. Killing Godwin enemies was the role of his twin.

"Of course I'll do it myself. He threatened my wife. You are a Godwin now, and no one gets away with threatening a member of this family."

Trepidation, uncertainty, and doubt constricts my heart like a vise. It suddenly feels difficult to breathe. "Today? You are going to do this today?"

Apollo must sense my chaos of conflicting

emotions, because he turns his head and looks at me with tenderness in his eyes. "When would you like me to?"

"I'm not sure... Not today. I mean, I want it done. I do, but..."

He doesn't say anything. He simply watches me.

"I'd like to talk to my sister first. Not warn her it's being done or anything. But... I just feel I need to speak with her first." Scared I may be missing my window of opportunity, I quickly add, "But I do want you to. I do. I just need a little time. If that is all right?"

He smiles. "You tell me when. It's your call."

Gratitude rushes over me, as well as...warmth. "Thank you, Apollo. I wouldn't ask if — thank you."

There's a long moment of silence between us. The air feels heavy, and I desperately want to be in his arms right now. I need his comfort, and I need to feel safe. And for the first time in my life, I truly feel Apollo has the ability to make me feel that. Secure.

There seems to be a crack in the air. A sizzle between us. An electric current that pulls us together, even though we've been drifting away as each day of our marriage went by. I've felt this powerful pull more and more since the accident. As if his near death has changed who he is and who we are. It's a gripping, suffocating hold over me, and I can't resist the way it demands me to just... be.

"Do you want out of the cage?" he asks, seductively hypnotizing me with his husky voice.

I remain silent and still, uncertain if his question is a trap of some sort.

"I have a lot of making up to do," he finally says.

"So do I."

"I think you've paid the last few days. Or at least coming damn close."

My body heats at the memory of all the ways I've paid. "Does that mean the cage and the punishment is over?"

"I'll tell you what," he says. "You can stay in that cage, roll over and get some sleep. I will leave you alone even though my cock is hard again and I want to fuck you until you scream my name." He presses up on his elbows, revealing his rippled abs. "Or you can crawl out of that cage and come sit on my face so I can lick you. We can end this punishment once and for all right now." He smiles. "The choice is completely up to you."

TWENTY-SIX

Apollo

"The cage is locked," she says with a sly smile.

I instantly sit up and walk toward the cage. "Ah, that it is. Would you like me to unlock it so we can end this punishment?"

"My choice?" she asks with wide eyes but a smirk on her face.

"Your choice," I parrot.

She nods. "Unlock the cage. Punish me."

I do so and step out of the way so she can crawl out and stand before me.

"I want to fuck you," I say, stepping closer as I wrap my arms around her waist, pulling her against me.

Her body is warm, even though she's surrounded by cool metal bars.

"Turn around," I demand, spinning her to face the cage.

Daphne does as instructed, allowing me to press her up against the metal bars. Pushing her long hair to one side, I kiss a warm path over her skin, loving how I can see visible chills on her body.

I hear the soft, sweet sigh of delight spill from her lips. She sounds angelic. My fingers caress down her arms, over the smoothness of her skin as I squeeze her hand.

"Lift your arms up," I say, guiding them up into the air. "Keep them there," I add with a tinge of warning.

I bring my hands up to caress her face, pulling her closer, capturing her lips with mine.

Hungry. Desire. Passion sparks between us like a lightning storm at sea, rough and turbulent. This is wrong. This is right. This is everything it shouldn't be, and yet it is absolutely perfect.

I don't want a pet anymore.

But I want her.

I don't need her as my captive anymore.

But I need her.

Somehow, we cross the line of forbidden, and I'm not turning back.

I back her against the bed, her knees hitting the surface. "Lie down," I say, telling her what to do, guiding her onto her back. Controlling my hunger, I tower over her as I gaze upon her beauty.

Daphne leans up, her fingers reaching out to

caress my chest. I climb on top of her body. We are nowhere near finished from earlier even though I desperately tried. I failed. I epically failed. If I can spend all day and night curled in her embrace, I will never get up from the bed again.

I have somehow become her captive instead of the other way around.

My breath hovers and teases over her flesh, intended to tingle on her skin and make her grow restless as my mouth grazes just above her thigh. My fingers climb back up her body, hovering above her breasts teasingly as I bring my lips down, crushing hers, desiring to feel her warmth and need for me in a simple kiss.

Her hands tangle in my hair and then down my back, smoothing over my spine, moving lower over and across my ass.

"I need you inside of me," she all but purrs. Her words are like music, a sweet melody that makes my heart strum louder in my chest.

I fucking need to be inside of her too.

I kiss a warm path down her neck, sucking the sensitive skin, listening to her moans of pleasure. I want to touch her and taste the sweet juices that flow from her pussy. I also don't want to rush the moment, as I truly want to savor every single minute with this woman.

My breath caresses her breast, pinching a nipple with one hand as my mouth meets the other. I could suck on her tits all night.

Daphne shifts beneath my weight, her soft purrs and moans filling the air. "I can't take it any longer. I need you. Now." Her hands move restlessly across and down my back while I continue sliding down her stomach, kissing over her navel.

My fingers gently caress the top of her mound as I look into her eyes silently.

Positioning myself between her thighs, I burrow my face into her folds, smelling her sweet womanly aroma while my tongue darts out to taste the signs of her arousal. With two fingers, I guide her lips apart, pleased with the smoothness as my mouth descends, tonguing and teasing her sex.

"Apollo," she gasps, her breaths filling the room with soft moans as I guide two and then three fingers into her tight hole. "I need your cock."

"I want you to be ready for me," I tease. "I want you coming the minute I shove my dick inside of you."

I stroke her warmth, wetness seeping out as I thrust my fingers in and out of her slick hole, diligently making her ready to explode the minute I enter her.

Her eyes slam shut, and I feel her fingernails graze across my back. She is getting close. Daphne's inner walls clench down on my fingers as she trembles beneath my weight.

Lowering my mouth again, I lick her some more, determined to have her scream out my name by the time the night is over. I have every intention of making her come for me over and over again. I need to hear my brother's name *rep*eatedly so she can help brainwash me into believing I am now Apollo. I need to become him. I need his name to be beaten into my body and soul.

Gradually, I climb back up her body, her eyes lazily opening as she refocuses on me.

"Do you want me?" I tease, my voice coming out heavy and thick.

"I do. I do," she begs. "I've never wanted you as badly as I want you right now."

Daphne's hand finds my cock, stroking the head, her thumb grazing the tip as it glazed with pre-cum. Her fist glides up and down over my shaft.

My hard cock aches with the need for release. The feel of her soft fingers and firm grip makes me struggle not to just fuck her brains out right then and there. I fight the urge to let her gain all control.

With her hand stroking me, I place my hand above hers, poising the head of my cock at her entrance.

She loosens her grip, allowing me to take over the moment I push slowly inside her tight little pussy.

"Bend your knees," I command, wanting to get balls deep in that body of hers.

Daphne does as I say, allowing me to move deeper at that angle. Her eyes shut and fingers claw at my back as I roughly thrust into her, nearly tearing that tight little hole of hers.

Slowly, I withdraw before sliding my cock further into her pussy, even deeper than before. "I want to keep you forever," I whisper against her ear.

"Do you forgive me?" she asks. "Is my punishment over?"

I lick a path down her neck to her collarbone. "Consider your penance paid. But never betray *your husband* again."

Daphne nods, her tightened grip on my back ceases, the pain from my deep thrusts turning to pleasure as she relaxes beneath my weight, curling her body around me, dragging her legs over mine, bringing me deeper into her warmth as she meets my thrusts with her own.

"Keep me. Keep your *loyal* wife forever," she pants as I drive into her with more force.

She leans up, crushing her lips against mine, her fingers tangling in my hair as my cock spreads her wide.

I feel her insides tighten around my shaft.

She's close.

She'll be screaming out my name.

Harder, I fuck her.

Harder, I push in and pull out.

Harder. Faster.

I reach down between us, two fingers stroking her clit, determined to set her tiny bundle of nerves on fire as I dominate her pussy.

Her insides shudder and her grip on me clenches

down, moaning as her head lolls back and she arches from the mattress.

"Apollo," she screams. "Apollo!"

I continue on.

I'm a greedy bastard and will not stop until she comes again.

I fuck her with more fervor than before. In and out. Punishing that tiny cunt of hers until she'll have to beg for me to stop.

Feeling her body coming undone a second time, I allow myself to let go, spilling my completion inside of her as she continues to murmur my brother's name.

My name.

TWENTY-SEVEN

Daphne

Waking up in a soft bed with fluffy white pillows all around my head is a luxury I'll never take for granted again. It's a far cry from waking up naked on the bottom of a cage.

The cage... It's gone.

I blink away my sleep to make sure I'm seeing what I think I see and scan the room to make sure I'm still in the room we've been in. Everything is the same except the missing cage. Turning my head to look at Apollo, I notice he is also gone. Even through a caffeine deprived mind, I see that I slept through both the cage and Apollo leaving the room.

Sitting up, not sure what to do next, I'm surprised and happy when I see a pair of my jeans, a white shirt, and flats waiting for me at the foot of the bed. Not only is the cage gone, but Apollo is not going to make me remain naked any longer.

After getting showered and ready, I decide to go find Apollo. I'm assuming he's still inside the manor, but I can't be sure of that. I'd find it shocking that he'd leave me alone without a note or waking me to tell me he had a meeting or something. Although I've been to Olympus several times for events, I've never really walked the halls or had free rein before. The place has always given me the creeps, and this time is no different. Portraits of dead ancestors line the hallways, the furniture all appears to be antiques, and there is a smell of...ghost in every nook and cranny. Most certainly this house is haunted. There is a ghost in the attic. I know it. I swear that every single family event outside on the expansive yard, I've seen the curtain in the attic window move. Every single time. None of the Godwins seem to mind the ghosts, however. I guess they have no reason to. They are all related.

As I approach the study, I hear Apollo speaking and can tell he's on the phone with work. He's talking numbers and budget projections, and I decide to not interrupt him. My stomach is growling in hunger, and I can guess that Apollo's may be as well. He's always been a man who can get lost in his work and forget to eat. Knowing there isn't any staff to assist us, I know I need to fend for ourselves. I'm not a good cook. I've never been taught, and once I married Apollo, there was never a need for my culinary skills. We had staff or we dined out. I also don't have any idea if there is any food in the kitchen since the manor has been empty.

As I make my way to the kitchen, there is a deafening silence to the house. It's polar opposite of what I'm used to when visiting Olympus. The Godwins are loud, and their friends even louder. This large place does not feel like home. But then again I don't really know what a home feels like. I've yet to experience that comfort. Yes, I have a house. But it's just that. A cold and sterile house. No love. No family. Just me and Apollo who...hated each other.

In a near daze, I rummage the kitchen and shockingly find food and enough supplies to cook a basic meal. Standing in this unfamiliar kitchen staring out the window, I can barely see a large tree on the edge of a cliff overlooking the sea due to the thick fog that's set in. My mind sifts through my own thick fog of confusion and lust. I can't even put what has occurred in words if I had to.

Apollo kidnapped me.

He had locked me in a cage.

Apollo punished me. Repeatedly.

He had me question if I'd live or die, and if my sister would be pulled into it.

Apollo fucked me, and not like a husband would fuck a wife.

He had humiliated me, humbled me, and forced me to face animalistic...desires.

And I had loved every single minute of it.

Everything about what happened since arriving on Heathens Hollow is wrong. Inappropriate for a Godwin. Apollo could go to jail for years for what he's done to me. But all of Apollo's discipline has accomplished one thing. I won't ever try to go to the authorities again. I won't make that mistake twice.

Hearing the water boiling over, I rush over to the pasta I'm cooking us for breakfast. There aren't any eggs or breakfast foods, and I only really know how to make pasta, so it will have to do. I can't remember the last time I actually prepared anything that required me turning on a stove.

I chuckle to myself at the fact that I'm clearly a fish out of water in the kitchen. But I'm having to adapt, and I should be grateful that I'm at least out of that damn cage so I can. So much has happened in a short time that it feels like my time in Seattle was a lifetime ago. So much has changed. He's changed.

Finishing up dishing up our breakfast which I suppose is more of a lunch, I'm not sure if Apollo wants me to bring him his plate or not. No doubt he's already been in the study for hours catching up with work and has been on phone calls that appear to be heated. But he needs to eat—

As if reading my mind, Apollo enters the kitchen and walks toward the small table by the window. "It smells good," he says as he takes a seat at the table as if this is our normal.

Nothing about cooking and having a meal across from each other at a kitchen table is normal.

Taking his lead, I bring our plates to the table. "I made pasta with red sauce," I say, trying not to remember The Vault and how we ate a similar meal there. "I hope it's okay." After the years of marriage, I still don't know what this man likes to eat. Not really. I haven't really tried to know, and I take that accountability now. I should have. Our marriage wasn't bad just because of him. I played a part. I know this.

"I really like your cooking," he praises. He looks up at me, studies my face, which must reflect my shock in his statement, and adds, "I mean, I know we've always eaten out and all the parties...but I like *this*."

"There wasn't much to choose from in the pantry," I say as I sit down to join him. "But it surprised me to see it stocked with anything at all. When was the last time anyone stayed here? I thought the Godwins only came here for big parties or family holidays."

"We like it to be ready for spontaneous trips." He takes a large bite of his pasta and chews as he stares directly into my eyes. Swallowing, he continues, "If there is something you need, let me know. I'll have it delivered to us."

"How long are we staying here?" I ask. "Now that the punishment is over, as you said, I assumed we'd be going home soon."

He shakes his head as he takes another mouthful.

When he's finished chewing, he says, "I sold the house."

I freeze mid-chew, not sure if I had heard him correctly. "What? You sold our house? Why?"

"It didn't feel like a home. It held...memories. Memories that I figured you and I both wanted to forget. And I—"

"You just sold our house without even mentioning it to me?" I interrupt. "What about all our belongings?"

"It's all been placed in storage." He looks up at me and smiles. "Don't worry. We'll get a new house. One that feels like a home to you, and to me. We need a fresh start."

"You loved that house," I point out, shocked by his impulsive act. He's never been one to just make such a huge decision without months of research and planning.

He shrugs. "I think a new house will be good. As for the belongings... It's all materialistic stuff, right? We can just buy new." He looks at me. "You like shopping, right?"

"You know I don't."

He stops chewing and then nods. "That's right. But maybe if we do it together, it won't be so bad." He returns to eating his pasta. "Anyway, we'll stay here at the manor until we find a new place. But I was thinking I'd call the agent and have us fly into Seattle tomorrow to meet with her. Maybe we could have her show us some houses. Start the process."

"Okay..." This all seems so unlike Apollo, but I will not question a good thing. I always hated that house. Apollo wanted it. Not me. "What kind of house do you want? Do you have a neighborhood in mind?"

He shrugs again. "What do you want?"

He's never asked me that question before. I had always just assumed I should be grateful that I had a roof over my head and was no longer living in a shack with no power on the Eastside of Heathens Hollow.

"The truth?" I ask as I place down my fork.

His brow rises at my question. "Of course. Why would you ask that? I always want the truth from you. Always."

I take a deep breath and decide to confess something I told no one. "When my sister and I were old enough to explore the island and beyond without being questioned, we took the ferry from the island to Seattle. Well...actually, we snuck onto the ferry since we didn't have any money. We had been so excited because it was our first trip to the city. We lucked out when we got there because the busses ran that day for free, so we didn't even have to pay for that." I pause and take a sip of water, pausing to see if Apollo tries to stop me or rush along my story. But he only stares at me, giving me his full attention. I decide to continue on. "We didn't know our way around the city or where anything was but decided to get on the bus and see where it took us. We ended up getting off in the Queen Anne district, and I instantly fell in love with the houses. The old craftsmen homes were everywhere, and I loved the neighborhood with all the landscaped and perfectly groomed yards. But there was this one house in particular that stood out to me. It had beveled windows with a large stainless glass heart hanging in the center. Plants lined up along the sill and you could see into the dining room from the street where we stood. There was a simple four-person table with a chandelier hanging above. Not an overly fancy one, but a fixture with clean lines and casting warm light below. I had imagined myself sitting in that house, at that table, and fantasized what it would be like. I promised myself that I would someday live in a craftsmen house in the Queen Anne district." I take another drink of water. "I was a big dreamer as a kid."

"Then the Queen Anne district will be our first stop," Apollo says simply. His smile is so warm that I'm tempted to reach out and hold his hand. For some odd reason, I long for the connection.

"When I suggested it before, you said the area is for upper middle-class people. It was beneath us."

Apollo grimaces, swallows hard, and stiffens his spine. "You must have caught me on a bad day. I apologize." He places his fork down on his plate, dabs his mouth with his napkin, and adds, "I'd like to explore the district with you. I like the idea of a craftsmen as well."

Excitement shoots through me. "Really? You mean it?" The thought that a possible dream of mine could actually come true seems unreal.

"If the idea makes you smile like that," he stands from the table and walks over to me, "then I'd love to see what actually walking inside of them will do." He lowers his mouth to mine and gives it a quick peck. "I'll go make the call now and set it up. I then have some more work to do. Will you be all right for a bit without me?"

"Apollo," I say softly, hating to break this *sweet,* and very uncharacteristic of Apollo, moment. "Can I ask a favor?"

"Yes, what?"

"Do you mind if I use the phone to call my sister?"

"Call your sister? Of course." His eyes darken at the mention of her, and I know why. He's waiting for the signal for him to act. A signal I'm not sure when I'll be able to give.

"I haven't touched base with her in a long time. I don't have my cell phone though."

"Sure," he says, as he reaches for his phone and then gives it to me. "It gets the best signal in the main room, but it works great from the study too. Do you want me to work in another room so you can use the study for privacy?"

"Oh, no," I say, bolting toward the door. "I'll go in the main room. Thank you."

TWENTY-EIGHT

Daphne

My sister and I had spent our entire lives mastering the ability to communicate through code. Ani was only two years younger than me, so we had always been close. We only had each other. My memory of my mother is very limited, and Ani's is non-existent. But we both remember my father and always will. He was an awful, abusive man who we had the misfortune of having to live with. Our only way to survive was by creating a secret code language so that we could communicate in times that we didn't want him to know what we were saying. A tug of an ear meant beware. I braid of our hair meant dad had over five drinks and was approaching the stage of drunk where he'd pop us for no reason. Biting the lip meant one of us found food so we could sneak a meal in and not starve that night. And a yawn meant for us to get out of the house as fast as we could and meet at a lean to shelter we had built. But once my father died, I never imagined we still needed to speak in code. But we do.

I let the phone ring twice and then hang up. It's the code needed for Ani to feel the vibration in her pocket and then to go find a place she can speak in private without Mark knowing of her secret phone. I wait five minutes and call again, hoping she'll pick up, which isn't always a given. This time, she does.

"Hi," she says, but I hear sadness in her voice. It isn't the first time I've called and heard the tone.

"Are you all right?" I ask.

There's a pause. "No."

She's never said no. She's never said anything other than trying to convince me that everything is fine when I know it's anything but.

Alarm bells are going off. I force myself to take a seat so my knees don't buckle. "What happened?"

There's another pause. I can hear her breathing. I hear a sniffle.

"Ani? What's wrong? What happened?"

"Mark... He went on a two-day bender. When he got home, he started accusing me of awful things. He claimed the baby wasn't his. He beat me."

That's it. The man is dead. I wasn't sure I could actually give Apollo the green light to actually kill a man. It had all sounded good in theory, but being faced head on with deciding whether a man lived or died. But now...the fucker is going to die.

"Where are you? Are you at the house? I'm coming to get you." I've offered to do this repeatedly and Ani always says no. She always refuses. I've even considered just showing up and not giving her an option, but I know my sister. She's stubborn, and if she says no, then her answer is set in stone. But this time is different. I'm not four hours away. I'm close, and I'm coming. "I'm on Heathens Hollow now. I'll be there in twenty minutes. Get your stuff ready."

"The baby..." she continues and breaks down into a sob. "I lost the baby."

It was as if Mark had the ability to reach through the phone and beat the shit out of me too. I fell back against the chair and let out a winded gasp.

"I'm calling the police. Do you need an ambulance?" I somehow got the words out, but I'm not sure since I still couldn't inhale a breath of air.

I can hear her cry on the other end. "No. No. Don't call anyone."

"Where is he?"

"Sleeping off the bender. He should be asleep all day. Please don't call anyone. Don't."

"Will you leave with me?"

There's a pause.

"Apollo and I are here at Olympus. Can we come and get you? Please, Ani. Please. Apollo and I won't allow anything to happen to you. I promise."

There's still silence on her end other than the occasional hiccup and sob.

"Ani?"

"Yes... Come and get me."

Apollo

I kill alone.

I've never had a partner. I've never even spoken of the exact time and method of when or how I'd kill someone. Solo. I've always been solo.

But there was no way I was going to leave Olympus Manor without Daphne. Even locking her in a cage wouldn't have worked, because my hysterical wife was determined to rescue her sister with me.

We rode in silence for the entire ride. I wasn't sure what to say or what to ask. The little she told me through her shaking and tears was enough to know the man needed to die. And if she hadn't looked me in the eyes and said, "Kill him now," I would have done it, regardless.

"The trailer's up this dirt road," she says, pointing to a washed-out path that isn't passable by vehicle.

"Can we make it on foot?"

"I think so. I've only been here once. But I remember it not being too far up in the woods."

The rain coming down is going to make the hike up the path muddy and uncomfortable. I want to tell Daphne to wait in the car, but her sister doesn't know who I am, and me arriving alone most likely won't go well. Daphne doesn't give me time to consider any other options, because she hops out of the car and starts running into the trees. I have no choice but to get out and chase after her. I don't blame her for her sense of urgency. If it were my sister up there, I'd be doing the same.

Fortunately, the muddy path is actually more of a driveway. It doesn't take us long to reach a trailer the color of piss. Ani must have been looking out the window, because she walks out the door with a blue Adidas duffle and enough bruises on her face to match the bag perfectly.

I clear the distance between us as fast as I can, take the bag from her, scan her face and head for severe injuries that require any immediate first aid, and then hand the bag to Daphne when I feel her sister is safe enough to travel. "Go down to the car with your sister and wait for me."

Ani looks over her shoulder at me. One of her eyes is already swelling shut. "You aren't coming?"

"I'm not coming."

"Don't go in there." Ani turns her head to Daphne. "Don't let him go in there. Mark is sleeping and he won't know I'm gone until tomorrow at the earliest. Don't go in there and wake him up." She points at the bag. "I have all I need."

Daphne puts her hand on her sister's arm, and then her sister's belly that is no longer carrying a baby. "He's not going to leave you alone. You said it yourself to me over and over again. He won't just let you leave."

Daphne looks up at me and nods her head. I can see it in her eyes that she still wants me to follow through with the plan.

"What are you going to do?" she asks. There's panic in her voice. "Going in there and kicking the shit out of him isn't going to do anything but piss him off more. Let's just go. I can leave the state, maybe. I can just run and hide, and he'll never find me."

Daphne shakes her head. "No."

"What do you mean no?" she asks her sister, clearly not having any idea what Daphne and I both know is going to be the outcome of the day.

It's raining harder now, and both women are soaked all the way through. "Wait for me in the car. I won't be long."

"He's just like Dad, Ani. You know it."

Daphne's words finally are what it takes for Ani to catch on with what's going to happen next. She shakes her head vigorously and takes a few steps back to the trailer. "No. No! You are not going to kill him. We can't just go in there—"

I take a step forward so I'm blocking the trailer from Ani. "*We* aren't doing anything. I am. You and Daphne need to go to the car and get warm. I'll be there soon."

Ani shakes her head, but then suddenly stops when the front door of the trailer opens and a man wearing nothing but faded boxers blinks against the rain. "What the fuck is going on here?" he demands. "Ani, you get your ass inside here now." He then squints against the falling rain and sees Daphne. "I told you to stay the fuck away from your sister. I told you that I'd kill you if you stepped foot on my land again, you stupid bitch." When he sees that Ani hasn't made a move to do as he asked, he repeats. "Get in the fucking house, Ani!"

I've seen the eyes of many people right before they meet their maker, and I've never seen the kind of fear like what I see in Ani's eyes.

Mark glares at me. "And who the fuck are you?" He starts walking down the stairs to confront me.

Stupid, stupid man.

"I'm the fucking Grim Reaper," I say as I punch him right in the Adam's Apple.

His eyes bulge as he reaches for his throat with a sickening croak escaping from his contorted lips. He falls back, slipping on the last step and splashing into the mud. His wheezing for air mixes with the sound of the storm. The drops of the rain hit the metal roof of the trailer with more intensity, and I know a torrential downpour is coming and it's time to act before all these hillbilly backroads get washed out.

I'm happier that he confronted me. He entered this fight and now I'm going to finish it. I didn't like the idea of killing a man in his sleep, and I didn't want to act like a silent assassin. No, this fucker walked right up to me and stared directly into the eyes of his killer.

Daphne runs up to Ani and takes her by the arm. "We're leaving. Now."

I don't know if it's the fact that Ani is too shocked to argue and resist any longer, or the fact that seeing the man who caused her to lose her baby laying in a puddle of mud was the last straw, but she does exactly as Daphne ordered, and the two women leave for the car.

Now it's just me and this piece of shit.

Mark somehow scrambles to his feet, though I can see that he's still struggling to breathe. He doesn't have enough air to scream. He can't beg. He can't do anything but gasp through the final minutes of his life.

"You beat my wife's sister." I take a step toward him as he climbs the stairs of the trailer on all fours. "You killed her baby. You called my wife a bitch. And you *threatened* my wife. You threatened a Godwin." I take hold of his hair and yank him off the stairs, throwing him back down in the mud. "And for that, you are going to die. But I don't just kill. I kill slowly."

Though I've been trying to be Apollo Godwin ever since waking up from my accident, right now, this very moment... I'm Ares Godwin. And this fucker is about to see what that means.

THIRTY

Apollo

Daphne knocks on my door as I finish getting ready to start my day. "Good morning," she says.

"How is she doing today?" I ask, having checked on Ani myself a couple of times, but she had been sleeping every time. It's been a couple of days of recovery, and it's nice to see some of the swelling go down as well as some of the bright blues and purples begin to fade.

"She's doing much better," Daphne says. "Her ribs are still giving her some trouble, and she is having nightmares still..."

"Do you want me to have the doctor come back to the house?"

Shaking her head, she says, "No. He said she just

needed time to heal. And I'm feeling confident she is. Slowly, but she is."

"I've tried to leave you two alone," I say. "I figured you needed some time together. To talk about what happened."

"She doesn't really want to talk too much, and I'm respecting that. I think she's just processing right now. She has healing to do on the inside too. The wounds there are worse than the ones we see."

"I think that can be said for everyone. We all have wounds on the inside that need to be healed." I take her in my arms, feeling the need to have her close.

She looks up at me. "True. But what you did... You helped heal a very large one inside of me."

"I should have done it sooner."

"But you did it now. Thank you. I know I keep telling you that. But I mean it. I can never say those words enough. When you first asked me to marry you, you said that you'd always keep me safe. That you'd protect me. You gave me my very own Cinderella story." She releases an unsteady breath. "But my glass slipper had thorns. Until now."

"I should have plucked out every fucking thorn for you," I declare, hating the visual of how my brother had caused such pain. Sharp, stabbing pain to a woman who didn't deserve it.

Although if he were still alive, I want to believe he'd eventually do as I did. I want to believe that he was that kind of man. He wouldn't have been able to look into Daphne's eyes for long and resist.

I sure as fuck can't. I'm growing more and more obsessed over this woman as each day goes by.

"You and I haven't really had a chance to speak since everything happened," she says, looking down at her feet and fiddling with her fingers. "I told Ani that you," she swallows hard, "took care of everything."

"I did." I tilt my head to examine her face in order to try to read her. "Do you want to know how? The details?"

I've never told anyone the details after a job. Not even my father. I do the deed, I clean up after myself, and we never speak of it again. But I'll make an exception for Daphne if she needs it. Or if her sister needs it.

"No," she says. "I feel like talking about that man, even the way he died or where his body is, gives him too much of our breath. He's not worth it. I think it's best to forget the man even existed. He's nobody."

"He's nobody," I agree.

I know Daphne has a lot on her mind right now with her sister, but she doesn't turn away when my mouth lowers toward her. I haven't kissed her since Ani arrived. We haven't slept together since she's been sleeping by her sister's side this entire time.

I've missed her. I've missed...my wife.

Our lips touch, a fleeting hint of what's yet to come. I press her close, then closer still, so that the soft curves of her body meld to the hardness of my cock. I kiss her again, as her arms lift to encircle my neck. Our kiss intensifies, leaving our bodies tense for more.

I want to approach things slowly, to not let my desire be mastered by my passion. But when Daphne moans against the thrust of my tongue and her hands frantically remove all of my clothing, I know the battle is lost.

The level of chemistry between us is consuming, making me want her with an intensity I never experienced with anyone else. When she makes it known she's willing and wanting to accept my claiming of her body, I almost explode with lust.

Her physical response leaves me no doubt that the woman feels the same pull I do. Sensual, erotic, and tantalizing sex can easily become our form of communication and connection. Passion always mixed with our day and night is my ultimate goal for this marriage of ours. It's what and who we are becoming, and I plan to keep it that way.

She rubs herself intimately against me, the action making my cock grow even harder. I want to sink into her, to lose myself in her slick, wet heat, to drive us both hard and fast to orgasm. I can't wait to hear her scream out my name.

It's what we both want—more important, what we need. But this time, I'm determined to give her something different, to offer her something more. Not just a sexual experience, but a promise. I want to communicate security in the way we make love. Yes, I said it. *Make love.* I want to make sure she feels safe in the fact I'm here. I am going to shelter her from any storm that comes her way.

My cock presses against my pants to the point of pain. I can't free myself from the restraints of my clothing fast enough. She does the same and lowers her dress, her panties, her bra... This woman... this goddess before me literally makes me grow weak in the knees. Such sweet delicate features, and also such luscious and alluring curves. I have to have her. I have to have her now, and I pray to God that I can be gentle since I have already been firm and truly pushed her boundaries.

Shedding the last of my clothes as she sits on the edge of the mattress, I approach the bed and run my palm up Daphne's leg, enjoying her not flinching, but moaning in response to my touch. She lays back on the bed completely naked and doesn't conceal herself at all. Her eyes never leave mine, as if she's attempting to hypnotize me with her seductive and needy stare.

"I want to look at and touch every part of your body. I want to memorize every curve, every dip and valley, and every inch of your skin," I say so she has no doubt of what's coming.

Without waiting for a response, I spread her legs wide, watching the seam of her pussy open for me. Beneath her pussy, I see her anus, so small...so tight. Her tiny hole just begging to be entered, but I want to go easy today. I want that sweet pussy of hers milking my cock dry.

Running my finger along the puckered and delicate flesh, I watch how she presses her ass against my hand, not resisting my touch.

"This time isn't meant to be a punishment. I don't want to hurt you. I only want you to feel pleasure," I say the words as I run my fingers to the seam of her pussy.

I can barely contain my hunger to be buried so deep inside of her. Soaking up her juices glistening on her pussy with my fingertip, I lick, tasting her arousal. With as much care as I can, I press my wet finger into her pussy and ease my way in. Daphne gasps and tenses, but then relaxes when I slowly move my finger in and out of her tight channel. I lean down between her legs and kiss her smooth mound, inhaling the musky scent of her desire.

"It feels good," she whispers. "So good."

"Yes, princess," I coax as my finger glides in and out. "I need to get this body of yours ready for me. You know I'm not a small man, and I don't want this to hurt more than it already will when I can't fuck nicely." When her legs relax open and her hips thrust up to meet my mouth, silently begging for more of my kisses, I whisper, "That's my good girl. Let me prepare you to become my perfect and most cherished wife in all ways."

My name catches in her throat when a moan overpowers it as my tongue flicks her clit, nipping it between my lips. Her hands run down both sides of my head, driving my face into her pussy as her moans intensify.

"Apollo... Apollo? This feeling. I feel..." Panic laces her words.

"Come for me, my wife. Let it in." I add a second finger and pump with more force, driving deeper inside.

Her head thrashes side to side, and her breathing becomes ragged. A deep moan fills the room as her pussy constricts around my fingers.

"Come for me. Fill my mouth with your sweet cream. Release and let go of all those restrictions holding you back. Let that orgasm rock the inner walls of your pussy."

Her hips buck as her moan turns into a tiny scream. Her pussy quivers around my mouth, and the taste of her release coats my tongue. I lap up every last bit of her completion as her body shakes on the tail end of her climax.

Not wanting her to fully become sated, I moved up to her breasts and circle my tongue around one nipple, and then move to pay the same attention to the other. Molding the flesh of her firm and perky mounds with my hands, I no longer fight the hunger. I need my cock buried deep inside of her and can't wait any longer.

I place my lips at the shell of her ear and groan out, "I'm going to fuck you now. It is going to hurt, Daphne. It's going to hurt bad, but also hurt so, so good. I don't know how to fuck soft. I only know how to fuck hard."

"Yes, yes, please," she begs. "I want this. I do."

Placing the head of my dick at her entrance, I slowly ease in, pausing when her body tensed with resistance. This is the time when I will fully claim her. I'm not punishing her ass. I'm not taking her body. I'm not spanking her into submission. My wife is giving it.

Forever mine.

Forever to play with as I choose.

"Take a deep breath and relax," I order as I push all the way in and begin pistoning in and out at a rapid and unforgiving pace. "Shhh..." I pause for a moment so she can adjust to the intensity of the fucking and to the sensation of being stretched. "I know this hurts."

"You're just too big. Just too hard." Her eyes are wide, and her voice quivers as she says the words.

"You *will* take all of me. You have no other choice."

Wanting to be gentle is one thing. Actually being able to is another. Gentle and sweet when it comes to fucking and claiming what I consider mine just isn't in my nature.

Raw, hard, aggressive is who I am. And though I am pretending to be Apollo, I can't change this primal fact about me no matter how hard I try.

I launch another steady rhythm of pushing in and out, only being fueled by her soft little mewls. A steady staccato of my cock pulling out just enough to spread her opening even wider, and then plummeting back inside, so deep the walls of her pussy constrict around me. In and out, I claim her in one of the most animalistic and lust-filled ways. In and out, she gives herself to me. Mine.

Not being able to hold back my pleasure any longer, I allow the surge of my ecstasy to take over, filling my seed deep within her.

"Apollo," she calls out, the sound so sweet on her pouty lips.

"Yes?"

"Will you ever let me go?"

"Never. Never. You are mine, and I am one stingy son of a bitch."

CHAPTER
THIRTY-ONE

Apollo

It's been three weeks? Maybe a little under a month? I've completely lost track of time, which is completely unlike me. Godwins march to strict order and timelines. I can't remember the last time I didn't follow some order issued by my father. My days and nights were full, overflowing so. But since waking up in that hospital room, something inside of me is different.

I'm married.

I have Daphne, and I want Daphne. I can't get enough of the woman. If I'm not fucking her, I want her to stay in my presence just so I can look at her whenever I want, or smell her, or touch her, or fuck her all over again. It seems my cock remains in constant need of attention, and the only way to cure the ailment is having it buried deep inside of this woman...my drug.

But one thing remains the same. I am not Apollo. No matter how hard I'm trying to convince the world that I am indeed my brother, I wonder if I'm living this lie on borrowed time. I'm a Godwin, and we are masters at deceiving and can lie without so much as a flinch, but this time is different.

This lie involves Daphne.

She deserves better than me. I'm not my brother, and I don't know how to be married. I don't know how to give her much more than sex. I try to stop working for our meals so I can give her some attention and learn about the woman I can't get enough of, but my mind struggles to focus. I have yet to do anything with her that couples would do. There is no wining and dining. No sweet gifts. No "honey I'm home." My life consists of fucking and working. Olympus Manor is giving us a bubble of security from the rest of my family, and I'm loving the seclusion. Not a terrible life for me, but I also believe Daphne deserves better.

I have to keep thinking about what Apollo would do. Not what I would do. No doubt he'd do more than just fuck and work. Though it sounds like they weren't doing a lot of fucking. Regardless, I need to remind myself that I am a married man and need to act accordingly or there is a chance Daphne may discover my dark secret.

"Daphne," I call out, finally deciding that it's time I take a break.

She must have been near the study because she pads barefoot into the room holding a dishtowel in her hand. She wears jeans and a white t-shirt and has never looked sexier. Casual and comfortable is a good look on her.

With one eyebrow raised, she asks, "Do you need something? Dinner isn't for a couple of hours. I still need to start it."

"Don't," I say. "Let's go into town. It's about time I take you on a date."

"A date?" she asks as a smile grows on her face. "Really?"

"We haven't gone into town unless you want to count The Vault. Have you ever eaten at Ghost Pines?"

"No never. It's so... Ghost Pines was too expensive for me to ever go when I lived here."

"It has the best seafood I've ever had. It also has a prime rib that is to die for. We can share a bottle of wine and make a romantic evening out of it."

"Yes!" she replies fast. Maybe a little too fast, which tells me that the poor girl is desperate for some attention, and probably to get out of the house. She and I had taken some walks together on the grounds, but I'm sure she's getting a bit stir-crazy. "You don't think it's raining too badly to drive?"

I glance out the window to see that a steady rain is falling. "It's fine. I don't think the heart of the storm is supposed to come in until tomorrow night. This is minor. Do you think your sister can be left alone for a bit?"

Daphne smiles. "It's cute that you worry about her. And yes, she'll be fine. Maybe we can bring her home a piece of cheesecake or something."

I look at her bare feet. "Go get some shoes on. We'll leave now."

I don't have to say another word. Daphne spins on her heels and runs upstairs. I hear her excitement as she sprints up the staircase, and it reminds me of a child running down to a tree with presents underneath on Christmas morning.

The drive into town is fairly quiet. I hadn't turned off my brain yet and am still, unfortunately, thinking about how I'm going to deal with my father and Athena when I see them. Fortunately, they both have left me alone, allowing me to deal with Daphne and to process everything that happened since the accident. I know they are doing it for two different reasons. Athena is giving me space because I asked for it. My father is giving the time I need to figure out how to keep this lie of becoming Apollo from blowing up in my face.

It's getting easier by the day with Daphne. I've also been able to convince the staff at work via phone and email that I'm Apollo. Not an easy feat since numbers are not my strong suit, and I feel like I'm drowning in spread sheets and tax questions I have no idea how to answer. But I've yet to have to face anyone from our lives besides at the funeral, and I'm not sure when I'll be ready.

When it comes to Daphne, I try to just listen to her talk. I try to take it all in. She's caught me on a few more things that I've had to claim memory loss on, but for the most part, I'm able to fake my way through conversations. But we also haven't really been in an intimate situation like sitting in a car by each other heading to a date. So, I've just been driving and allowing silence to swarm around us. Though it doesn't seem that Daphne minds. She just sits in her seat and listens to music as the foggy forest passes us by. The roads aren't bad, and nothing my Jeep can't handle. I have no concerns that we have to rush back. We can enjoy a nice evening out. We both deserve it.

"I should have taken you here for this dinner sooner," I say as my eyes quickly lock with hers. "I apologize for that."

"No need. We only came to Heathens Hollow for family gatherings and parties. It's not like we had the opportunity."

"But is it something you would have liked to do?" I ask as I put my eyes back on the road.

"Of course. Ani and I used to fantasize what it would be like to eat there. It's fancy, but not snooty. Ghost Pines was sort of that marker for people. If you could afford to eat there, then you made something of yourself. I—"

"I wish you would have told me this. Your

dreams should be granted," I interrupt. "Especially something as simple as taking you to a nice seafood and steak restaurant."

"I've never been good at opening up," she confesses. "Sometimes dreams need to just stay dreams."

I glance over and reach for her hand. "Not anymore. You're my wife and the very least I can do is start granting some of them."

When we reach Ghost Pines, I pull up at the entrance to drop Daphne off so she doesn't have to walk through the parking lot in the rain. "I'm going to park. Go ahead and put our name in."

THIRTY-TWO

Daphne

I've never eaten prime rib before. I don't want to admit this fact to Apollo. High society women in Seattle—and I'm assuming the rest of the world—seem to only eat dainty fish dishes, salads, or maybe the occasional chicken breast. No woman I ever met would dare sit at a table and eat a big slab of fatty meat. But that's exactly what I'm doing. Apollo hadn't given me much of a choice since he ordered for the both of us. But I can't say I'm upset by that fact. Growing up an Eastsider, eating at Ghost Pines was never an option. Not even on a special occasion could we even dare walk into a place like this.

I had considered trying to get a waitressing job here at one point. One night's tips would no doubt be a month's worth of bills paid. But I wasn't even up to their standards for *serving* their clients. Ghost Pines was simply an illusion for the poor like me. It catered to the wealthy who had vacation homes on Heathens Hollow, or flew in on their sea planes or helicopters from Seattle. No true locals could afford a place like this.

"They have great prime rib, right?" Apollo asks as he places another piece of meat into his mouth.

"It's so good," I say as I take in every savory taste.

The restaurant isn't exactly fancy by Seattle standards—at least not white tablecloths and candlelight—but it does have a roaring fire, leather booths, and the rustic charm of the decor makes the entire place feel warm and inviting. For Heathens Hollow, this is as fancy as this fisherman town will get. I love it, and I love every minute of this date with Apollo.

"So, I'd like to ask you something," he says as he sips from his wine. "But I don't want to hurt your feelings by admitting I can't remember something."

"You won't hurt my feelings. I know that memory loss is going to be an issue. The doctors had warned me it could be much worse than it seems to be. You really are recovering at break-neck speed."

"Okay, but this could hurt you."

"Hurt me? How?"

"I don't really remember us meeting and how we became married. What I do know almost feels...like it's a story that's been told to me. I lack the details. You've mentioned that I saved you from the island.

You make me feel as if I did something more than just asking you to marry me." He pauses as he chews his meat and then swallows, never breaking his stare. "How did we meet? I'd like to hear it from you."

I divert my eyes and shrug. Does it bother me he doesn't remember our beginning? Maybe. But maybe I'm bothered even more that I don't really want to talk about it. "It's the classic Cinderella story. Poor girl. Rich man. You brought me into your life so I could no longer be an Eastsider."

"Did we meet here on Heathens Hollow or Seattle?"

I pause from eating, observing the way he asks the question. He really doesn't remember. "We met at the pier. I was a fishmonger. One of my many jobs that would pay me in cash so I could eat or pay whatever pressing bill was demanding to be paid. You were walking along the pier and we met. For some crazy reason, you and I seemed to form a connection. Regardless that I smelled of fish and poverty. You asked me to dinner, and then three months later we were married." I rushed the story, but hopefully it's all he'll need to trigger his memory.

I take a drink of my wine and stare at the fireplace nearby. I don't want to talk about my past, and even though Apollo and I seem closer than ever, I'm uncomfortable talking about our past as well. It's almost as if a trip down memory lane will pop the perfect bubble we've been in.

"Tell me more," he says, clearly not picking up on

the fact this topic is like picking a scab. I don't want to bleed when I feel like I've started to heal.

"Like what?"

"Did you know I was a Godwin when you met me?"

I chuckle. "Did I know I was having dinner with someone who owned the entire island of Heathens Hollow?" I laugh again. "No, or I wouldn't have had dinner with you, no matter how hungry I was. I'd be too scared you'd ask for back rent we owed you. We were squatting on your land." I smile, but it's not exactly funny.

"What made you fall in love with me?"

I shrug. "I came from poverty, abuse, and neglect. My father was an alcoholic and my mother was dead —or at least that's what he told my sister and me. So when you came along with all your money and promises, it felt like I had found my happily ever after. My fairytale I had hoped for was now a reality. But—"

"It wasn't exactly a fairytale," he finishes for me.

"Not at all. I had no idea what marrying you and becoming a Godwin would be like." I see that he isn't eating any longer, and I feel like I need to lighten the mood. I don't want this dinner date to become a bashing session. He's trying to make amends, and I need to allow him to be able to do so. I *want* him to do so. "But you still saved me from the Eastside, and I'll forever be grateful."

"Do you still want out of the marriage?" he asks.

I take a bite of meat so I have time to think about his question as I chew. He waits and watches me as I swallow. "I know it's not an option. Your family never hid that fact from me. I know what I was marrying in to. I signed that contract with blood. So...no. I no longer want out of the marriage. A deal is a deal."

"Is that how you see us? A deal?"

"How do you see us?" I counter, not wanting to really dive in and divulge all the conflicting emotions I've had since the accident, the betrayal, the punishment, and then what he did for my sister.

"You're my wife. I'm your husband," he begins. "Call it what you want, but I'm fucking obsessed with you. I can't imagine ever letting you leave."

"I'm not leaving," I say softly, drinking my wine as I look over the table with hooded eyes. "I may like this *obsession* you speak of too much to leave."

Apollo leans forward, his elbows resting on the table. In a low voice, he says, "I'm going to take you home, and I'm going to fuck you hard. I'm going to fuck you until you scream out my name. Not cry. Not moan. Scream."

CHAPTER

THIRTY-THREE

Daphne

"That was the longest car ride home," Apollo says as we both enter the kitchen. "Maybe I should have pulled the car over and fucked you in the back seat like two horny teenagers."

The blush takes over my entire body without warning. I walk to the kitchen table and take a seat in order to try to regain my composure. This man now has a way of making me feel like a giddy little schoolgirl, and I hate it. But I don't hate him. No, my feelings are the polar opposite of hate, but just as powerful.

Apollo smirks. "I like the way you embarrass so easily. Now that it's just you and me, alone here, I'm noticing all the little things about you, and I'm finding I enjoy them all."

I turn my head to look into Apollo's smiling eyes. The soft wrinkles at the edges give his sexy charm a sense of maturity. He keeps my stare locked within his for what seems like an eternity. His gaze single-handedly melts my heart. I ooze from the inside out. He has a power over my emotions that I'm not used to allowing. His strength, his intoxicating dark demeanor, his aura just screams out, 'Man.'

Without looking away, Apollo slowly walks to my side of the table and leans in toward me, with his mouth only inches from mine. "I want to feel your lips on me."

He isn't asking permission, yet announcing his intent. The actions of a Godwin.

I look down at his mouth and then back into his eyes and softly whisper, "I'd like that."

He places a hand on each side of my head and softly presses his lips to mine. The touch sends tingles through my entire body. Never has a simple kiss given me such a powerful, intense reaction with anyone else, and not even with him. It's just a kiss, and yet so much more.

The power this man has over me... When he never had this control before...

His lips move slowly along mine until his tongue lightly presses past my lips. The warmth and the wetness increase the desire building inside my core. His fingers caress my hair softly as his tongue continues to explore. A kiss, a high-inducing kiss, is more than I can imagine. I can smell Apollo, taste

Apollo, and feel Apollo. I hunger for more. I want the kiss to last forever—never wanting his lips to leave mine.

"You feel so right," Apollo murmurs between our entwined breaths.

The sound of his voice, muffled by the kiss, provokes an involuntary gasp, revealing how locked in his hold I've become. Never would I have thought I'd feel so much power from a simple kiss. At this moment, the only thing I want is for him to never stop.

His hands move down my back, and he pulls me to standing so we can be closer. My breasts press firmly to his rock-hard chest with only thin layers of cotton between us. As our bodies merge, our kiss becomes more frenzied. Apollo presses his tongue deeper into my mouth. I respond by parting my lips wider and dancing my tongue with his. My breath mixes with his, my gasps swallowed by the kiss.

The all-consuming, most mind-blowing kiss.

A kiss I never knew could exist. With one kiss, my husband—a man I never thought I'd love again—has captured my heart even more than it has already been possessed by our passionate sex before.

Slowly pulling away, he looks deep into my eyes. His own glazed over as desire courses across his face. He runs a single finger along my jawline and traces it along the edge of my needy lips. A small, seductive smile forms as he leans forward and kisses the tip of my nose.

We both stare at each other for a few moments, scanning each other's face, searching for a peek into our souls.

"This has never been us. We rarely kiss...well, this is just not like us." I feel the need to discuss this, confused that I like the kiss as much as I do. That deep down, I don't want it to stop.

"This might not be how we kissed before, but it's how we kiss now." He smiles.

I take a deep breath before speaking. "This is different, Apollo. You and I both know it. So different."

Apollo lowers his mouth to mine again, silencing my words. He kisses with more passion this time, and with more excitement than before. His mouth continues to claim mine as I feel his desire building —my desire building. I inhale at the sudden change but pull him closer with my hands clinging desperately to his back.

"I don't want you to think of the past. Of the way we were. Only focus on right now." Apollo pauses from his onslaught of kisses to examine my face. "It's just you and me right now. Right now."

I smile at the look of determination mixed with passion on his face. "I want that, too. Right now. Only focus on now. I don't know why. I don't know how this happened. All I know is that I want to feel you inside of me."

"Daphne," Apollo moans.

He moves his mouth to my neck and places soft

kisses there, while his hand slowly works its way under my shirt and bra. His palm cups my breast, and I arch my back to meet his touch. His lips move to my ear, and he lightly nips. I hear his ragged breathing and feel his body tense with pent-up passion.

I lower my hand to his bulging erection pressed against his pants. When my fingers make contact, Apollo groans in desire.

"Fuck! I want to be soft. I want to be gentle... But you are driving me crazy."

I undo his belt buckle, unbutton and unzip his pants in one fluid motion. "I don't want soft. I don't want gentle. I want you to take me. Take me hard," I demand as I wrap my hand around his throbbing cock.

He grabs and pushes me hard up against the wall. Reaching for my hands, guiding them above my head, holding them firm with one hand, his other rips off my clothing. He yanks, he tugs, and he has me naked before I can even take my next breath. His lips press against mine with such force, such fierce command.

I have never felt such strength, such domination before with this man. Something changed as of late, but I'm trying to do as he asked. Only focus on the now. But still... First with the spankings, the cage, the forced sex, and now with this round. This time is different, however. We seem to be going into this with eyes wide open.

Apollo moves his lips to my neck and kisses, sucks, and bites. With my arms still pinned above my head by his massive hand, I have no choice but to allow Apollo to do as he wishes.

I feel the sting of his teeth on my neck and mewl, trying to not focus on the fact that I stand completely naked before him once again.

He picks me up and carries me to his room—*our* room—before I can fully comprehend what is happening. I'm in his arms. His chest is flexing beneath me. I can hear his heavy breathing, thick with desire. I can smell his intoxicating scent. My head spins; I am consumed with lust, drunk with passion.

Before I can regain composure, he throws me down onto his bed. I see him grab a black satin ribbon from a bedside table. I wonder what other wicked items he has inside that table. He grabs one hand and ties it to the bedpost, and then he does the same with the other. I have never been tied, never been defenseless by a simple ribbon. I tug to see if I can escape, pull to see if this is for real. With a mixture of fear and desire, I allow myself to trust Apollo, but at the same time, take delight in the sizzle of fear that courses through my veins. I am helpless. There is nothing I can do to fight him off. I can't stop what will happen next. And yet, even as my heart skips, I love the feeling. The complete abandon. Knowing he is now fully in control.

He stands before me and takes off all of his

clothes in the same rush and fury that has landed me naked and tied to his bed. His ripped, tight body stands before me in all its glory. With hungry eyes, he stares down at my body stretched out on his bed and seductively smiles.

"I plan to make this a habit of my day. To feed my hunger."

I smile. "We must keep that appetite satiated."

"It's now your job."

"I plan to be an overachieving employee," I tease back.

Apollo reaches for more ribbon, grabs one of my legs, and ties one ankle to the bedpost and then secures the other, spreading me wide open. In mere moments, I find myself sprawled out on the bed, in Apollo's control. I try to move, try to test the strength of the bonds. A shiver runs down my spine when I can't move. I am his. Yes, I am his.

"Apollo..." I moan.

He kisses one breast and then the other. He sucks each nipple, slightly nipping with his teeth. I gasp. I moan. I have never been restricted before and am not able to hold on to someone during sex. The feeling of being defenseless is terrifying but electrifying at the same time.

"Please. I want to hold you," I beg. The need to touch his skin consumes me.

Ignoring my plea, he continues his descent down my abdomen with kisses. He reaches his final destination, his lips caressing every ounce of flesh, licking my entire mound until I'm desperate for more. I am dying to feel his tongue delve into me. I want to feel the invasion, the penetration. The man has a way of intensifying every emotion and sensation in my body. I need him. I hunger for him. I crave everything about him. Yet, I know the ultimate power is his, and he will lead this delicious dance as he sees fit.

"Apollo!" I scream when his tongue connects with my clit. A surge of sensation steals my breath. "I want you," I plead as I test the ties again. I'm aching to touch, desperate to have some control back.

My body frantically searches for release any way that I can as I shamelessly grind my pussy against his face and mouth. I need to come. God, I hope he'll make me come. But I need more than his mouth. I need his cock in me, and just as I'm about to demand he fuck me, he moves away from my needy cunt and lowers his body on top of mine. I try to reach for him. I try to embrace his body. But the constraints of the ties hold me in place.

"Untie me," I beg.

He simply shakes his head and slowly eases his way in between my legs. As his cock spreads me wide, he captures my gaze and never releases it. He stares deep into my eyes, linking our souls, connecting our energy.

He presses deeper with every gasp from me, as if my sounds of pleasure fuel the energy and desire inside of him.

I moan.

He presses on.

I cry out.

He fucks me harder.

His own moans become my soundtrack to the most amazing sex of my life.

Apollo pushes deep within and suddenly stops. Without either of our bodies moving, I feel nothing more than Apollo rooted within me. Taking the moment of stillness does something to me. I feel a connection and closeness I didn't know possible. I look into his eyes and just smile. It begins with just my lips, but staring into Apollo's face, I know my pleasure is reflected in his eyes.

"I'm yours," I admit freely.

"I wanted nothing more than to hear those words."

"Untie me. Let me show you how much I'm yours. Let me prove how much I want to belong to you," I whisper.

Apollo touches his lips to mine, pulls his cock out of me, and then slowly unties one hand and then the other. He takes his time and after each bond is removed, he kisses and licks the reddened area to soothe the sting. I didn't realize how much I fought against the restraints until he does so.

Once all the ties are removed, I crawl into his lap, press my lips to his neck, and take the moment to be held and feel protected. I enjoy the soft, the calm... The love. I move my lips to his and kiss him until I feel that our lips have melted together. His breath is mine, my breath is his. I feel his tongue lightly move along, his hands caress, we embrace.

He eases me onto my back and slowly rubs his cock along my throbbing clit. The sensation sends an emotion through me that nearly brings tears to my eyes. I become whole, so complete. Having him so close to me feels...right.

He moves the tip of his dick at a slow and sensual pace. He caresses my hair and smiles softly while looking into my eyes. "I can't do soft any longer. I need to fuck you hard before I explode," Apollo confesses.

A growl works its way past his lips as he grabs me by the hips and, in one hard thrust, drives himself deep within the warmth of my body. I wrap my legs tighter around his back and thrust my hips to drive him even deeper. I moan at the feeling of him spreading me, further inside me than I ever imagine possible. I crave more. I want him to drive in and out at a rapid pace.

I feel like a sex-crazed vixen beneath him as he pumps in and out with a force and speed that brings an impending orgasm near. He grabs me by the hair and pulls my lips to his again. He drives his tongue deep within my mouth, never letting go of his grip. He dominates me with the pull, with the thrust of his hips, and with the power he has over the building explosion of pleasure begging for release.

"Let go for me. Let go, princess," he demands with a deep, sensual voice.

As if knowing I should never go against one of Apollo's commands, I let the climax take over. The fire works its way from my toes all the way to my head. My moan becomes louder, louder until it becomes a scream.

With the sound of my release ringing throughout the room, he pumps hard one last time, filling me with his seed. Claiming me. Marking me. Forever his.

CHAPTER

THIRTY-FOUR

Daphne

I snuggle up next to him the next morning after wine-infused sex that blew my mind as every time with Apollo does of late, wondering if I should seduce him and go for round two. I don't want to wake him... Okay, I totally want to wake him. But will he be mad if I do?

My answer comes when our lips meet, a pull neither can resist any longer. Our hunger is never satiated. His heart beats against mine as he arranges my body closer. The single kiss has the power to forever bind. The kiss is the exclamation mark to the sentence. One kiss speaks volumes of what is meant —a demand, a command, an order of love and passion.

I want him.

I want him this very second... again.

Now.

Apollo sucks my breast, then moves to the other to give it equal attention. Lowering his hand to my mound, damp with fresh arousal, he dips a finger to my clit and applies pressure as he rouses an overwhelming longing that has me gasping for air. Moving from my clit, he presses his fingers past my folds and pushes one, then two digits into my sex. I force my hips up to drive them inside my pussy even deeper. They aren't enough. I want to feel the small bite of pain as his cock stretches me as he claims what is now his. I want to feel him so badly that the hunger changes who I am.

I am an animal.

I am a stalker in search of its victim.

I am a woman who needs to be fucked hard by her man. Her man who has been missing in most of our marriage but now is found.

Not being able to hold back the fever that scorches me, I beg, "Please, Apollo. Please..."

"Please what?" he asks as he dances his fingers inside my core. "Say it, Daphne. Tell me what you want."

"I want you," I pant, desperately wanting to feel the orgasm that rests just beneath the surface, begging to be set free. But I need Apollo's cock to make that happen.

"Say it, Daphne. Say what you really feel."

"Fuck me!" I blurt out as a moan follows my command. "I want you to fuck me hard and make me remember the feeling between my legs for days. Make me sting. Make me hurt. Fuck! Fuck me!"

I am absolutely desperate at this point as his fingers hit a spot inside my pussy that has me gyrating uncontrollably. I need more! I need him so badly that I could lose my mind in a wild thirst for more if he doesn't mount me and take me right now.

Merciful as he is, he does just as I need. Feeling his weight on top of me, I'm soon rewarded when his cock presses up against my opening and easily slides in with the aid of my wetness. Wrapping my legs around him, I hold on in fear that I'll cede complete control over to the lust.

I am so hungry.

I have such a craving and an urge that only he can quench.

And with a forceful shove of his hips, he drives his thick cock all the way in, claiming me completely. Yes, yes, yes... I am his.

In and out he thrusts, deeper and deeper with each pounding action. My moans blend with his as our bodies merge as one. He is my commander in this war of lust, and my body will forever be his to order, to master, to lead toward completion.

"Fucking mine," he groans as he powers into me, his muscles taut, his eyes glazed over. "Cry out for me, princess," he demands. "Cry, princess, cry."

As if I need the command, like a dutiful soldier, I

do just as he ordered. A wave of warmth that has rested on the cliff since he took my nipple into his mouth finally releases. Pure carnality shakes through my body as I cry out his name... crying in the only way I ever want to cry again.

Tears of lust rather than tears of pain.

Moaning with each pulsation of decadence that attacks my pussy, I truly melt into an abyss of sexual heaven. With a few more thrusts, Apollo adds his own pleasurable moans, and he, too, joins me in our own utopian paradise.

Slipping my arms around his neck, I pull away enough to stare into his eyes. There is so much I want to say. So much I want to tell him. But right now, right this second, I enjoy the silence.

Apollo's phone vibrates on the nightstand...and then again.

This time, he doesn't ignore it, but reaches for it with a groan.

"I need to call my father," he says as he flings his legs over the bed. "He's been trying to reach me, and his patience is going to only last so long."

My heart sinks. I want more cuddle time. I want more of him. "It's Sunday. Can't you take one day off from Medusa? Maybe we can go into town for shopping and lunch or something. I've never been to any of the little shops on Main Street. It'll be weird to go inside with the ability to buy something and—"

"I can't," he says, walking toward his closet as he

reads the text on his phone. "I need to deal with some business. Why don't you go do that with your sister?"

I don't like his answer. I hate his answer. It's reminding me of our life before. Before the accident. His father always came first, Medusa came second, and everyone else *besides me* came next.

"My sister will be fine. She's still recovering and has visible wounds to her face. She won't want to go out in public for a while. But I do. Please? It's sunny out. And you said a storm is coming soon, so shouldn't we go out and enjoy the nice day while it lasts? We may be cooped up inside for a while." I lower the blanket to reveal a breast on full display to tempt him. "Apollo," I say as he turns to look at me. "Come back to bed. Let's play."

It's completely unlike me to be so flirty and sexually open, but I'm having fun with it. The man turns me into an animal.

Apollo looks away, as if my tease does nothing. He pulls on his pants and pulls a sweatshirt on as if I'm not lying here naked in bed, willing and waiting. His attention is back to his phone as he texts something urgently with a scowl.

"Apollo..."

"Daphne," he snaps, walking toward the door. "I need to go deal with this. I'm sorry." Without saying another word, or even walking over to the bed to give me a simple kiss goodbye, he leaves and heads to the study...again. Just like every single damn day of our marriage before we came to Olympus Manor.

The pang in my heart from his hasty rejection quickly turns to anger. The anger turns to rage. The rage turns to defiance.

All right, fucker! You don't want to go into town, then I'll go by myself!

Yanking my own clothes on in a fury, not paying attention to what I actually put on, I then storm out of our room to go check on my sister. Peeking my head into her room, my anger dissipates a little when I see her tiny and beaten body in a deep slumber, sleeping away her nightmare. It doesn't take long for my anger to return when I leave her room and head downstairs. Apollo hurt my ego, my feelings. I asked for one damn day off and practically threw myself on him, only to be cast aside for his damn father. The Godwin family always suffocates.

"We need to talk. Athena is on the chopper heading this way," Apollo says as he comes out of the study with an empty coffee cup in hand.

Son of a bitch! Did he not even see that I'm mad? I don't give a fuck who in his family is coming.

"Have fun visiting with her," I snap. "My sister is still asleep, and I'm going into town before the storm comes in."

"What?"

"Did I stutter?" I'm being a bitch, but I don't care. My temper has blown and there is no pushing it back in once I get going on a rampage.

"What the fuck has gotten into you?" He takes a few steps toward me. "And you're not going into town right now. It's important you and I have a discussion about that text I got."

"Oh, *now* you have time to spend with me," I say, rolling my eyes. "I guess Daddy Dearest doesn't need you any longer?"

"I don't like how you are speaking or acting," he says with warning laced throughout every syllable.

"Well, I feel the same way. I don't exactly like how you're acting either," I counter as I put my hands on my hips and take a step toward him as a predator would slowly stalk its prey.

"And how is that?" he asks, pausing as if he's genuinely baffled that I would be angry at all. "How exactly am I upsetting you? Because I said I had to do some work and respond to my father?"

I say nothing, but that is answer enough for him.

"I haven't been in the office since we got here. I'm trying to deal with a shitload of work remotely, and my family is still reeling from the death of my brother and your—"

"Yes, I know! My betrayal! They want me dead—"

"Yes. They do. For which I'm essentially buying us time to figure it the fuck out," Apollo interrupts, acting much more calmly and in control than I am. "But that text that has you so pissed off was them telling me that they don't feel as if I'm handling things any longer, so now they are sending Athena to take care of it."

"We are all one big happy family now, right?" My stomach coils and I almost want to throw up. The truth of the matter is I hate this family. I truly do. His father interrupting our perfect morning is just a small taste of what's coming the minute we reenter *real life* and have to live in Seattle again. "It doesn't matter what you do or say. I'm the enemy now, and you know it. But I won't sit here and think about that today. So, I'm going out. Your sister will just have to kill me on another day."

Apollo storms toward me and grabs my arm firmly. "You are not going anywhere. So stop this nonsense before you piss me off."

I snatch my arm away from him and take a few steps away. The pain in my gut nearly suffocates me when I realize he doesn't even try to deny that his family wants me dead, nor does he try to reassure me that my life isn't in danger. It's what I feared. Apollo may have forgiven me, and my penance may be paid with him. But the rest of the Godwins will want vengeance.

"I know you were supposed to bring me to Olympus to kill me. And just because you changed your mind, doesn't mean they have. It's why we're still here, right? You were stalling because you know it's true. We can't just return to Seattle like nothing has happened. And we can't just stay here forever either. Athena isn't coming to just have a chat with us, or to threaten me, or to just—"

"Daphne, take a deep breath and calm down."

I am out of control. I can feel it. But I don't care anymore. My inner beast has been unleashed, and she is wounded and bloody and wants to flee. I have to protect myself. I'm not going to just let a Godwin kill me. I'm not going to just sit here as ready prey.

"My sister and I need to leave. I want to leave."

"We'll leave as soon as I can—"

"I'm no longer talking about going to town or even going back to Seattle. I mean, that my sister and I need to truly leave. Leave Seattle, maybe even leave the country. We need to go somewhere where your family can't find us," I say. This is the first time since Apollo kidnapped me and took me to Heathens Hollow, that I'm actually coming up with an escape plan. An escape plan that doesn't involve... my husband.

"Absolutely not." Apollo never raises his voice once.

"You know I have to. You know Troy will kill me."

Apollo shakes his head. "No, he won't."

I smirk. "You're right. *He* won't. But Athena will. That's why she's flying here right now. She has her marching orders. She's the new hitman now that Ares is dead."

"Neither one of them are going to kill you because I have a plan," he says.

"A plan? What?"

He takes my hand and brings me into the study. He then walks over to the desk and pulls out a thin box and hands it to me. "It may be too soon. And maybe it hasn't happened yet. But there's a chance. And even if it hasn't happened yet, we're going to stay here at Olympus until it does."

I peer at the box, not understanding why he's handing me it, although my gut starts churning as if in preparation for the hurricane coming.

"A pregnancy test?" I croak out.

"We haven't been using protection, and we've definitely been trying." He gives a smirk, but I'm not finding this funny in the slightest. "So go see if you are."

"Why?" I'm staring at the man but not seeing him. My knees lock so they don't completely buckle as they're threatening to do.

"Because if you're carrying my child—a Godwin child—neither my father nor my sister will harm a hair on that beautiful head of yours. They won't allow a Godwin to grow up without a mother. They will want the best for that baby. For the heir." He points to the door. "Go take the test."

I don't know how I am able to will my feet to walk, or how I can steady my hands enough to take the test, but I somehow do. And as I walk back into the study where Apollo is anxiously waiting, I extend my hand to him with the test.

"Well?" he says, rushing to me to take the test to see for himself.

I don't say anything. I need to see him read the results to make sure what I saw was correct.

"Two lines! Two lines means pregnant right?" He looks at me with a wide grin that shows off every possible laugh line on his face. "You're pregnant!"

THIRTY-FIVE

Apollo

Daphne doesn't appear happy. She doesn't appear upset. There's zero emotion on her face. It's as if she has stared at Medusa herself and turned to stone.

I lean forward and kiss her lips, noticing that she doesn't kiss me back. She's stunned, which I guess can be expected since she wasn't in on my plan of trying to get her knocked up so my family will consider her off limits to murder. Having a child with Daphne is the only way to bind this family back together. It is also the only way to truly make her mine. She may have been Apollo's wife, but she is now the mother of my child. *My* child. Not Apollo's.

But we never used protection once. She had to know we were taking a chance. I already knew she wasn't on birth control because I had her doctor records sent to me the minute we arrived at Olympus, and I began to put this plan in motion.

She shakes her head from side to side slowly. "No. I can't be pregnant."

I hold up the test. "It says different." I give her a smile. "Which is great news. You're going to be an amazing mother and—"

"It's impossible."

"I know this is shocking, but it's fantastic news."

Her eyes narrow. "You can't have children, Apollo."

"What?" I take a step back from her so I can get a clearer view of her entire body. "What are you talking about?"

"You can't have children." Her voice raises. "There's no way that I can be pregnant. We went to doctors. We saw the best specialists. They couldn't have all been wrong. And you aren't standing here claiming it's a miracle so..." Her eyes widen as she puts her shaky hand to her mouth. "*You* can't have children. But... Oh my god. *Apollo* can't have children..."

I'm seeing spots as the air is sucked out of the room. Her realization is punching what little air I have left to breathe out of me. I just fucked up. I *really* fucked up.

"*Ares?*" Her question—my name—comes out hoarse, almost inaudible.

My mind spins as I try to come up with a solution to the impending chaos. Do I deny? Do I say that I had doctors fix my infertility? Do I try to convince the woman standing before me she's got it all wrong?

"Oh my god. You aren't Apollo. You're Ares." Her eyes haven't blinked once.

I can't look her in the eyes. I can't tell this woman something she already knows.

As if a lightning bolt had struck a damn, destroying it to pieces, the wave of anger flows over as she charges me, punching my chest with both her fists. "Where is my husband? Where is *Apollo*?"

I take hold of her wrists and answer, "Dead. He was the one who died in the accident. Not me."

But she already knows this. She knew it the minute I handed her the pregnancy test. I know this now. I should have read it in her face, but I didn't. Maybe I could have rebounded quicker. Maybe I could have figured out a way out of this and kept the lie going. Maybe—

Snatching her wrists away from me, she storms to the other side of the room, spinning on her heels to face me as fire burns in her eyes. "Why would you pretend to be your *dead* brother? Why would you want to be Apollo?"

"You know why," I say calmly, wishing I had a way to defuse the bomb going off inside of her.

"No, I—" she freezes. "So you wouldn't have to go to jail?"

I simply stare at her, letting her put all the pieces of the story together herself.

"You were just going to step into his life and be

him. Remain married to *me*." Her breath hitches as it's clear the memories of everything that has happened since the accident flood in. She flinches with each memory. She inhales and exhales with shaky breath. Her eyes dart side to side. Her hands clench at her sides, and then land on her stomach. "You had sex with me. You made me think you were him!"

"I did." I will not deny anything anymore. Nothing but honesty from this point on.

"And you aren't apologizing?" Her voice raises another octave. "You don't even seem like you are sorry."

"I won't apologize. I made a decision and stand by it."

"To sleep with your brother's wife? I didn't agree to have sex with *you*! I thought you were my husband."

I nod, taking in her words and hating the pain and betrayal she must be feeling. "You have every right to be angry."

"And you aren't even going to apologize for that?"

I remain silent.

"Does everyone know but me?" she asks. "Am I the only fool in this fucked up and twisted Godwin game?"

"Only my father knows. He figured it out at the hospital. This was all his idea at first."

"Of course it was," she hisses with a roll of her

eyes. "And that's why he let you take me to Olympus. He had no doubt you'd be able to kill me because you are *Ares*." She tilts her head and studies me. "So why didn't you kill me? I'm not your wife? And it was because of me you were going to jail."

I had just told myself that I was going to be honest and not hold anything back, and I'm a man of my word. "Because I developed feelings for you. Because…I wanted to keep you as my wife. My brother had his time. Now it's mine."

It's as if my confession slapped her in the face. Her head reels back, her lips part, and her hands start to shake as they hold her belly that now carries my child. "I can't stand here and look at you. I can't—" I see the tears in her eyes glistening and threaten to fall, but before they do, she runs out of the room as fast as she can.

THIRTY-SIX

Daphne

The sound of the helicopter landing on the Godwin property spins my mind in mayhem even more. I'm pacing the bedroom I just spent the night in having sex with Ares, holding my hand on my belly, trying not to throw up.

I'm pregnant. I have a baby inside of me. I'm going to be a mother. These are all things I had given up thinking were even a possibility when we discovered Apollo couldn't have children. I had grieved that part of my life I'd never experience, and just like that... I'm now going to be a mother.

With *Ares's* baby!

When the helicopter's motor turns off, signaling that whoever arrived is going to stay for a while, I realize Athena is here to kill me. I may actually never become a mother if in fact Apollo, correction, *Ares*, didn't underestimate Athena's rage. Just because I'm pregnant doesn't guarantee the woman won't kill me. I wouldn't put it past her ruthless self to kill an unborn child if it belonged to me.

My thoughts quickly turn to my sister. Would Athena then kill my sister? Yes, I think that's fair to say as well. But I doubt Apollo—Ares would tell her Ani is asleep in the other room, so if I say nothing before she kills me, then all is good. I scan the room for a weapon. I sure as hell plan on putting up a fight.

Before I can find anything, however, a rich, sultry voice penetrates the room. "Well, well. It looks like you took my advice and spread your legs." Athena's eyes cast to my belly. "I suppose I should say congratulations."

I stiffen my spine and push my shoulders back. Athena doesn't respect weak women, and I'm not going to even show the slightest bit of fear. "Did you come here to kill me?"

"Yes." She enters the room all the way and steps toward me.

I don't cower back, even though I want to.

"But then your dear husband informed me of your news. It seems you've both had a little second honeymoon in the family manor." She looks around and scowls. "Sort of sick if you ask me. This house is like a gothic museum that smells of grandfather's dentures. But whatever gets you turned on, I suppose. It's about time you and Apollo get knocked up. Someone needs to keep the Godwin name going. It's not going to be Ares, obviously. Phoenix just masturbates to himself forever alone, and I sure as fuck am not popping out a baby."

"But you were going to kill me if I wasn't pregnant?"

She gives a wicked grin. "Most definitely." She shrugs and crosses the room to look out the window. "No offense, of course."

I give a sardonic laugh. "Why would I be offended?"

"Apollo assured me you were punished, and that you won't even dare consider betraying the family again." She looks over her shoulder. "Did he take you to the tree of forgiveness? Did he make you kneel on rice while he whipped you with the leather strap?"

"No," I say, not willing to give her any details of exactly what her brother did do to me as a punishment.

"Shame. Then he let you off easy." She returns her attention to the window, her eyes staring down at the tree in the distance. "I figured he would go light on you. Ares was the stronger brother. *He* would have never let you get away with what you did."

Chills run down my spine as the realization that Ares is the man who is standing downstairs, and Athena has no idea. And Athena is right. Ares was the stronger brother. And the fact I'm actually standing in this room alive says something.

But what does it say?

What does it mean?

He said it was his turn now. He said that he had developed feelings for me. He wanted—

"I hope you're aware that you can't even think of divorce now," she says to me with a glance over her shoulder. "Now that you have that baby inside you, you are more of a Godwin than ever before. So get those ridiculous ideas about leaving out of your head." Her attention goes back to the tree of forgiveness. "Apollo is going to need you. He's going to need that baby. I know how I feel about losing Ares, and he wasn't my twin. I can only imagine what losing your other half feels like."

I'm taken aback by the softer version of a true viper before me. It doesn't last long, however, because she turns on her heels and heads to the door to leave. "Do you love him? Even the slightest?"

If she would have asked me this question before the accident, the answer would have been no. But now...

"I don't know," I answer.

"He told me downstairs he loves you."

"He did?" Was he only telling her that so she wouldn't kill me? "A lot has happened since we've arrived at Olympus," I confess. "It's complicated."

"Complicated defines us perfectly," Athena says with a smirk and then opens the door. "If you even so much as dare try to betray my family again, I will kill you in the most tortuous of ways. If you hurt my brother, or you don't raise that baby to the best of your ability, I will make you scream for mercy." She pauses, smiling wickedly. "But if you are ready to really be part of this family, then... Welcome."

CHAPTER

THIRTY-SEVEN

Apollo

I enter the room without knocking in fear Daphne wouldn't let me inside anyway. I resist the urge to march over to her and take her in my arms. But I know that as much as I want to fix this, and make it right, I'm not sure I can.

"You just missed your sister," she says.

"I know."

She fidgets with her hands in front of her and continues to reposition her weight from one foot to the other. "I guess you were right about getting me pregnant." She looks around the bedroom, then back to her hands. "Your sister told me it's the only reason she didn't kill me herself."

"I know."

Her eyes connect with mine, and I take a few tentative steps toward her.

"Having this baby has now officially made me a Godwin," she informs. "But I guess you knew that too."

I nod. "One thing I understand is the twisted vines of this family tree. Extending the bloodline goes far with the Godwins."

Whatever my sister must have said seems to have calmed Daphne down from when I last saw her. She's no longer shaking. She's no longer looking at me as if I'm the devil.

"I came up here because I realized that you wanted something from me when we were downstairs. You kept expecting an apology that I wouldn't give." I inhale sharply. "That was wrong. I should have. I'm sorry. You are owed that and more. I am sorry."

"Godwins don't apologize," she replies with a smirk.

"We do if we seriously fucked up and hurt someone. And if our intent was to never actually cause pain. I'm sorry, Daphne. You didn't deserve to be lied to."

"Even when the reason you had to lie in order to not go to jail was because of me?" she asks. "Because I understand why you decided to become Apollo. I do. I get it, and frankly it was smart. Why should Apollo die and you go to prison forever? If everyone mistook your identity and... It was really good luck.

It's almost as if Apollo was looking down on you and turning the fates around." She chuckles. "If anyone could do it, it was him."

"I've never told anyone this," I begin. "But I think Apollo saved my life."

Her eyes widen but she doesn't say anything.

"I don't remember the crash," I continue. "And based on the wound on my head, I think I was knocked unconscious. There's no way I could have undone my seat belt and got out of that helicopter before it sank all the way down. I think Apollo sacrificed himself and unfastened me just in time for me to get out and get to the surface. I think he gave his life for me."

"Just as you were willing to give your life for him," she adds.

"I hope I didn't betray him by doing what I did with you. It eats at me."

"Our marriage was dead. There wasn't any love there, and there wasn't anything between us until... well until the accident," she confesses.

"I don't deserve your forgiveness, but—"

"You're forgiven," she cuts in. "I understand why you did what you did. I forgive you just as you forgave me."

"A betrayal for a betrayal," I say with a grin and a wink. "What all healthy marriages are built on."

"Are you ever going to let anyone know about you?" she asks. "The real you? If Athena knew, she didn't let on to me she did."

I chuckle. "If she knew, you'd be the last to know. That woman holds secrets and information until she can use them to her advantage. But no, I don't think she knows."

"I won't tell her. I won't tell anyone. I haven't told you that, and well... after what I did to Apollo and you, I at least owe you this. Your secret is safe with me."

I nod again, pleased to hear she intends to keep this secret quiet. "Why?" I ask. "Afraid of what I might do? Afraid of what my family would do?"

She shakes her head. "No. It's ours. Our secret. No one else's business." She smirks and crosses her arms. "Plus, you are the father of this baby. And you are still...my husband."

I return the smirk. "We are married. Until death do us part."

She breaks my stare and looks down at the ground. "Apollo and Daphne were married." She looks back up at me. "And death *did* do us part."

"So technically you are free, but—"

"I know," she interrupts as she places her hand on her belly. "I'll never be free from the Godwin family now."

I'm relieved that she understands exactly what having my child inside of her means.

"Yes. Breaking away from the Godwins is not possible. Ever." I take a deep breath. "But my father knows the truth. If you really want to break away from *me*, we both can make that happen. Because you're right. You vowed to be with Apollo until death. Not me."

Her eyes widen. "You'd let me go? Even though I have your baby in me?" She rolls her eyes. "Ha! Stop acting like the valiant, self-sacrificing hero in this story. I know you wouldn't just let me go. Neither would your father."

"No." I laugh, appreciating the fact that this woman can not only see my shit but call me out on it. "You're right. You aren't going anywhere. You're smart to see that, and to know that."

Her eyes narrow. "What about after I have the baby?"

"You're still mine," I answer.

There is stillness between us as I can see she's processing the information.

Finally, I slice through the awkward silence. "That baby inside of you is mine. Which means I will forever be in your life, and you in mine. That fact can't change. But...to what degree I'm in your life is up to you. I won't force a real marriage, if that's not what you want. We can live together but separately, if you know what I mean."

"Like the marriage I had with Apollo," she says.

"If that's what you want."

She now takes a step toward me and extends her hands. "But if I don't want it? What if I don't want to repeat what I had with Apollo? What if I want a real marriage...with you?"

CHAPTER
THIRTY-EIGHT

Daphne

To my surprise, he takes me in his arms and holds me close. Never once does he speak while I'm in his embrace. Never once does he stop showing me an unfamiliar love, kindness, and comfort.

Ares Godwin.

It's Ares who blankets me in his warmth as a second chance lover would. Or is this a new love rather than a second chance? The definition is muddled, but I no longer care to make sense.

I'm not sure how long I rest against his chest, but eventually he pulls me back so he can look me in the eye. He says nothing. He doesn't need to. I can see his thoughts. I can see that his entire soul crumbling to pieces inside. He doesn't want to be here with me as Apollo, and at the same time, he has to.

Stroking his face with my palms, I whisper, "Do I call you Ares or Apollo in private?"

I see pain flicker in his eyes. "I feel like I'm betraying my brother by saying what I know I need to say." Taking me by the hand, he says, "I can't ask you to call me Apollo, and yet it's what I need from the people in my life who know. I'm Apollo. I'm forever Apollo. But I also know it's not fair to expect you to live this lie of mine."

I shake my head. "It's not just your lie now. It's ours." The thought of being alone without this man for another second sends a panic through me. I never want to be without *my husband*. "I didn't want this marriage before. You know this. I didn't love him. But I do love you." I look up at him with desperation pumping through my veins. "Don't plan this life— living as Apollo—without me."

"Even though I shouldn't say this. It tears at my soul admitting this, but I love you. I do," he says. "I didn't go into this plan with that intention. I didn't mean to bring in the emotions. But I don't want to live my brother's life without you, either. I want you by my side."

He leads me over to the edge of the bed and sits us down. I curl up next to him and press my cheek to his chest as he hugs me tight.

"What are you thinking?" I ask, which isn't really a fair question. If he were to ask me the same words, I wouldn't be able to answer because my thoughts are racing at rapid speed.

He looks down at me and makes eye contact. His expression gives nothing away.

"About us," he begins. "About what our next step is. I'm thinking about my brother and wondering if he'd ever forgive me for this. You were his. Not mine. But now that I want to make you mine... will he haunt our asses forever? Are we crossing a line that we both can't live with?"

My heart skips a beat knowing that he's considering me in his future plans, but that he's also considering not having me in them either to honor his brother. "What are you saying?" I interrupt, needing more clarification. "Do you think the fact that I was married to your brother will prevent you from... being with me?"

He swallows hard and takes a deep breath. "I've been loyal to my family my entire life. I'd throw myself in front of The Reaper himself for any of them. But this one time in my life, I want to be selfish. I want to do what will make myself happy."

"And what will make you happy?"

"Making you truly mine. Holding on so tight you can barely breathe. Obsessing over you, protecting you, and doing the same for that child of ours. I don't want the life Apollo had with you... I want us to start our own. But one thing I know is I want you. Mine."

"Yours?"

"Mine." He stands up and pulls me from the bed. He wraps his arms around my frame, trapping me against his body. "I feel so much more than the dark, angry emotions of before. It's as if my heart has grown. My entire being has changed. I feel pain, I feel the loss of the thought of not having you in my life, and yet I feel emotions such as hope and love. Love for you. I don't feel like Ares anymore. He truly died in that crash right alongside Apollo."

I look up into his eyes and allow the tears to fall. His words are all I have ever wanted to hear. He loves me. He openly admits his feelings for me. No one in my life, other than my sister, has been so free with expressing love to me. No one has made me feel this way before.

"I don't deserve your love in return," he says. "I've done awful things in life. I've killed, and to be honest with you... I won't be able to change who I am. There is nothing I won't do for my family and Medusa. And now when it comes to you and our baby, I'll kill anyone who dares try to harm you. I've lied, and I'm now expecting you to lie forever as well. I'm a bad man, but a bad man who is in love with a woman and the idea of what a future with her could be like. But I also want to earn your love. I want to prove to you I can give you and our baby what you need. I can honor the memory of my brother by protecting and caring for you like a true Godwin would do. I'll try to be everything a man and provider should be."

"I have no doubt you will." I stroke his face and give him a soft kiss before adding, "You aren't a bad man. You may have done bad things, but that's your world. It's a world I understood when I entered this family. You only do what was in your nature as part of that world. Yes, I want the good in you. But I won't refuse the bad either. I want every part of you and won't expect you to change. Be Apollo. Be Ares. Be good. Be bad. Be whatever you want."

His eyebrow rises, and a devilish grin spreads across his face. "Are you telling me I can be the villain *and* the hero?" He lightly places his palm on my neck. "Be careful what you say."

"I don't have to be careful when I'm around you. I know you'll keep me safe."

"But who will keep you safe from me?" He dips his hand past the waistband of my pants and caresses my mound.

"I'm not needing saving. I happen to like the villain in the story. He's just misunderstood."

He puts his lips so close to mine that I can feel his heavy breath. "And if I told you I want to fuck you right now, what will you say?"

"I'll say no. Just so you can fucking take me anyway."

I smile up at Ares—Apollo, and we both know the time has come. When I try to offer assistance in shedding my clothing, he slaps my hands away. Effortlessly, he rids me of my clothing, never breaking his stare with mine. When he removes his own clothing and stands before me in all his nude glory, I can't help but moan in anticipation.

"Ares—"

"Apollo," he corrects. "From now on, the only name you ever call me is Apollo."

"Apollo—"

"Don't talk," he interrupts as he lowers me back to the bed and climbs on top of me, lowering his mouth to mine. "Do only what I say." He kisses me long and deep. He tastes of life, and hope, and sweetness, but there is also the sting and the spice. He strokes his hands up and down my body, batting away my hands every time I reach for him.

"Don't make me chain you, princess," he hisses. "Only move when I tell you."

Moving lower down my body, he cups my hot-skinned sex in his hands, clearly pleased to find me wet with my legs spread wide. I'm ready for him. I don't think it's possible to ever deny him. Never turn him away. I will never truly ever be able to say no.

Breaking his rule, I reach for him. He's thick and hard, the massive girth of his cock swollen and leaking. Just for me.

"Let me suck on you," I plead. "I want to taste you."

He grants me my wish and straddles my neck, so his cock rests in front of my face. Moving fast, I suck him deeply into my mouth, running my tongue along the tip, luxuriating in the heady taste of him. I want more.

I rake my nails down his chest and pull him into my throat until he bottoms out, delightfully gagging me with his size. Still, I try to take more, until I gag again, and my mouth salivates. My lips spread wide; he's too big, but I love it. I'll never get enough of him. His smell and taste are drugs working on my system. The heat of his body, the comfort of his solidity, a balm to an existence that has become fraught, rocky, and confusing.

This man stands at the center of my universe, rigid and impregnable. Constant. Reliable.

"Come for me, *Apollo*," I mumble around his hard flesh, eager for the flavor of his release. I like the way his name sounds on my lips now. He groans when I palm his sack, squeezing gently. "Give me your come. I need to taste you."

He thrusts against my throat, his hips working, pushing deeper.

"I need you." I try to say it, but it comes out muffled. He doesn't care, and neither do I.

His fingers dig into my scalp as he pulls my face tighter against his groin. Speech is impossible, so I just hum around him.

The pre-cum of his desire coats my tongue, thick, heavy, and sweet. I moan as the serum's aphrodisiac works through my body, setting nerves tingling. I swallow him down, sucking until he would have no choice but to release fully into the back of my throat. But he resists.

"No, I want to fill your pussy with my seed."

Frantically, he lowers himself down and reaches for his cock to guide the brutal length of him between my thighs, pressing past my slick folds, claiming me once again. He raises his hips and slams back down, pounding into me with everything he has.

One of his hands close over my breast, fingers strumming my nipple. I groan as I arch my back, silently begging for more. I want him deeper. I want to feel his possession so deep that I'll truly feel as if we blend as one. I can't get enough of him. It's as if my body is starved and it's this man who gives me life.

"Deeper," I moan.

He groans out a wordless answer, deep in his throat, and my stomach coils tight at the rasping sound. Flipping us over, he lies on his back and has me straddle him, riding his cock. I bob up and down as his eyes watch my tits bounce. I like having the power to give him pleasure. I can see it in his black eyes. I can feel it coming from his flesh. I please him, and that very knowledge brings on a wave of euphoria as a tidal wave comes crashing down.

I arch my back as his cock drives deep inside and scream out his *new* name. Over and over again. *Apollo. Yes. Apollo.*

He grabs me with a rough hand to the neck, pulling my face down. He sucks at my tongue, swallowing my orgasmic groans. I bite his lip, tasting his blood and buck my hips, milking the last wave of my release.

I rear up, gasping, reveling in the big cock that slams deep inside of me with every thrust of his hips.

My husband looks wild, the thick muscles of his abdomen and chest rippling, his hair curling around his ears. I have never seen a more perfect man. My man.

I dig my fingers into his chest, and he groans again. My thighs burn. I don't care. None of it matters. All that matters is giving Apollo the pleasure I so desperately want to give him.

I lean back, resting my hands on his corded, muscled thighs so I can get a better angle. His eyes burn into me, dark and probing, hard and hot, as if he sees into my soul. Every time he looks at me, I feel our bond grow stronger and stronger.

The orgasm coils tight within me again, drawing close.

"Apollo," I cry.

He nods. "Yes, say *my name* as you fucking milk my cock."

He slips a hand down to stroke my clit, and I allow him to throw me over the edge as he thrusts his final release into me with a deep growl. I scream as a flood of sensation knocks the wind out of me. Wave after wave of heat courses through my veins as Apollo pumps his seed inside of me.

When the shocking erotic delights dim enough that I'm able to open my eyes fully, I breathe out, "That was amazing." He lay beneath me with a light sheen of sweat on his skin.

"That was just round one," he says with a chuckle. "More's coming, *my wife*. So much more."

CHAPTER

THIRTY-NINE

Daphne

I enter my sister's room, not sure how much of what's just happened I need to tell her. I touch my belly and consider sharing the good news but feel it's not time yet. The pregnancy is still early, and she just lost her baby. Her wound still has to be extremely raw. The time will be right soon enough, but not now. And as for Apollo and his true identity... she doesn't need to know that either. She's still asleep which makes all my decisions easy. I don't want to lie to her, but she doesn't need to be pulled into the Godwin web any more than she already is.

Tip toeing out of her room, I make my way to Apollo's study.

Apollo hangs up the phone and kisses me firmly on the mouth. "Good morning."

"Good morning," I answer with my eyes still closed as I slowly pull away from the kiss. A girl could get used to spending her mornings greeted this way.

I always imagined a marriage to be this way but gave up hope of that pretty early on after saying our vows.

"That was our agent. I needed to reschedule since we canceled on her when we went to get your sister. She's got some houses that she thinks will be perfect for us to see today."

"Today?"

"Why not? We can't live here forever, and I'm looking forward to starting our future. Whatever that future is."

The idea of a future with this man terrifies me but also excites me. "I like that idea," I say, still not wanting to get off his lap. Never wanting to get off his lap. "I guess I better get ready."

He tugs my wrist toward him, giving me no choice but to stumble up against his chest.

"Kiss me," he orders in a gruff whisper.

I follow his direction gladly. I want nothing more than to feel his lips against mine.

Everything is so uncertain in our lives now that we have to start new. We have to build from scratch. But the one thing that my new husband and I have is the intense chemistry that makes it almost impossible to keep our hands off of each other. When in doubt, fuck. I think that may be the new motto we live by. At least for now until we figure out who exactly we are to each other and what that means moving forward. But as the man kisses me, I have no issue at all with this new motto.

"Remove your clothes," he orders again.

Without hesitation, something I now know he appreciates—immediate compliance—I stand back and with as much grace as I can muster, remove each item as seductively as I can. It's a dance I am performing for my audience of one.

Apollo sits back on his desk and crosses his arms against his chest, clearly enjoying the display.

"Stand naked before me," he orders once all my clothes are removed.

I do so without protest.

"Spin and allow me to see that ass of yours."

I do as he asks, turning my back to him.

"Bend over so I can see you on full display."

I pause for a moment but follow his request. "Your demands are dark and twisted."

"You have no idea how true that statement is. Spread your cheeks for me. I want to see the asshole that I plan to claim again and again," he orders.

My heart skips, but I reach behind me and pull apart the fleshy mounds of my ass. The cool air of the room invading the most intimate of spots sends shivers down my spine. He says nothing for seconds, but it seems like a lifetime. I remain in position, almost feeling his stare. The juices that form between my lips are also on display, and I'm sure he can indeed see that fact. I can smell my scent of need and wonder if he can smell me as well as see exactly what his authoritative words do to me.

I hear the motion of him getting off the desk. I remain in position, determined to stay that way until he gives the command to move. I hear him rummaging through a drawer and fight the temptation to glance over.

I jump slightly when I feel his palm on my ass. "Keep them spread," he directs. A cold liquid touches my anus, and I tense and nearly let go of my cheeks. "I want to take you here. I want my cock buried in the depth of your ass again."

My heart beats so hard, I can feel the pulse in my temples. I swallow back the lump in my throat, trying not to jerk up and run out of the office. Panic mixed with a forbidden desire to have him do just as he pleases rumbles within me. I liked it last time. In fact, I loved it. But it still makes me nervous as I await the biting stretch.

He continues to spread the lubrication all around my anus and presses it past the puckered hole with his finger. He coats every inch of my hole, preparing it for entry.

He moves me to the edge of the desk and presses me down to lie on my stomach against the cool surface. "Have you fantasized about me taking your ass again?"

I nod, realizing that subconsciously I must have. The idea of anal sex has always been off limits with us before, and yet, here I am with this man, excited… craving it more than once. I want it as part of our marriage for so many reasons, and even reasons I'm not sure of. My body says yes, even though my insecurities may say no.

"I will be gentle, but it will take some time for you to adjust. Just because it happened before and I've played with that hole of yours, doesn't mean you'll get used to the bite. I need you to trust me, relax with my touch, and completely give me your submission."

"Is it going to hurt just as bad as last time?" I ask in my most innocent voice. I'm enjoying this little game. I want his cock buried in my ass again more than anything, and I know he wants the same. But the innocent anal virgin game is fun.

"You know it will. Just the way you like it, princess."

I nod. I can't say anything more if I try. My breathing comes in ragged pants, and my body hums with a sensation I'm new to experiencing.

He lowers himself over my back and softly kisses the side of my neck, my shoulder, my earlobe—each kiss sending tingles to my throbbing pussy. His cock presses against the crease of my butt.

"I'm scared," I lie. The only thing I'm truly scared of is him stopping.

"I'll take care of you. Just breathe and trust me."

"I'm scared it'll hurt too much," I continue.

"You'll feel a bite of pain as my cock enters you.

But as your little hole relaxes, it will allow me better entrance. You just have to relax the best you can." He kisses my neck and nibbles my ear. "But the pleasure I give you will be worth the bite of pain."

He reaches down with his hand and guides his cock to my tight back entrance. Slowly, and with so much control, he presses the tip of his dick past the tight ring. He pauses so I can get used to the initial shock.

"Relax. Open yourself to me," he purrs in my ear, following the words with soft kisses to my neck.

He pushes further, causing me to gasp. The bite, the stretch, the erotic feeling, all become too much. I shake my head. "You're too big for me. I think I'll tear."

Apollo whispers in my ear, "You've thought that before, and you took me just fine. Might have hurt, but hurt so fucking good. Take a deep breath." I do as he asks. "Take another one and relax your muscles. You need to trust that once I am fully inside you, it will feel good. Submit your fear, your tension, and your body to me."

He reaches a hand around my front and finds my clit. He circles his finger around, causing me to moan in delight. I focus my attention on the arousal his finger gives me and can ease the muscles of my anus. Doing so allows his cock to press completely into my ass.

"That's it, princess," he praises as he slowly

pumps his length in and out. "Let me claim that ass of yours. Let me make you mine."

My hole stretches to impossible levels, but my body heightens with each move of his cock. It's a different type of pleasure than with my pussy, but it's still pleasure.

Having Apollo's cock fill my ass and pump in and out gives me a sense of belonging. At that very moment, I am his. I give myself completely.

"I want to come in your ass," he moans.

"Yes, yes!"

His gentle thrusts become a little more aggressive. Each push goes slightly deeper than before. Tingles in my ass become sparks of ecstasy. My dark channel pulsates around his cock, and I scream out his name.

My sound of pleasure brings on a few more driving thrusts, and Apollo ends the fucking with a roar. I feel his shooting seed fill my hole.

We rest on the desk for quite some time. I listen to his deep breaths as I gather my own.

"I could do this all day," he finally says.

"We could..."

He sighs. "The agent is waiting."

I wiggle my ass as his cock finally pulls out of me. "Yes, I suppose we should get ready."

"As soon as we get back to Seattle, I'll need you to go into Medusa really quick to sign some contracts." Apollo's words are like cold water being poured on me.

My heart sinks. I'm not sure if it's because he speaks of going back to our normal reality without even mentioning what that means for us, or that a part of me desperately wants to never leave Heathens Hollow. I'm afraid of what will change between us. I'm afraid of what will change with him. But then I should be excited. He said we're going to look at houses. To start fresh. To embark on a new future. But hearing the word *Medusa* sends a shiver and sense of dread through me.

"Okay," I whisper, trying to not make it obvious how unsettled I am. "What time did you want to leave today?"

"Let me finish responding to these emails. If you don't mind letting your sister know we're leaving. Also let her know that I have the housekeeper and cook coming back to help her out while we are gone. I'll join you as soon as I get done. Then we can head to Seattle."

I get off his lap, pick up my clothes, and walk toward the door feeling like my entire life is in chaos. I can't decide if it's good or bad or a mixture of the two.

FORTY

Apollo

Daphne hasn't said more than a couple of words the entire boat ride back to the city. I had chartered a boat this time so we could take the opportunity to see the orcas swim around us as we make our way to Seattle. I had hoped it would be a romantic gesture, but it seems to have fallen short. She stares out at the scenery and is clearly lost in thought. And to be fair, I'm pretty zoned out myself. I'm trying to really think out what truly being a husband and father means. Troy Godwin isn't exactly the best role model, and yet, he isn't the worst either. Family is everything to this man. He's brought us all up to know that and to live by that belief. We may be ruthless, even evil at times, but the one thing remains true... we will forever be family

"You all right over there?" I ask.

"Yeah," she answers, but she doesn't look away from the passing beauty. She's looking, but I don't think she really *sees* anything.

"Awfully quiet."

"Yeah."

I reach across the seat and take her hand in mine. "Are you afraid of real life? Of what's ahead? I am."

"Yeah."

"I think we can pull this off, if you're worried about that. Apollo and I are identical, and the accident and the head injury gives me a buffer if I forget something, or don't recognize someone only Apollo knows. Plus, I have you to help guide me. We got this."

She shrugs, but still hasn't looked away from the water, and her hand lays limply in mine. Something is clearly wrong.

"Daphne, what's going on? What's on your mind?"

"Just thinking, I guess."

"Okay, care to tell me about what?" I prod.

"Well..." I glance over at her and see her lip quivering. "It's nothing really. Just sad leaving Heathens Hollow." She smirks. "I can't believe those words just left my mouth. I never thought I'd ever be sad to leave the island."

I squeeze her hand. "We went through a lot there."

She nods, and I see her lip still quivers. My gut tells me something else is going on.

"Your sister is fine at Olympus. I hired our housekeeper and cook to return full time," I begin, wondering if she's worried about her sister's future. "And when she's healed and ready to leave the manor, we'll find her a place in Seattle. We'll help her start over," I add with a smile.

For the first time, she looks away from the sound and stares at me. She appears as if she's going to say something but turns her gaze back to an orca's tail crashing down on the waves.

"Daphne—"

My phone rings, interrupting me. I pull my hand away from Daphne's and answer the call.

"I have the walkthrough all lined up," the real estate agent says. "Text me when you arrive, and I'll pick you up at the pier."

"Great. Is it the house I wanted to see?" I ask.

"Yes," the agent says. "All the details are worked out. I have other houses ready to go to be seen too, if you want."

"I think we'll only need to see the one," I answer, maybe a little too quickly. I should make the agent sweat a bit before giving in just for fun. She needs to earn her commission.

As I end the call, I still see sadness in Daphne's eyes and her body seems to slump down in the seat.

"The agent will be waiting for us." I pause, noticing how cold she is in the way she doesn't ask any questions about the house, the agent, or care about what we are about to do. "Okay, enough. Tell me what's going on. I can feel it. I can hear it. I don't want to keep asking." My tone grows firm, but I feel I have no other choice. We're getting closer to the city, and I don't want to start the day on a sour note. Something is off, and there is something Daphne isn't telling me.

She sighs deeply, her shoulders rising and falling in what appears to be defeat. "I just didn't want to leave the island. To leave... you."

"Me? You aren't having to leave me. Last I checked, I'm on this boat right beside you." I reach for her hand again, but this time, she pulls it away.

"We're heading back to Seattle. To Medusa. To that life."

"What do you mean by *that life*?"

"Dinners. Parties. Working at all hours. Lonely days, and even lonelier nights."

"I'm not him," I say a little harsher than I intend. "Don't assume I'll be him."

Her lips purse and then she finally snaps. "No, you'll just be out killing people rather than crunching numbers. But everything else will be the same. You're still a Godwin. Family first." She rolls her eyes. "Family always comes first."

"You aren't being fair..." I feel my jaw tighten, and I take a deep breath of my own to steady my temper. My patience is growing thin, and I don't want this to turn into a fight and it to allow either of us to push what I feel could be a really good thing between us away.

"What's that stupid saying? Life isn't fair." She looks at me and gives a fake smile. "But don't worry. I know how to be the perfect Godwin wife."

"Daphne…" I warn. "I have no idea what is going on, but I'm not liking this tone or how you're acting."

Finally she snaps. "Oh, I'm sorry," she seethes between clenched teeth. "Am I not being a respectful wife? Am I not being a good and dutiful wife? I guess I should be kidnapped and locked in a cage again. I suppose I should be punished into submission."

"Is this what has you so upset?" I ask. "What I did to you?"

She crosses her arms against her chest and doesn't say a single word.

"I'm not going to apologize for what I did," I begin. "It was either that or death, and I much prefer you alive."

"It's not about the goddamn cage!"

"Then what? Because I'm having a hard time following you."

"Everything is changing!" she snaps back as she scoots herself to the edge of the seat like she can't get far enough away from me.

"Yes," I say calmly. "Some things will change now that we're heading back in the city."

"But I don't want it to. Don't you get that? What you and I had at Olympus was… I don't want it to change. Medusa has the power to turn our lives to stone. I don't want that!"

"Daphne, you need to calm down."

"I'm calm. Perfectly." A lone tear falls down from her cheek, and her pain nearly breaks my heart.

"I don't know what's going on, or why you think that you and I—"

"I don't think anything," she interrupts again. "I know," she shouts as the tears fall. "If we go back to that life, we won't survive."

Her words are like a punch to the gut. "We will." I pause to take hold of her hand. "Look at me." I wait until she does. "We will survive. I already had my brush with death. And losing you would be the same as dying."

"Promise me," she breathes.

"You know I do."

"I don't know what's going on with me," she says as she wipes at her tears. "I feel so out of control. I think these baby hormones are messing with me."

I chuckle. "And I'm here to ride the wave of them every single day."

She looks up at me and smiles. "I'm excited for today. I am. And I'm sorry to have snapped. I'm just scared of what comes next in our story."

"You need to remember something," I say as I touch her belly. "You and this baby are Godwins. I will die for my family. There is nothing I won't do for you. I give you my vow of a Godwin."

Daphne

I watch the scenery change from a city feeling to a more residential one. Even though my hormones are raging, and I've already cried multiple times today, I can't help but feel excitement as we get closer to the Queen Anne district. The rows of snugly fit houses in the hilly neighborhood are truly to die for. It's the best part of Seattle.

We pull up to a house, and my breathing stops.

It's the house. *The house.* The house I saw when I was a young girl and fantasized about. Apollo had listened to my story, and he acted. We are parked in front of my dream home. It still had the stained glass and even the little potted plants in the window.

Tears well up in my eyes, and my damn lip, I can't seem to control today, quivers. "This house is for sale?"

"Not exactly," the agent answers. "But your husband is very convincing." Glancing at Apollo and then at me, she takes her cue and says, "I'm going to see if they are ready for us." She exits the car and leaves us alone.

"Is this the house you told me about?" he asks.

"Yes. But how did you—"

"Your sister helped me. I told her I wanted to buy it for you."

"Are you serious?" I ask, not believing that he'd do something so... so romantic.

"If you like the inside and not just the outside, then yes. I'm serious."

My heart beats so hard that it seems to be stopping itself. "It's smaller than any house we've ever had. Are you sure it's good enough for you?"

He smiles. "*We've* never had a house before. And yes, if it's good enough for you, then it is for me."

"I can't believe you did this. I've never had anyone..."

Apollo reaches out and runs his fingertips down the side of my head, tucking a piece of hair behind my ear. "Let's go inside and see this dream house of yours."

He leans in close enough that he can take hold of the back of my head and pulls me into a kiss. He claims my mouth just as he has so many times before. Before, when we were locked away in Olympus. When our reality could be cloaked by the fog of Heathens Hollow. Before real life stepped in. Before I have to return to a life that I so desperately want to leave behind me, never to return to.

As his tongue dances with mine, I lean closer to him, wanting him to desperately bring us back to Heathens Hollow. Back to the only place that ever felt like home.

"I didn't want to leave the island," I mumble against the kiss. "But then you show me this."

He pulls away just enough that he can look into

my eyes again. "We can live anywhere in the world you want to live in." He gives me a quick peck to end the more passionate kiss and adds, "But before you decide, let's go see the house."

"I love you," I say softly. "You." I want him to hear me say it. I love him. The perfect and amazing man that he is.

The biggest smile forms on his face, not only with his mouth, but with his eyes. "I like hearing those words from your lips. Lips I want to kiss over and over again. But first..." He gets out of the car, walks around to my side, and opens my door. "Let's go see if we found our new home." He stares up at it proudly. "I can see us living here."

I get out of the car feeling overwhelmed with what's about to happen for us. A house, a baby, a new beginning. This family tree is so rooted and old, but for us, we are just beginning this family saga. We are about to start our own branch of the Godwin tree.

CHAPTER 41

ANI

I wake slowly, feeling disorientated with soft sheets luxurious against my skin. There is a feeling of stillness in the air, and the room is lit by a soft night light kept on at all times. I can hear the ticking of a clock somewhere in the distance and feel a faint chill.

I don't even know what time it is. I've been sleeping more than I've been awake, but the darkness of the night has deepened, and I feel curiously removed from the world around me. I've been in this mansion for days—maybe even a week or two. Each day has blended with the next, and I feel as if I'm living in an odd purgatory between the hell I was once in and a potential future of better times ahead now that *he's* gone.

My phone vibrates on the nightstand beside me, and I wonder if that is the sound of what woke me. Seeing it's my sister calling has me quickly answer, knowing if I don't, she'll start to panic.

"Hey," I say, reaching for the glass of water beside my bed to drink. My voice is scratchy, and I don't want Daphne to worry even more that I may be getting sick or something.

"Did I wake you?"

"I really need to start sleeping on a regular schedule. I'm losing all sense of time."

"You're healing. Your body went through a lot," Daphne says, softly. This isn't the first time she's given me this reassurance. Every time I bring up how I should leave and get out of her hair, I receive this same lecture.

"I know. But I'm feeling better. The bruising is fading. Nothing I can't hide with a little makeup." I leave out the fact that I have the kind of makeup that covers the bruises back at my trailer and have done this multiple times.

"You aren't ready to leave Olympus," Daphne says, clearly reading my mind. "I don't want you in that tin can any longer."

"That tin can is my home."

"It doesn't need to be. I can help you—"

"I'm not taking your money," I interrupt.

"Ani…"

"I'm serious. You and Apollo have already done far more than I'm comfortable with."

This argument my sister and I have has been going on ever since she married into the Godwin family. Just because she has access to money now doesn't mean I do. I don't take charity or handouts and never have. Never will.

"Tell me about the house you saw today," I say, changing the subject. "I'm assuming you've seen it by now."

"It's so pretty. Everything inside is what I imagined it would be. It's perfect. Apollo said we can buy it. It has three bedrooms, so if you want to move—"

"I'm not moving in with you guys," I interrupt. "No way. Don't even think that's a possibility."

She sighs heavily on the other end of the phone but doesn't argue any further. Instead, she says, "Thank you for remembering this house and giving the information to Apollo. It was by far the most romantic thing I could have experienced. A true Cinderella story."

"You deserve it," I say, and she does. My older sister has always done whatever she could for me, and it's time for her to put herself first.

"We're going to stay in Seattle for a couple of days while Apollo does some work for Medusa and also does what it takes to buy the house. Do you think you'll be okay?"

I suppress the urge to groan from my bruised ribs as I sit up all the way, peering into the darkness. The furniture of the room is opulent—a four-poster bed, a vanity, and a tall armoire all dominate the room. An ornate rug spreads out across the floor, and expensive tapestries hang on the walls. Despite the luxuriousness of the room, there is something vaguely menacing about it. The shadows seem to lurk in the corners, and the objects that decorate the room appear to be watching me.

I always feel watched.

"I'll be fine," I reassure.

"Apollo told me that a housekeeper and cook will arrive tomorrow. He wants the house to be staffed again, so you won't be on your own completely."

"I really need to get back to my home," I say. "There's no reason for Apollo to pay to have people here just for me."

"Ani…" I hear Daphne take a calming breath. "A few more days, okay. Then we can revisit this conversation. That's all I ask."

I can sit here and try to argue, but I know my sister. She'll win. She always does.

"Fine. A few more days. But then I'm serious. I need to get home and deal with my mess of a life."

There's silence on the other end, which tells me that Daphne isn't going to just agree to let me go, but I'm not going to battle this out yet. I'm going to need a plan of action to even have a chance of convincing her I'm going to be alright, and I don't have it yet.

"It's getting late. We'll talk tomorrow," she finally says. "There's food in the kitchen and—"

"I can fend for myself," I cut in. "But thank you. I appreciate it. Love you," I say.

"Love you."

When I hang up the phone, my stomach growls

at the mention of food, and I decide I do indeed need to find something to eat in the kitchen downstairs. As I get out of the bed, an ominous creak echoes down the hall, and I shiver. It's not the first time I've heard a creak, or a bump, or shuffle of what I swear are feet when no one is supposed to be in the manor.

Godwin ghosts are everywhere, and I have to keep telling myself that they're harmless, even though I know living Godwins are anything but.

Throwing on a borrowed robe, and stepping out into the hallway, my heart pounds in my chest, no matter how much I'm telling myself that I'm being ridiculous. But when I hear another bang at the end of the hallway, I know it's not just my imagination. Daphne said the housekeeper and cook don't arrive until the morning. The house should be empty... and quiet.

Olympus Manor is old and drafty, and the darkness seems to stalk me as I move down the hallway. Still feeling as if I'm being watched, I peer into each of the empty rooms as I pass them but see nothing. I'm not sure what exactly I'm expecting to see. The Boogie Monster, a ghost, or maybe it's just bats in the attic fluttering around that I hear.

I reach the end of the hallway where a staircase leads up to the attic. I hesitate, suddenly feeling very foolish in the darkness. This is how people in horror stories die.

I can hear the creak again, coming from the attic.

Something inside of me wants to go up, but I can't help but feel like I'm trespassing if I do.

But then again, maybe I can put my mind at ease by checking it out. It could help me know that all thoughts of monsters are simply in my head.

Taking a deep breath, I start up the stairs, my footsteps echoing in the darkness. As I reach the top, the creaking becomes louder and more insistent. I step into the attic, my heart in my throat...

Are you ready for more from the
Godwin family?
Continue reading with
MONSTERS ARE HIDDEN...

ABOUT THE AUTHOR

Alta Hensley is a USA TODAY bestselling author of hot, dark and dirty romance. She is also an Amazon Top 10 bestselling author. Being a multi-published author in the romance genre, Alta is known for her dark, gritty alpha heroes, sometimes sweet love stories, hot eroticism, and engaging tales of the constant struggle between dominance and submission.

She lives in a log cabin in the woods with her husband, two daughters, and an Australian Shepherd. When she isn't battling the bats, and watching the deer, she is writing about villains who always get their love story and happily ever after.

Facebook: https://www.facebook.com/AltaHensleyAuthor/
Amazon: https://www.amazon.com/Alta-Hensley/e/B004G5A6LI
Website: www.altahensley.com
Instagram: https://instagram.com/altahensley
Bookbub: https://www.bookbub.com/authors/alta-hensley

TikTok: https://www.tiktok.com/@altahensley
Join her mailing list: https://landing.mailerlite.com/webforms/landing/c9b6n3

Also by Alta Hensley

Gods Among Men Series:

Villains Are Made

Monsters Are Hidden

Vipers Are Forbidden

Secret Bride Trilogy:

Captive Bride

Kept Bride

Taken Bride

Wonderland Trilogy:

King of Spades

Queen of Hearts

Ace of Diamonds

Dark Pen Series:

Devil's Contract

Dirty Ledger

Dangerous Notes

Top Shelf Series:

Bastards & Whiskey

Villains & Vodka

Scoundrels & Scotch

Devils & Rye

Beasts & Bourbon

Sinners & Gin

Evil Lies Series:

The Truth About Cinder

The Truth About Alice

Breaking Belles Series:

Elegant Sins

Beautiful Lies

Opulent Obsession

Inherited Malice

Delicate Revenge

Lavish Corruption

Gold In Locks

Sick Crush

Secret Bride

Spiked Roses

Captive Vow

Ruin Me

Delicate Scars

www.ingramcontent.com/pod-product-compliance
Lightning Source LLC
Chambersburg PA
CBHW021335150726
47989CB00005B/1996